THE ALGERINE
CAPTIVE

Royall Tyler

The Algerine Captive

OR,

The Life and Adventures of
Doctor Updike Underhill:
Six Years a Prisoner Among the Algerines

Introduction and Notes by Caleb Crain

THE MODERN LIBRARY

NEW YORK

2002 Modern Library Paperback Edition

LIBRARY OF CONGRESS CATALOGING-IN-PUBLICATION DATA
Tyler, Royall, 1757–1826.
The Algerine captive, or, The life and adventures of Doctor Updike Underhill,
six years a prisoner among the Algerines / Royall Tyler ; introduction and notes
by Caleb Crain.
p. cm.—(Modern Library classics)
Includes bibliographical references.
ISBN 978-0-375-76034-1
1. Americans—Algeria—Fiction. 2. Slave trade—Fiction. 3. Physicians—Fiction.
4. Captivity—Fiction. 5. Algeria—Fiction. I. Title: Algerine captive. II. Title:
Life and adventures of Doctor Updike Underhill, six years a prisoner among the
Algerines. III. Crain, Caleb. IV. Title. V. Series.

PS855.T7 A44 2002
813'.2—dc21   2002019642

Modern Library website address: www.modernlibrary.com

Printed in the United States of America

15 14 13 12

ROYALL TYLER

Royall Tyler—American playwright, novelist, poet, and essayist—was born William Clark Tyler on July 18, 1757. His parents, Royall and Mary Steele Tyler, raised their family in the thick of pre-Revolutionary Boston, where the young Tyler attended South Latin School for seven years. After Tyler's father died in 1771, he took his name and was known thereafter as Royall Tyler. In 1772 he entered Harvard University, where he received his bachelor's degree in 1776, and then enlisted in the army under Major General John Hancock. Although Tyler rose to the rank of major and participated in an unsuccessful attack at Newport, Rhode Island, on the whole, he saw little military action. He studied law during these years and received a master's degree from Harvard in 1779; in 1780, he was admitted to the Massachusetts bar.

The law was Tyler's chosen career. He set up practice in Braintree, Massachusetts, and moved within the town's top social circles. There he met and fell in love with Abigail Adams (nicknamed Nabby), the seventeen-year-old daughter of future president John Adams. Although the courtship continued for years, in 1786 Nabby married someone else. Spurned, Tyler returned to Boston and was soon swept back into military action during Shays's Rebellion. He traveled as a negotiator to New York in March 1787, where it is likely that his creativity was stirred by the theater, then prohibited in Boston. One month later, Tyler wrote his own play.

The Contrast debuted at New York's John Street Theatre on April 16, 1787. The play, depicting Yankee humor and expounding patriotic themes, was favorably reviewed; it became well known as the first professionally produced comedy by an American playwright. For Tyler, writing had been a mere hobby, and he attempted to remain an anonymous author, ascribing authorship of his play to "A Citizen of the United States." Nonetheless, his reputation as a writer grew, and he quickly followed *The Contrast* with a musical comedy, *May Day in Town; or, New York in an Uproar,* later in 1787.

In 1790, Tyler returned to his legal practice and moved to Vermont. In 1793, he published a 108-line poem, "The Origin of Evil," one of the many pieces of verse, published and unpublished, that Tyler produced during his lifetime. He was elected state's attorney for Windham County in 1794. That year, Tyler married Mary Palmer, and he also began collaborating with friend Joseph Dennie on a series of amusing sketches and essays that appeared in various newspapers under the pseudonymns Colon and Spondee.

Tyler wrote his first novel during the next few years. *The Algerine Captive; or, the Life and Adventures of Doctor Updike Underhill: Six Years Prisoner Among the Algerines* was published anonymously in 1797. Purporting to be a true captivity narrative, Tyler's topical novel combines native color with foreign adventure; it is also a social commentary on the institution of slavery. Tyler was identified as the author of the well-received work, and it would remain his only finished novel. *The Georgia Spec; or, Land in the Moon,* a comedy by Tyler which is now lost, was performed in Boston in 1797. Three other plays that may date from this period are attributed to Tyler: *The Farm House, The Doctor in Spite of Himself,* and *The Island of Barrataria.* In 1801, Tyler was elected to the Vermont Supreme Court, and he moved his family (which would eventually include eleven children) to Brattleboro. As a circuit court judge, he traveled often, but he found time to contribute many columns and poems to *Port Folio* magazine, then edited by Joseph Dennie.

In 1807, Tyler became Chief Justice of the Vermont Supreme Court. His careers merged briefly in 1809 and 1810, when two volumes of his legal reports were issued as *Reports of Cases Argued and Determined in the Supreme Court of Judicature of the State of Vermont*. Also in 1809, Tyler completed a collection of fictional (and anonymous) letters about traveling titled *The Yankey in London*.

Tyler's defeat in an 1812 campaign for the United States Senate was the first of many setbacks suffered over the next few years. In 1813, he lost his position as chief justice, and his eldest son died. His three-year professorship at the University of Vermont ended in 1814. He was appointed register of probate for Windham County in 1815, but his financial situation remained bleak. However, he did not abandon writing. In 1817, Tyler worked on an unfinished essay, "The Touchstone, or a Humble Modest Inquiry into the Nature of Religious Intolerance." In 1824 and 1825, he completed three sacred dramas, written in blank verse: "Joseph and His Brethren," "The Judgement of Solomon," and "The Origin of the Feast of Purim," which were published posthumously. He also composed a 744-line poem titled "The Chestnut Tree," which was not published until 1931.

Suffering from cancer of the eyes for many years, Tyler slowly became blind. He attempted to revise *The Algerine Captive*, renaming it *The Bay Boy*, but it remained unfinished at the time of his death on August 26, 1826. Dedicated to the rise of a native literature, Royall Tyler used patriotic themes and skillful characterizations in drama, fiction, poetry, and essays to encourage and record early American art and culture.

CONTENTS

THE ALGERINE CAPTIVE

VOLUME 1

VOLUME II

LIST OF ILLUSTRATIONS

These copperplate illustrations accompanied *The Algerine Captive* when it was serialized in *The Lady's Magazine: or Entertaining Companion for the Fair Sex, Appropriated Solely to Their Use and Amusement* (London: Robinson and Roberts) in 1804. They appeared in volume 35, facing pages 198, 249, and 348.

INTRODUCTION

1

In 1824, two years before his death, Royall Tyler wrote "The Chestnut Tree," a long poem about Vermont in the late twentieth century. Tyler guessed that even after 175 years, his home state would still have flirts, dandies, lawyers, soldiers, Quakers, drunkards, hunters, paupers, and bachelors. In a serious stanza, he worried that factory labor would blight the health of children. And in a lighthearted stanza, he joked that anyone still reading his books in the 1990s would be wearing clothes just as dated.

His only fans would be antiquarians, he wrote, and their pleasures would be desiccated ones:

> The Bookworm's features scrawl a smile
> While gloating on the musty page;
> As we admire some ruined pile,
> Not for its worth, but for its age.

Alas, Tyler turned out to be more or less correct about his twentieth-century readers. They read him because he was one of

America's earliest playwrights and novelists. It is not clear they laughed at his jokes.

Will he fare any better in the twenty-first? By way of an answer, consider "The Origin of Evil: An Elegy," which Tyler published anonymously in 1793. It begins with a thick Augustan shrubbery of learned quotation, and this hedge has no doubt deterred some readers and misled others. The reader is then invited to "Weep the *fall* of *Eve* and *Adam*, / From their first state of Innocence," which would seem a pious enough task. But the subject matter quickly ceases to be appropriate for Sunday school:

> *Eve,* the fairest child of nature,
>   In naked beauty stood reveal'd,
> Exposing every limb and feature,
>   Save those her jetty locks conceal'd.
>
> Light and wanton curl'd her tresses
>   Where each sprouting lock should grow,
> Her bosom, heaving for caresses,
>   Seem'd blushing berries cast on snow.
>
> *Adam,* got by lusty nature,
>   Form'd to delight a woman's eyes,
> Stood confest in manly stature,
>   The first of men in shape and size!
>
> As *Eve* cast her arms so slender,
>   His brawny chest to fondly stroke;
> She seem'd an ivy tendril tender
>   Sporting round a sturdy oak.
>
> . . . As her arm Eve held him hard in,
>   And toy'd him with her roving hand,
> In the middle of Love's Garden,
>   She saw the Tree of Knowledge stand.
>
> Stately grew the tree forbidden,
>   Rich curling tendrils grac'd its root;
> In its airy pods, half hidden,
>   Hung the luscious, tempting fruit.

> ... Softly sigh'd the rib-form'd beauty,
> "How love does new desires produce?
> This pendant fruit o'ercomes my duty,
> I pant to suck its balmy juice."

Readers with an appetite for more should consult Marius B. Péladeau's edition of *The Verse of Royall Tyler* for the climax, omitted here. Attentive students of the complete text will be reminded, at line 80, that circumcision was not routine in America until the twentieth century.

There is nothing else like "The Origin of Evil" in early American literature. Tyler himself did not write anything so bawdy ever again, and it might be considered a cruel tease to quote the poem in a preface to *The Algerine Captive,* a novel that keeps its buttons properly fastened. But although ribaldry may be irrelevant to Tyler's novel, his capacity for it is not. "The Origin of Evil" gives decisive evidence of his character as a writer: sly, alert to pleasure, and unconstrained by decorum or orthodoxy. He knew how to be juicy, which is why he deserves readers without too much dust on them.

2

Tyler was not altogether comfortable with the wiliness of his own mind, and he struggled all his life to use it in the service of conservative politics. He succeeded, but given the nature of his talent, one might say he succeeded in spite of himself, or in spite of a part of himself, at least.

He was born in Boston in 1757, the youngest of four children, and was christened William Clark Tyler. His father, Royall Tyler (1724–71), was an importer and retailer of English goods, with a reputation as a weather vane in politics. The elder Tyler was aggressive about committing paupers to the workhouse and fiery against the British after the Boston Massacre. It was said that he bragged about his skill at ingratiating himself with working-class voters. "You would sometimes laugh your soul out, if you was to see how I work them poor toads," he reportedly boasted. His nickname was Pug Sly.

Young Tyler was sent to Boston's South Latin School in 1765. In May 1771, his father died. The attending physician was accused of malpractice—an episode that may have colored Tyler's view of the medical profession. Fortunately, Tyler's father left the family a considerable sum, at least four thousand pounds, perhaps much more. In April 1772, at his mother's request, William Clark was renamed Royall by an act of the General Court. He enrolled at Harvard in July.

At Harvard and during his legal studies afterward, the young Tyler had money to burn, and he ran a bit wild. (Late in life, when tempted to become a preacher, Tyler would decide not to because "a consciousness of having lived too gay a life in my youth made me tremble lest I should bring in some way disgrace upon the sacred cause!") While fishing for a piglet from an upper-story window, he and a roommate instead snagged the wig of the college president; they were punished by rustication in Maine. After Tyler graduated in July 1776, he studied law in Cambridge and Boston, where he socialized with the smart set surrounding the painter and poet John Trumbull. Several young men in the circle, including Tyler, were examined by the Harvard faculty for drunk and disorderly conduct in October 1777. The following year, Tyler served in the Revolutionary army as an aide to General John Sullivan, but after Sullivan's forces were routed by the British in the Battle of Rhode Island, he returned to his legal studies. In June 1779, Katherine Morse, "a sweeper for very many years in the [Harvard] college buildings," gave birth to a boy she named Royal. According to a note found in the papers of a nineteenth-century historian of Harvard, Royal Morse was Tyler's bastard.

Despite his evident relish for urban pleasures, in 1780 Tyler moved to the countryside—the first of several abrupt, mysterious decampments that would shape his adult life. He tried to launch his legal career in what is now Portland, Maine. Perhaps it bored him. In 1782 he gave up and returned to Massachusetts, where he rented a room in the Braintree home of Richard and Mary Cranch, who had an attractive seventeen-year-old niece. Now allegedly a serious young man, Tyler began to court her.

The niece in question, Abigail "Nabby" Adams, came with a forbiddingly distinguished pedigree. She was the daughter of John Adams, future president of the United States. By December 23, 1782, Nabby's mother, Abigail, felt obliged to relay news of her daughter's new suitor to her husband, then in Paris negotiating the infant nation's peace with Great Britain. To judge from the tone of her report, mother, like daughter, was charmed:

> Loosing his Father young and having a very pretty patrimony left him, possessing a sprightly fancy, a warm imagination and an agreeable person, he was rather negligent in persueing his business in the way of his profession; and dissipated two or 3 years of his Life and too much of his fortune for to reflect upon with pleasure; all of which he now laments but cannot recall.... His mamma is in possession of a large Estate and he is a very favorite child. When he proposed comeing to settle here he met with but little encouragement, but he was determined upon the trial. He has succeeded beyond expectation, he has popular talants, and his behaviour has been unexceptionable since his residence in Town; in concequence of which his Business daily increases. He cannot fail making a distinguished figure in his profession if he steadily persues it. I am not acquainted with any young Gentleman whose attainments in literature are equal to his, who judges with greater accuracy or discovers a more delicate and refined taste....
>
> What ought I to say? I feel too powerful a pleader within my own heart and too well recollect the Love I bore to the object of my early affections to forbid him to hope. I feel a regard for him upon an account you will smile at, I fancy I see in him Sentiments, opinions and actions which endeared to me the best of Friends.

John Adams was unmoved by his wife's evocation of their courtship and nonplussed by what she had to say about Tyler. On January 22, 1783, he rebuked her for having indulged the romance:

> I confess I dont like the Subject at all. My Child is too young for such Thoughts, and I dont like your Word "Dissipation" at all. I dont know

what it means—it may mean every Thing. There is not Modesty and Diffidence enough in the Traits you Send me. My Child is a Model, as you represent her and as I knew her, and is not to be the Prize, I hope of any, even reformed Rake. . . . A youth who has been giddy enough to spend his Fortune or half his Fortune in Gaieties is not the Youth for me, Let his Person, Family, Connections and Taste for Poetry be what they will. I am not looking out for a Poet, nor a Professor of belle Letters. . . .

This is too serious a subject to equivocate about. I dont like this Method of Courting Mothers. There is something too fantastical and affected in all this Business for me.

A week later, Adams repeated his objection. "I dont like the Trait in his Character, his Gaiety. . . . That Frivolity of Mind, which breaks out into such Errors in Youth, never gets out of the Man but shews itself in some mean Shape or other through Life."

This was sniffy, but it cut to the heart of the matter. In early national America, it would have been hard to find a more potent symbol of alliance with the establishment than marriage to the daughter of John Adams, the most arbitrary and least democratic of the Founding Fathers. Though kindly in the domestic sphere, in public life Adams was so rigorous about virtue as to verge on authoritarianism. There was no politician of stature to the right of him, except perhaps Hamilton. And Adams was correct about Tyler: A prodigal never leaves behind his waywardness of spirit. From a prudent father's point of view, the passion of the young man's wish to join the Adams family was a further argument against him—more evidence of Tyler's failure to judge the world accurately and control his impulses accordingly.

Nabby was promptly removed from Braintree to Boston, and she and her mother began planning to join Adams in Europe. As the mileage separating Tyler and Nabby grew, John Adams relented somewhat. When mother and daughter embarked for London in the summer of 1784, Tyler was entrusted with management of the family accounts and given the run of Adams's personal library. In October, Nabby sent her miniature portrait across the Atlantic to Tyler.

To the Adamses' credit, they were giving Tyler a chance to prove his love by overcoming the traditional challenges of distance and delay. He failed. During the first year that Nabby was abroad, he wrote her only four letters. During the same period, Mary Cranch—his landlady and Nabby's aunt—wrote unfavorable reports of his behavior at every opportunity. In August 1785, Nabby returned Tyler's miniature and canceled their engagement. She married Colonel William Stephens Smith, who had been working with her father in London as secretary of legation, in June 1786.

Tyler was so demoralized that he retreated to his mother's house in Jamaica Plain. In order to impress the Adamses, he had undertaken to buy a handsome estate in Braintree, and after the engagement was broken, he fell behind in his payments and lost it. He also neglected the Adams family account books and had to surrender them, too. Meanwhile, in the autumn of 1786, a western Massachusetts man named Daniel Shays became so angry about the government's unwillingness to ease the debt burdens of small farmers that he took up arms. Shays planned to attack the federal arsenal at Springfield in January. At loose ends after his failure to marry into what would eventually become America's greatest political dynasty, Tyler enlisted, in order to help put down the rebellion.

3

Because of his training as a lawyer and his skill as a public speaker, Tyler's service during Shays's Rebellion consisted largely of diplomacy. After most of the rebels were seized, he pursued Shays into Vermont. But instead of capturing him, Tyler spent his time there smoothing relations between Vermont and Massachusetts authorities. He had a knack for it, and in March 1787, the governor of Massachusetts sent him on another diplomatic mission, this time to New York City, the nation's capital.

Tyler had never been to Manhattan. Within three weeks, he had written a play. Within five weeks, he had seen it performed.

It was the sort of achievement that biographers feel they ought to explain away, lest they be suspected as gulls. Nonetheless, *The*

Contrast did debut at the John Street Theatre on April 16, 1787, and it was a hit: It was a commercial success, and it was beloved. Five years later, when Tyler made an unannounced, highly abbreviated visit to his future wife, who was staying with her aunt and uncle in upstate New York, the breach of visiting etiquette was instantly forgiven when Tyler was revealed to be the author of *The Contrast*. The play was "the only thing Uncle had read except the newspapers," the young woman later recalled. In 1790, George Washington was listed first among the subscribers to the published play, and even though Tyler's name was, in accordance with genteel convention, absent from the title page, it was in all the newspapers.

In *The Contrast* was all the frivolity John Adams had foreseen. There was even a touch of sympathy for "the sturgeons," to use the name that Jonathan, the play's malapropistic Yankee backwoodsman, gives to the followers of Shays. The contrast of the play's title is between Billy Dimple, a simpering, inheritance-squandering Chesterfieldian with designs on three different women, and Colonel Henry Manly, a scrupulous, altruistic, and impoverished veteran of the Revolutionary War. But the wittiest lines go to Manly's sister Charlotte and her friend Letitia—rivalrous young women who know it's wrong to choose husbands for their fashion sense, money, and propensity to die young, but don't see why they shouldn't try to get away with it anyway.

The humor is durable because it derives from character. You can imagine a different outcome for the play, but the personalities in it would always be at cross-purposes. And the writing is unburdened by moral propaganda. Tyler knew that virtue can be a bore, and that naughtiness can be a way of holding on to options. He had the kind of plain insight that is as comfortable writing children's verse ("I'll tell a tale—how Farmer John / A little Roan colt bred sir") and drinking songs ("The monk, who mopes in cloister'd cell, / May write, and rave, and bellow; / At night, with rosy, romping Nell, / He's quite another fellow") as it is writing a drawing-room farce.

A month after *The Contrast*, a second play by Tyler was performed in New York. It does not survive. Perhaps it was no good, because just as suddenly as it had begun, his New York theatrical career was over. Tyler became depressed and again retreated to his mother's house.

While wooing Nabby Adams, Tyler had rented a second bedroom for himself in the Beacon Street home of Joseph Pearse Palmer, for occasions when business kept him in Boston overnight. Now he boarded with the Palmers once more, renewing his friendship with the family as a whole and with Joseph's daughter Mary Hunt Palmer in particular. Eighteen years his junior, she would eventually become his wife, but she could not yet be an anchor for him. In the spring of 1789 she left to stay with her aunt and uncle in upstate New York, and in the summer the Palmers as a family abandoned Boston for Framingham. Left to his own devices, Tyler announced in 1790 that he was moving to Vermont.

Like Portland, Maine, the small town of Guilford, Vermont, was an odd choice for a man who flourished in cities and probably harbored political as well as literary ambitions. One motive may have been a quarrel with his mother about his choice of Mary Palmer as wife. Tyler's biographer, G. Thomas Tanselle, attributes the move to depression, and it does have the air of deliberate restriction and self-chastening typical of that disease.

Tyler and Palmer were secretly married in May 1794. She remained in Framingham while he continued to live in Vermont. In her memoir, *Grandmother Tyler's Book* (New York: G. P. Putnam's, 1925), Mary recalled that this arrangement was inconvenient and eccentric, but at the time Tyler's "reputation as an author was high, and his genius covered a multitude of faults." The secrecy may have had something to do with the dispute between Tyler and his mother. The rupture between the two was permanent. "Although I often in years after urged him to visit her," Mary remembered, "he would turn away and, looking grave, preserve a profound silence." In the spring of 1800 Tyler would learn of his mother's death by reading about it in a Boston newspaper.

In December 1794, Mary and Royall's secret came out: Mary gave birth to the first of eleven children. But she had to wait another winter to join her husband. It was customary in those days for a new bride to remain in her parents' home for an interval before "going to housekeeping." Most waited six weeks; some waited nearly a year. Not until February 1796 was the snow thick enough for Tyler's two black horses, Crock and Smut, to draw a sleigh carrying Mary, her baby, and her luggage from Framingham to Guilford.

Tyler's maturity in Vermont was productive but prudent. As he explained in 1800 to a publisher eager for more of his writing but reluctant to pay for it, "From certain disgusts perhaps uncharitably admitted, I . . . renounced the ambition of authorship. . . . If writing for the public is attended with no more profit, I had rather file legal process in my attorney's office, and endeavor to explain unintelligible law to Green Mountain jurors." He earned his living as state's attorney for Windham County until 1801, when the family moved to Brattleboro. For the next twelve years, he was elected to Vermont's supreme court; he served as chief justice from 1807 to 1813. After he left his position on the supreme court, Tyler maintained a private law practice until 1822, when a skin cancer on the left side of his face forced him to retire. Despite his distinguished career, he died poor.

Though in middle age Tyler insisted that literature was no more than a hobby to him, he continued to write. Starting in 1794 he and Joseph Dennie collaborated on a popular series of satirical essays and poems published in various newspapers under the pseudonyms Colon and Spondee. Tyler's brother managed the Federal Street Theatre in Boston, and through him, Tyler continued to have plays performed. He published *The Algerine Captive* in 1797, a faux travelogue about England entitled *A Yankey in London* in 1809, and two volumes of reports of Vermont Supreme Court cases in 1809 and 1810.

In almost everything he wrote, Tyler showed his talent and willingness to please. *A Yankey in London* is breezy and amusing. Tyler's impersonation of a tourist disguises as casual and effortless what was in fact the synthesis of a lifetime of reading about English politics and culture. In his light verse there are sharp knocks and impressive fluency. The love poem "Almoran to Eliza," probably given to Nabby Adams along with an ice sculpture in the shape of a heart, hinges on an elegant and poignant conceit. But the only work by Tyler that matches *The Contrast* in ambition is *The Algerine Captive,* his novel about an American schoolteacher turned doctor, who was captured by pirates and sold into slavery in North Africa.

4

The novel's two volumes—the first set mostly in America, the second in Algiers—differ so markedly in tone that they could be thought of as two distinct books. Volume 1 is a satire and a picaresque. At the start of it, the joke is usually on the hero and narrator Updike Underhill, so earnestly devoted to his Puritan ancestors and the study of the classics that, much like Washington Irving's Ichabod Crane, he looks ridiculous to women and defenseless to bullies. As a doctor exposed to a spectrum of fraudulent colleagues, Underhill acquires more savvy, and by the time he tours the South, he has become more knowing than those around him. His encumbrance there is not naïveté but "a certain staple of New England which I had with me, called conscience." After all, as a New England Federalist who believed in the natural alliance of commercial prosperity and social progress, Tyler could not imagine that even the most hapless son of New Hampshire would be shown up by slaveholders.

The prevailing tone of volume 1 is irony, even when Underhill is not the butt of it. But then Underhill loses his innocence by taking a job on a slave ship and is himself enslaved. Irony vanishes, with an abruptness not unlike its subsidence after September 11, 2001. When the novel turns to the slave trade, Algiers, and Islam, it joins Underhill in earnestness, and it never goes back.

The shift in sensibility is not altogether pleasing. Slavery goes from being an instance of Southern fatuousness to a moral catastrophe, and the reader cannot help but notice that Underhill's alteration of attitude tracks his self-interest rather closely. This is a human weakness, however, and in Underhill's defense, it should be noted that although the quality of his attention to slavery varies, he never thinks well of it. Furthermore, it might be considered a sign of Tyler's respect for the facts that he suggests a parallel between slavery in America and slavery in Africa but does not force it. As the reader is allowed to observe, Underhill's condition as a slave is much milder than that of African slaves in American hands. (Tyler describes the misery of new black slaves so vividly that one suspects he had read Olaudah Equiano's 1789 narrative of his enslavement and struggle for liberation, or some other firsthand account.) Not only is the treatment that Underhill receives less brutal, but his status as a slave is not immutable. As the mullah accurately reports in volume 2, chapter 7, any Christian slave in Algiers who converted to Islam would be set free. Though Tyler doesn't cite any, statistics show the disparity between the American and African cases even more starkly: In total, fewer than 700 Americans were captured by the Muslim nations of North Africa between 1785 and 1815. In fact, slavery in Algiers was in decline: The country had 25,000 slaves in 1650; only 3,000 in 1750; and less than 1,000 in 1788. By comparison, the 1790 census counted 694,000 slaves of African descent in the United States, and the slave population would reach nearly 4 million by 1860.

In 1798 a letter to the editor of the *Farmer's Weekly Museum* suggested that in his novel Tyler was too quick to blame Southerners for and exonerate New Englanders from complicity in the slave trade. This seems astute, even though the writer to the *Farmer's Weekly Museum* wished Tyler had been uniformly forgiving where we would probably prefer him uniformly indignant. Yet although the modern reader may wish that Underhill's Algerian experience would spark additional American insights, in Africa Tyler's hero faces a culture and a set of circumstances violently unlike his own, and it is understandable that the details themselves absorb him. Nor is Underhill the only American to find it difficult to relate the events in Algiers to those at home. Until recently, the episode seemed distant from the central concerns of American history, as if it were a poorly integrated subplot in the national narrative. A comprehensive and authoritative history of the Federalist era published in 1993 makes almost no mention of the American hostages in North Africa.

Today, of course, it no longer seems incidental that America was challenged and troubled in its first decades by a group of Islamic nations who routinely violated international law. Then, as now, Americans were startled to discover how little they knew about the people attacking them. Pirates supported by the Barbary nations—Algiers, Morocco, Tunis, and Tripoli—had harassed shipping in the Mediterranean and Atlantic for centuries. They persisted because European countries with the naval power to stop them chose not to. Instead they negotiated exemptions for the ships of their own nations only, so that the pirates would continue to raid their competitors. Once America declared independence, its vessels were no longer protected by Britain's agreements with the Barbary states.

One of the first to appreciate America's new vulnerability was the emperor of Morocco. He announced his readiness to negotiate, then grew impatient when the United States failed to present gifts promptly. On October 1, 1784, Morocco seized the American ship *Betsey* and its sailors. Thanks to Spanish intervention, however, the seamen were freed within a year.

Meanwhile, the British consul Charles Logie saw to it that the dey of Algiers also understood America's weakness. According to the memoirs of James Leander Cathcart, enslaved in Algiers for more than a decade, Logie informed the dey "that the United States were no longer under the protection of his Master [Great Britain], and, that wherever the Cruisers of Algiers should fall in with the vessels of the United States of America, they were good prizes and [he] wished them success." A 1785 treaty with Spain allowed Algerian corsairs to pass the Straits of Gibraltar and reach the Atlantic, where they soon took two American prizes: the *Maria* on July 25 and the *Dauphin* on August 4. Twenty-one Americans became slaves; three were sent to work in Logie's house as domestics.

The United States government responded with confusion, inattention, and dithering. Adams thought paying ransom would be cheaper than waging war. Thomas Jefferson thought it best to feign indifference, in order to discourage the Barbary states from taking more hostages. In the spring of 1786, America sent a former mule trader named John Lamb to negotiate. He offered more money than Congress was willing to pay and succeeded only in irritating the dey. The failure seemed emblematic of the systemic weakness of America's government before the ratification of the Constitution. In the 1787 novel *The Algerine Spy in Pennsylvania,* Peter Markoe capitalized on the nation's anxiety by pretending to be an Algerian working undercover in the United States, willing to provide Daniel Shays and his rebels with an army of "one hundred thousand spahis and janizaries" in exchange for "a certain number of virgins."

Not until 1793 did Jefferson manage to appoint a second negotiator to Algiers: David Humphreys, then minister to Portugal, who had collaborated with Tyler's old friend Trumbull on a poem about Shays's Rebellion titled "The Anarchiad." But Humphreys never reached Algiers. In October, before he could set sail from Lisbon, Britain finagled an apparent truce between Portugal and Algiers. Algerian corsairs again sneaked past the Strait of Gibraltar, this time seizing twelve American ships and more than one hundred American sailors.

Through his diplomatic connections, Humphreys arranged for each American captive to receive a hat, a new set of clothes, and a monthly allowance. He was alarmed to learn that captives were dying of the plague. In July 1794, he wrote a letter inviting citizens to raise ransom money with lotteries, and it was printed in many American newspapers. President George Washington and his administration were somewhat embarrassed, because they considered it bad form to ask private citizens to take on a public responsibility, and because they did not want any money to reach Algiers until a treaty had been signed. Humphreys was reprimanded, quietly. The public, meanwhile, responded to his appeal with letters, sermons, donations, and the formation of benevolent societies.

On September 5, 1795, two American negotiators—Joseph Donaldson Jr. and Joel Barlow—finalized a treaty with the dey. In exchange for more than $700,000, Algiers agreed to release the Americans it held and not take any new captives. In July 1796, after Barlow borrowed funds from the Algiers-based Jewish bankers David and Solomon Bacri, the hostages embarked for America. Delayed by an outbreak of plague that forced them into quarantine in Marseilles, they would not reach Philadelphia until February 1797.

5

In choosing to write a novel about an American-born slave in Algiers, Tyler once again harnessed for literary ends his ambivalence toward the Federalists, the political party of his almost father-in-law, John Adams. The Federalists were known for their support of close ties with Britain, and in the Algerian crisis Britain had done its best to humiliate the United States. A hostage crisis in a part of the world where America had few allies and no military resources would have made any administration look blundering and impotent, and the administrations of Washington and Adams were not exceptions.

On the other hand, it was the Federalists who insisted on a strong American navy, and in the end, even their opponent Jefferson would rely on it to put an end to Barbary piracy. Despite his subversive humor, in all likelihood Tyler intended for the Federalist motto that concludes the novel—BY UNITING WE STAND, BY DIVIDING WE FALL—to be resounding.

The motto's resonance today is uncanny, considering the novel's subject matter. The crisis in Algiers was America's first encounter with a hostile Muslim nation. Tyler's is not the only book of the period to take advantage of readers' sudden interest in Islam and North African culture, but it is the most imaginative, and it is unusually open-minded in its perspective. In the debate between Underhill and the mullah, Tyler presents the tenets of Islam as he imagines a believer would have presented them—so persuasively that Underhill's only defense against conversion is his stubbornness. In 1803, a reviewer for London's *Monthly Review* charged that in these chapters of *The Algerine Captive,* "the author too feebly defends that religion which he professes to revere." Boston's *Monthly Anthology* repeated the charge in 1810, and Tyler tried to answer it in a preface for a proposed second edition:

> The Algerine Captive was reviewed in a Boston Magazine by some one who had the sagacity to discover that it savored of infidelity. The Author was prepared to meet severe criticism on his style; and various other imperfections; but certainly he never imagined it was objectionable on the score of infidelity, or even scepticism. The part objected to, as far as the Author recollects, was written with a view to do away with the vulgar prejudices against Islamism. He never thought that in adopting the liberality of the good Sale, the translator of the Koran, he was even jeopardising the truths of Christianity; for the Author considered then, and now considers, that, after exhibiting Islamism in its best light, the Mahometan imposture will be obvious to those who compare the language, the dogma, the fables, the monstrous absurdities of the Koran, with the sublime doctrines, morals and language of the Gospel Dispensation.

No one should rely on *The Algerine Captive* for an accurate account of Islam—some of the terminology and anecdotes are the novelist's inventions—but Tyler was a cosmopolitan who composed poems in the style of the Persian poet and mystic Hafez (whose name means "one who has memorized the Koran"), and it is no surprise that his novel is well researched and broad-minded.

For the real Algerian captive James Leander Cathcart, knowledge of Islam became a point of pride. One day, while eating dinner in the slaves' dormitory, Cathcart was called a "dog without faith" and ordered to yield his seat to a Muslim. Perhaps because he had had a little to drink, Cathcart bristled, then rashly boasted that he knew more about Islam than his bully. He proceeded to show off:

> Mahomed the great law giver, I said, was born at Mecca in the month called Mary, in the year of Christ 571, and died at Medina on the 12th day of the 3rd month of Rabi-a-thani A.D., 632, and the 11th year of the Hegira, being 63 lunar years old at the time of his death. He was succeeded in the government by Ayesha's father, Abn Beckir, who was

succeeded by Oman or Othman, who was succeeded by Ally, Mahomed's son-in-law, who married Fatima, his daughter, by Cadigha, and had the best right to the succession, but was opposed three times successively by Ayesha and her party, and when ultimately he succeeded in obtaining the government, she and her party took up arms against him, and was the cause of the ruin of himself and his house. This was not a little facilitated by the death of his wife Fatima, which happened only sixty days after the death of her father, and considerably weakened his party. He, however, is adored to this day by the Persians, and some sects both in Asia and Africa.

Even through the archaic spellings and transcribers' errors, Cathcart's speech is recognizable as a decent précis of Islam's early history. The crowd who heard him appreciated it. After his performance, they declared that he must have been raised a Muslim. Over the next twenty-four hours, only Cathcart's talent for placing bribes saved him from being put to death as an apostate.

Updike Underhill is just as vain as Cathcart and even more willing to admit to foolishness. He is an entertainer. Unfortunately, he isn't more than that. Although he moves from a comic world to one that is painful and confusing, the reader should not expect *The Algerine Captive* to be sublime. Underhill's tale and Algerian history have been thrown into a single pot, but the flavors haven't quite blended; as Tyler's biographer G. Thomas Tanselle observes, the novel fails to do for Algiers what Melville's *Moby-Dick* would later do for whales. It merely offers a portrait of a flawed America at a difficult time, addressed to the reader's curiosity and sense of humor.

———

CALEB CRAIN is the author of *American Sympathy: Men, Friendship, and Literature in the New Nation*. He lives in Brooklyn.

A NOTE ON THE TEXT

The Algerine Captive was first published in 1797 by David Carlisle. A second edition was published in England by G. and J. Robinson in 1802 in book form, and serialized by them there in *Lady's Magazine* in 1804. A second American edition appeared in 1816, published by Peter B. Gleason and Co. in Hartford. A facsimile edition of the English edition was issued in 1967; the first and only modernized text, edited by Don J. Cook, was published in 1970. This Modern Library Paperback Classics edition is set from the first American edition, as the other three published in Tyler's lifetime have no authority. Though, according to G. Thomas Tanselle in his biography of Tyler, the first English edition contains "nearly 250 alterations of wording—usually for the better—and many hundreds more of punctuation," it seems unlikely that Tyler was responsible for these changes. The serialized English edition more or less followed the first, with just a few more punctuation changes and the omission of one episode near the beginning of the book. The second American edition was also set from the 1802 edition; Tanselle notes that the further variants found in it, which typically are word or letter omissions, are accidental.

Errors noted and corrected on the errata slip of the 1797 edition have been silently corrected as well in this edition, and the following printer's errors have also been corrected:

p. 6, line 10: "diary" has been corrected to "dairy."

p. 7, line 6: "spectator" has been capitalized.

p. 18, line 31: "pessession" has been corrected to "possession."

p. 33, line 2: "Odessey" has been corrected to "Odyssey."

p. 37, line 7: "couching" has been capitalized.

p. 60, line 6: The "I" in "Inspects" has been lowercased.

p. 66, line 7: A comma after "facetious" has been replaced with a period.

p. 75, lines 6–7: "a" in "a man" has been capitalized.

p. 79, line 2: "sunday" has been capitalized.

p. 92, lines 12–13: The asterisk was moved from after "an" to after "wine."

p. 113, line 4: "suspened" has been corrected to "suspended."

p. 113, line 20: "of" has been corrected to "off."

p. 134, line 13: "passsed" has been corrected to "passed."

p. 134, line 16: "pent" has been corrected to "spent."

p. 135, line 32: A space has been inserted between "virtuous" and "here."

p. 149, line 16: "opperate" has been corrected to "operate."

p. 150, line 10: A comma has been replaced with a period after "believer."

p. 174, line 16: "poeple" has been corrected to "people."

p. 186, line 31: "de" has been corrected to "du."

p. 188, line 4: "Hudibrass" has been corrected to "Hudibras."

p. 193, line 2: "pronounced; it" has been corrected to "pronounced it;"

p. 197, line 6: "arrival" has been capitalized.

p. 206, line 10: A comma has been moved from after "birth" to after "Mecca."

THE ALGERINE
CAPTIVE

————By your patience,
I will a round unvarnished tale deliver
Of my whole course.————[1]

SHAKESPEARE.

TO HIS EXCELLENCY

DAVID HUMPHREYS, ESQ.[1]

MINISTER OF THE UNITED STATES
AT THE COURT OF LISBON &c.

In Europe, dedications have their price; and the author oftener looks to the plenitude of the pockets, than the brains of his patron.

The American author can hope but little pecuniary emolument from even the sale, and not any from the dedication of his work. To adorn his book with the name of some gentleman, of acknowledged merit, involves his whole interest, in a public address.

With this view, will you, Sir, permit a lover of the Muses, and a biographer of private life, to address to you (a Poet and the Biographer of a Hero)[2] a detail of those miseries of slavery, from which your public energies have principally conduced to liberate hundreds of our fellow citizens.

UPDIKE UNDERHILL

JUNE 20, 1797.

PREFACE

One of the first observations, the author of the following sheets made, upon his return to his native country, after an absence of seven years, was the extreme avidity, with which books of mere amusement were purchased and perused by all ranks of his country-men. When he left New England, books of Biography, Travels, Novels, and modern Romances, were confined to our sea ports; or, if known in the country, were read only in the families of Clergy-men, Physicians, and Lawyers: while certain funeral discourses, the last words and dying speeches of Bryan Shaheen, and Levi Ames,[1] and some dreary somebody's Day of Doom,[2] formed the most di-verting part of the farmer's library. On his return from captivity, he found a surprising alteration in the public taste. In our inland towns of consequence, social libraries had been instituted, composed of books, designed to amuse rather than to instruct; and country booksellers, fostering the new born taste of the people, had filled the whole land with modern Travels, and Novels almost as incredi-ble. The diffusion of a taste, for any species of writing, through all ranks, in so short a time, would appear impracticable to a Euro-pean. The peasant of Europe must first be taught to read, before he can acquire a taste in letters. In New England, the work is half completed. In no other country are there so many people, in proportion to its numbers, who can read and write; and therefore, no sooner was a taste for amusing literature diffused than all orders of country life, with one accord, forsook the sober sermons and Practical Pieties of their fathers, for the gay stories and splendid impieties of the Traveller and the Novelist. The worthy farmer no longer fatigued himself with Bunyan's Pilgrim up the "hill of difficulty" or through the "slough of despond;" but quaffed wine with Brydone[3] in the hermitage of Vesuvius, or sported with Bruce[4] on the fairy land of Abysinia: while Dolly, the dairy maid, and Jonathan, the hired man, threw aside the ballad of the cruel stepmother, over which they had so often wept in concert, and now amused themselves into so agreeable a terrour, with the haunted houses and hobgobblins of Mrs. Ratcliffe,[5] that they were both afraid to sleep alone.

While this love of literature, however frivolous, is pleasing to the man of letters, there are two things to be deplored. The first is that, while so many books are vended, they are not of our own manufacture. If our wives and daughters will wear gauze and ribbands, it is a pity, they are not wrought in our own looms. The second misfortune is that Novels, being the picture of the times, the New England reader is insensibly taught to admire the levity, and often the vices of the parent country. While the fancy is enchanted, the heart is corrupted. The farmer's daughter, while she pities the misfortune of some modern heroine, is exposed to the attacks of vice, from which her ignorance would have formed her surest shield. If the English Novel does not inculcate vice, it at least impresses on the young mind an erroneous idea of the world, in which she is to live. It paints the manners, customs, and habits of a strange country; excites a fondness for false splendour; and renders the homespun habits of her own country disgusting.

There are two things wanted, said a friend to the author: that we write our own books of amusement, and that they exhibit our own manners. Why then do you not write the history of your own life? The first part of it, if not highly interesting, would at least display a portrait of New England manners, hitherto unattempted. Your captivity among the Algerines, with some notices of the manners of that ferocious race, so dreaded by commercial powers, and so little known in our country, would be interesting; and I see no advantage the Novel writer can have over you, unless your readers should be of the sentiment of the young lady, mentioned by Addison in his Spectator,[6] who, he informs us, borrowed Plutarch's lives; and, after reading the first volume, with infinite delight, supposing it to be a Novel, threw aside the others with disgust, because a man of letters had inadvertently told her, the work was founded on FACT.

VOLUME I

Chapter I.

Think of this, good Sirs,
But as a thing of custom—'tis no other,
Only it spoils the pleasure of the time.[1]

Shakespeare.

Argument.

The Author giveth an Account of his gallant Ancestor, Captain John Underhill,[2] his Arrival in Massachusetts, and Persecution by the first Settlers.

I derive my birth from one of the first emigrants to New England, being lineally descended from Captain John Underhill, who came into the Massachusetts in the year one thousand six hundred and thirty; of whom honourable mention is made by that elegant, accurate, and interesting historian, the Reverend Jeremy Belknap,[3] in his History of New Hampshire.

My honoured ancestor had early imbibed an ardent love of liberty, civil and religious, by his service as a soldier among the Dutch, in their glorious and successful struggle for freedom, with Philip the second of Spain; when, though quite a youth, he held a commission in the Earl of Leicester's[4] own troop of guards, who was then sent to the assistance of that brave people, by the renowned Queen Elizabeth of England.

The extravagant passion, which that princess was supposed to entertain for various male favourites, which occasioned the disgrace of one, and the premature death of another, while it has furnished a darling theme to the novelist, and has been wept over in the tragic scene, has never yet received the sober sanction of the historian.

A traditional family anecdote, while it places the affection of the queen for Leicester beyond doubt, may not be unpleasing to the learned reader, and may benefit the English historiographer.

It is well known that this crafty queen, though repeatedly solicited, never efficaciously assisted the Netherlanders, until their affairs were apparently at the lowest ebb, and they in such desperate circumstances, as to offer the sovereignty of their country to her general, the Earl of Leicester. Captain Underhill carried the dispatches to England, and delivered them at the office of Lord Burleigh. The same evening, the queen sent for the captain, and, with apparent perturbation, inquired of him, if he was the messenger from Leicester, and whether he had any private dispatches for her. He replied, that he had delivered all his letters to the secretary of state. She appeared much disappointed, and, after musing some time, said, "So Leicester wants to be a king." Underhill, who was in the general's confidence, replied that the Dutch had indeed made the offer of the sovereignty of their country to her general— esteeming it a great honour, as they said, to have a subject of her grace for their sovereign. No, replied the queen, it is not the Dutch; they hate kings and their divine right; it is the proud Leicester, who yearns to be independent of his own sovereign, who moves this insolent proposal. Tell him, from me, that he must learn to obey, before he is fit to govern. Tell him, added the queen, softening her voice, that obedience may make him a *king indeed*. Immediately after Captain Underhill had taken the public dispatches, the queen sent for him to her privy closet, recalled her verbal message, delivered him a letter for Leicester, directed with her own hand, and a purse of one hundred crowns for himself: charging him to enclose the letter in lead, sink it in case of danger in his passage by sea, and to deliver it privately. On the receipt of this letter, Leicester was violently agitated, walked his chamber the whole of the ensuing night. Soon after, he resigned his command, and returned to England, animated by the brightest hopes of realizing the lofty suggestions of his ambition. With him Captain Underhill returned, and upon the decease of the Earl of Leicester, attached himself to the fortunes of the Earl of Essex,[5] the unfortunate successour to Leicester in the queen's favour. He accompanied that gallant nobleman in his successful attack upon Cadiz, and shared his ill fortune in his fruitless expedition against Tyronne,[6] the rebel chief of the revolted clans of England; and, returning with the Earl into England, by his attachment to that imprudent nobleman, sallying into the streets of London in the petty insurrection, which cost Essex his head,[7] he was obliged to seek safety in Holland, until the accession of King James, in one thousand six hundred and three, when he applied for pardon and leave to return to his native country. But that monarch entertained such an exalted idea of the dignity of kings, and from policy, affected so great a veneration for the memory of his predecessor, that no interest of his friends could procure his pardon for an offence, which, in this day and country, would be considered a simple rout or riot, and punished with a small fine, in that age of kingly glory was supposed to combine treason and blasphemy: treason against the queen in her political capacity, and blasphemy against her as God's representative and vicegerent on earth.

The Reverend Mr. Robinson, with a number of other pious puritans, having fled, from the persecuting fury of the English prelates, to Holland, in one thousand six hundred and three, he dwelt and communed with them a number of years. He was strongly solicited to go with Governour Carver, Elder Brewster,[8] and the other worthies, part of Mr. Robinson's church, to the settlement of Plymouth, and had partly engaged with them, as their chief military officer; but, Captain Miles Standish, his brave fellow soldier in the low countries, undertaking the business, he declined.

How he joined Governour Winthrop,[9] does not appear, but he came over to New England with him, and soon after we find him disciplining the Boston militia, where he was held in such high estimation that he was chosen to represent that town in the general court; but, his ideas of religious toleration being more liberal than those around him, he lost his popularity, and was, on the twentieth of November, one thousand six hundred and thirty seven, disfranchised and eventually banished the jurisdiction of Massachusetts.

The writers of those times differ, as to the particular offence for which he was punished. Some say that it was for holding the antinomian tenets of the celebrated Ann Hutchinson,[10] others that the charge against him was for saying, *That the government at Boston were as zealous as the scribes and pharisees, and as Paul before his conversion.*[11] The best account, I have been able to collect, is, that at the time when the zeal of our worthy forefathers burned the hottest against heretics and sectaries, when good Roger Williams,[12] who settled Providence, the pious Wheelwright,[13] and others, were banished, he, with about sixty other imprudent persons, who did not believe in the then popular arguments of fines, imprisonment, disfranchisement, confiscation, banishments, and halters for the conversion of infidels supposed that the christian faith, which had spread so wonderfully in its infancy, when the sword of civil power was drawn against it, in that age, surrounded by numerous proselites, needed not the same sword unsheathed in its favour. These mistaken people signed a remonstrance against the violent proceedings, which were the order of that day. William Aspinwall and John Coggeshell,[14] two of the Boston representatives, who signed the remonstrance, were sent home, and the town ordered to choose others in their room. Some of the remonstrants recanted, some were fined, some were disfranchised, and others, among whom was Captain Underhill, were banished.

It is said by some authors, that he was charged with the heinous crime of adultery, and that he even confessed it. The candid American author, above named,[15] has fallen into this error. As I am sure it must have given him pain *to speak evil even of the dead,* so I am certain he will rectify this mistake in the next edition of his invaluable history.

That author informs us, page forty three of his first volume, "That he, Captain Underhill, was privately dealt with, on suspicion of adultery, which he disregarded, and therefore on the next sabbath was questioned for it before the church; but the evidence not being sufficient to convict him, the church could only admonish him."—Page forty five, "He went to Boston, and in the same public manner acknowledged his adultery. But his confession was mixed with so many excuses and extenuations, that it gave no satisfaction."

The unwary reader would perhaps conclude, that actual adultery was intended, as well as expressed, in these extracts. The Reverend author himself did not advert to the idea, that the moral law of Boston, in one thousand six hundred and thirty seven, was not so lax as the moral law of the same place, in one thousand seven hundred and eighty four, as explained by the practice of its inhabitants. The rigid discipline of our fathers of that era often construed actions, expressions, and sometimes thoughts, into crimes; which actions in this day, even the most precise would consider either innocent, indifferent, or beneath the dignity of official notice. The fact is, that Captain Underhill, so far from CONFESSING, was never charged with committing actual statute book adultery. At a certain lecture in Boston, instead of noting the referred texts in his bible, according to the profitable custom of the times, this gallant soldier had fixed his eyes stedfastly, and perhaps inordinately, upon one Mistress Miriam Wilbore; who it seems was, at that very time, herself in the breach of the spirit of an existing law, which forbad women to appear in public with uncovered arms and necks, by appearing at the same lecture with a pair of wanton open worked gloves, slit at the thumbs and fingers, for the conveniency of taking snuff; though she was not charged with the latter crime of using tobacco. It was the ADULTERY OF THE HEART, of which my gallant ancestor was accused, and founded on that text of scripture, "Whosoever looketh on a woman to lust after her, hath committed adultery with her already in his heart."[16]

Chapter II.

The glorious sun himself
Bears on his splendid disk, dark spots obscure:
Who, in his bright career, denotes those strains?
Or, basely from his full meridian turns,
And scorns his grateful salutary rays?

AUTHOR'S *Manuscript Poems.*

ARGUMENT.

The Author rescueth from Oblivion a valuable Manuscript Epistle, re-flecting great Light on the Judicial Proceedings, in the first Settlement of Massachusetts: Apologizeth for the Persecutors of his Ancestor.

I have fortunately discovered, pasted on the back of an old Indian deed, a manuscript, which reflects great light upon my ancestor's conduct, and on the transactions of those times; which, according to the beneficial mode of modern historians, I shall transcribe literally.

It should be premised, that in the year one thousand six hundred and thirty six, the governour, deputy governour, three assistants, and three ministers, among whom was Hugh Peters,[1] afterwards hung and quartered in England, for his adherence to Oliver Cromwell, were entreated, by the Massachusetts' court, to make a draft of laws, agreeable to the word of God, to report to the next general court; and, in the interim, the magistrates were directed to determine causes according to the laws, then established, and where no laws existed, then as near to the word of God as they could.

(INDORSED)
BROTHER UNDERHILL's EPISTLE.

TO MASTER HANSERD KNOLLYS[2]—THESE GREETING.
WORTHEE AND BELOVED,

Remembrin my kind love to Mr. Hilton,[3] I now send you some note of my tryalls at Boston.—Oh that I may come out of this, and al the lyke tryalls, as goold sevene times puryfyed in the furnice.

After the Yulers at Boston had fayled to fastenne what Roger Harlakenden[4] was pleased to call the damning errours of Anne Hutchinson upon me, I looked to be sent away in peace; but Governour Winthrop sayd I must abide the examining of ye church; accordingly, on the thyrd day of ye weeke, I was convened before them.—Sir Harry Vane, the governour, Dudley, Haines, with masters Cotton, Shepherd, and Hugh Peters[5] present, with others.—They prepounded that I was to be examined, touching a certain act of adultery I had committed, with one mistress Miriam Wilbore, wife of Samuel Wilbore, for carnally looking to luste after her, at the lecture in Boston, when master Shepherd expounded.—This mistress Miriam hath since been dealte with, for coming to that lecture with a pair of wanton open workt gloves, slit at the thumbs and fingers, for the purpose of taking snuff; for, as master Cotton observed, for what end should those vaine opennings be, but for the intent of taken filthy snuff; and he quoted Gregory Nazianzen[6] upon good works.—Master Peters said, that these opennings were Satan's port holes of firy temptations. Mistress Miriam offerd in excuse of her vain attire, that she was newle married, and appeared in her bridall arraye. Master Peters said, that marriage was the ocasion that the Devil tooke to caste his firy darts, and lay his pit falls of temptation, to catche frale flesh and bloode. She is to be further dealt with for taken snuff. How the use of the good creature tobaccoe can be an offence I cannot see.—Oh my beloved, how these prowde pharisees labour aboute the minte and cummine.[7] Governour Winthrop inquired of mee, if I confessed the matter. I said I wished a coppy of there charge.—Sir Harry Vane said, there was no neede of any coppie, seeing I knew I was guiltee. Charges being made out where there was an uncertantie whether the accused was guiltie or not, and to lighten the accused into the nature of his cryme, here was no need. Master Cotton said, did you not look upon mistress Wilbore? I confessd that I did. He said then you are verelie guiltie, brother Underhill. I said nay, I did not look at the woman lustfully.—Master Peters said, why did you not look at sister Nowell or sister Upham? *I said, verelie they are not desyrable women, as to temporale graces.*—Then Hugh Peters and al cryed, it is enough, he hath confessed, and passed to excommunication. I sayd where is the law by which you condemne me. Winthrop said, there is a committee to draft laws. Brother Peters are you not on that committee, I am sure you have maide a law againste this cryinge sin. Hugh Peters replyed that he had such a law in his minde, but *had not* writtene it downe. Sir Harry Vane said, it is sufficient. Haynes said, *ay, law enough for antinomians.* Master Cotton tooke a bible from his coate and read whoso looketh on a woman, &c.

William Blaxton*[8] hath been with me privelie, he weeps over the cryinge sins of the times, and expecteth soone to goe out of the jurisdiction. I came from England, sais he, because I did not like the lords bishops, but I have yet to praye to be delivered from the lords bretherenne.

Salute brother Fish,[9] and others, who havinge been disappointed of libertie in this wilderness are ernestlie lookinge for a better countre.

> Youre felloe traveller in this vale of tears.
> JOHN UNDERHILL
> *Boston, 28th 4th month,[10] 1638.*

It is with great reluctance I am induced to publish this letter, which appears to reflect upon the justice of the proceedings of our forefathers. I would rather, like the sons of Noah, go backwards and cast a garment over our fathers' nakedness;[11] but the impartiality of a historian, and the natural solicitude to wipe the stains from the memory of my honoured ancestor, will excuse me to the candid. Whoever reflects upon the piety of our forefathers, the noble unrestrained ardour, with which they resisted oppression in England,

---

*When our forefathers first came to Boston, they found this William Blaxton in the possession of the site, where the town now stands. The general court, April 1st, 1633, granted him fifty acres of land, near where his house stood; supposed to be where the pest house in Boston formerly stood.—He afterwards removed to Rhode Island, and lived near Whipple's bridge in Cumberland.—He planted the first orchard in that district, the fruit of which was eaten of one hundred and forty years afterwards, and some of the trees are now standing.—He had been a minister of the church of England, preached often at Providence, and died in a good old age much lamented.

relinquished the delights of their native country, crossed a boisterous ocean, penetrated a savage wilderness, encountered famine, pestilence, and Indian warfare, and transmitted to us their sentiments of independence, that love of liberty, which under God enabled us to obtain our own glorious freedom, will readily pass over those few dark spots of zeal, which clouded their rising sun.

CHAPTER III.

The Devil offered our Lord all the kingdoms of the earth, when the condemned soul did not own one foot of the territory.[1]

ETHAN ALLEN.

ARGUMENT.

Captain Underhill seeks Shelter in Dover in New Hampshire: Is chosen Governour by the Settlers: Driven by the pious Zeal of his Persecutors to seek Shelter in Albany: Reception among the Dutch: Exploits in the Indian Wars: Grant of a valuable Tract of Land: The Author anticipates his encountering certain Land Speculators in Hartford: A Taste of the Sentiments of those Gentlemen: Farther account of his Ancestors.

When the sentence of banishment passed on Captain Underhill, he retired to Dover in New Hampshire, and was elected governour of the European settlers there; but, notwithstanding his great service to the people of Massachusetts, in the Pequod wars,[2] his persecutors in Boston would not allow him to die in peace. First, by writing injurious letters to those he governed; by threats of their power; and lastly, by determining that Dover was within the jurisdiction of Massachusetts, they forced him to flee to Albany, then possessed by the Dutch, under the name of Amboyna.[3]

The Dutch were highly pleased with the Captain, and after Dutchifying his name into Captain Hans Van Vanderhill, they gave him a command of one hundred and twenty men, in their wars with the natives. It is said that he killed one hundred and fifty Indians on

Long Island, and upwards of three hundred on the Main. The laurels of the famous Colonel Church[4] wither in comparison. The Dutch granted him fifty thousand acres of land, then in their possession. Although the English, when they took possession of that country for the Duke of York, afterwards James the second, had promised to quiet the claims of the settlers; yet Captain Underhill, or his posterity, have never availed themselves of the grant.— Mentioning this circumstance, sometime since in Hartford, some gentlemen immediately offered to raise a company and purchase my right. I candidly confessed that I was not possessed of the title, and knew not the particular spot where the land lay, and consequently was unwilling to sell land without title or boundaries. To my surprise they laughed at my scruples, and observed that they wanted the land to speculate upon, to *sell,* and not to *settle.* Titles and boundaries, in such cases, I understood, were indifferent matters, mere trifles.

My brave ancestor at an advanced age, died in Albany, leaving two sons; the youngest of whom removed to the mouth of Hudson, where some of his posterity flourish respectably to this day. The eldest son, Benoni, from whom I am descended, some years after his father's decease, after being the subject of various misfortunes, returned in impoverished circumstances to New Hampshire, where the family have continued ever since.

Chapter IV.

Nor yet alone by day the unerring hand
Of Providence, unseen directs man's path;
But, in the boding vision of the night,
By antic shapes, in gay fantastic dream,
Gives dubious prospect of the coming good;
Or, with fell precipice, or deep swoln flood,
Dank dungeon, or vain flight from savage foe,
The labouring slumberer warns of future ill.

Author's Manuscript Poems.

Argument.

The Author's Birth, and a remarkable Dream of his Mother: Observations on foreboding Dreams: The Author reciteth a Dream of Sir William Phipps,[1] Governour of Massachusetts, and refereth small Infidels to Mather's Magnalia.[2]

I was born on the sixteenth of July, Anno Domini, one thousand seven hundred and sixty two. My mother, some months before my birth, dreamed that she was delivered of me; that I was lying in the cradle, that the house was beset by Indians, who broke into the next room, and took me into the fields with them; that, alarmed by their hideous yellings and warhoops, she ran to the window, and saw a number of young tawny savages, playing at foot ball with my head; while several sachems and sagamores were looking on unconcerned.

This dream made a deep impression on my mother. I well recollect, when a boy, her stroking my flaxen locks, repeating her dream, and observing with a sigh to my father, that she was sure Updike was born to be the sport of fortune, and that he would one day suffer among savages. Dear woman, she had the native Indians in her mind, but never apprehended her poor son's suffering, many years as a slave, among barbarians, more cruel than the monsters of our own woods.

The learned reader will smile contemptuously, perhaps, upon my mentioning dreams, in this enlightened age. I only relate facts, and leave the reader to his own comments. My own opinion of dreams I shall conceal, perhaps because I am ashamed to disclose it. I will venture to observe that, if we inspect the sacred scriptures, we shall find frequent instances, both of direction to duty, and forewarning of future events, communicated by Providence, through the intervention of dreams. Is not the modern christian equally the care of indulgent Heaven, as the favoured Jew, or the beloved patriarch?

Many modern examples, of the foreboding visions of the night, may be adduced. William Phipps, a poor journeyman ship carpenter, dreamed that he should one day ride in his coach, and live in a grand house near Boston common. Many years afterwards, when he was knighted by King William the third, and came from England, governour of Massachusetts Bay, this dream, even as the situation of the grand house, was literally and minutely fulfilled. If the insect infidels of the day doubt this fact, let them consult, for their edification, the learned Doctor Mather's Magnalia, where the whole story, at large, is minutely and amply related.—*It was the errour of the times of monkish ignorance, to believe every thing. It may possibly be the errour of the present day, to credit nothing.*

Chapter V.

'Tis education forms the common mind,
Just as the twig is bent, the tree's inclin'd.[1]

Pope.

Argument.

The Author is placed at a private School: Parental Motives to a College Education: Their design frustrated by family Misfortune.

In my childhood I was sent, as is customary, to a woman's school, in the summer, and to a man's, in the winter season, and made great progress in such learning as my preceptors dealt in. About my twelfth year, our minister, who made it his custom to inspect the schools annually, came to our district. My master, who looked upon me as his best scholar, directed me to read a lesson in Dilworth's spelling book,[2] which I recited as loud as I could speak, without regard to emphasis or stops. This so pleased our minister, who prided himself on the strength of his own lungs, that, a short time after, coming to my father's, to *dicker,* as they stiled it, about a swop of cattle, and not finding my father sharp at the bargain, he changed the discourse upon me; observing how delighted he was with my performances at school. What a pity it was such a genius was not encouraged. Mr. Underhill, you must put Updike to learning. My father pleaded poverty. When I went to Harvard College, replied the minister, I was poor indeed. I had no father with a good farm to assist me; but, with being butler's freshman, and ringing the bell the first year, waiter the three last, and keeping school in the vacations,

I rubbed through, and am now what I am; and who knows, continued he, but when Updike has completed his education, he may make a minister, and possibly, when my usefulness is over, supply our very pulpit.

My mother here interfered. She was a little spare woman. My father was a large bony man; famous, in his youth, for carrying the ring at wrestling; and, in his latter years, for his perseverance at town meetings. But, notwithstanding my father's success in carrying points abroad, my mother, some how or other, contrived always to carry them at home. My father never would acknowledge this; but, when a coarse neighbour would sometimes slily hint the old adage of the gray mare being the better horse, he would say to his particular friends that he always was conqueror in his domestic warfare: but would confess that he loved quiet, and was of late tired of perpetually getting the victory. My mother joined the minister; observing that Updike should have learning, though she worked her hands to the bone to procure it. She did not doubt, when he came to preach, he would be as much run after as the great Mr. Whitfield.[3] I always thought, continued she, the child was a genius; and always intended he should go to college. The boy loves books. He has read Valentine and Orson,[4] and Robinson Crusoe. I went, the other day, three miles to borrow Pilgrim's Progress for him. He has read it through every bit; ay, and understands it too. Why, he stuck a skewer through Apollyon's eye in the picture, to help Christian beat him.[5] My father could not answer my mother's argument. The dicker about the oxen was renewed; and it was concluded to swop even, though my father's were much the likelier cattle, and that I should go that week and study Latin with the minister, and be fitted for college.

With him I studied four years, labouring incessantly at Greek and Latin: as to English grammar, my preceptor, knowing nothing of it himself, could communicate nothing to me. As he was enthusiastically attached to the Greek, and had delivered an oration in that language, at the commencement at Cambridge, when he took his first degree, by his direction, I committed to memory above four hundred of the most sonorous lines in Homer, which I was called to repeat before a number of clergymen, who visited him at an annual convention, in our parish. These gentlemen were ever pleased to express astonishing admiration at my literary acquirements. One of them prognosticated that I should be a general, from the fire and force, with which I recited Homer's battles of the Greeks and Trojans. Another augered that I should be a member of congress, and equal the Adamses in oratory,[6] from my repeating the speeches, at the councils of the heathen gods, with such attention to the cæsura.[7] A third was sure that I should become a Witherspoon in divinity,[8] from the pathos, with which I declaimed Jupiter's speech to all the gods. In fine, these gentlemen considered the classics the source of all valuable knowledge. With them dead languages were more estimable than living; and nothing more necessary to accomplish a young man for all, that is profitable and honourable in life, than a profound knowledge of Homer. One of them gravely observed that he was sure General Washington read Greek; and that he never would have captured the Hessians at Trenton, if he had not taken his plan of operation from that of Ulysses and Diomede seizing the horses of Rhesus, as described in the tenth book of the Iliad.

Thus flattered by the learned, that I was in the high road to fame, I gulped down daily portions of Greek, while my preceptor made quarterly visits to my father's barn yard, for pay for my instruction.

In June, one thousand seven hundred and eighty, my father began seriously to think of sending me to college. He called upon a neighbour, to whom he had sold part of his farm, for some cash. His creditor readily paid, the whole sum due, down in paper money, and my father found, to his surprize, that the value of three acres paid him the principal and interest of the whole sum, for which he had sold seventy five acres of land, five years before. This was so severe a stroke of ill fortune, that it entirely frustrated the design of sending me to college.

CHAPTER VI.

Heteroclita sunto.[1]

LILLY'S GRAMMAR.

ARGUMENT.

This Chapter containeth an Eulogy on the Greek Tongue.

What added to the misfortune, mentioned in the last chapter, a worthy divine, settled in Boston, passing through our town, told my father, in a private conversation, that all the Greek I had acquired, was of no other service than fitting me for college. My father was astonished. He was a plain unlettered man, of strong natural abilities. Pray, Reverend Sir, said my father, do they not learn this Greek language at college? If so, why do such wise men, as the governours of colleges, teach boys what is entirely useless? I thought that the sum of all good education was, to teach youth those things, which they were to practise in after life. Learning, replied our enlightened visitor, has its fashions; and, like other fashions of this world, they pass away. When our forefathers founded the college, at Cambridge, critical knowledge in the mazes and subtleties of school divinity was all the mode. He that could give a new turn to an old text, or detect a mistranslation in the version, was more admired than the man, who invented printing, discovered the magnetic powers, or contrived an instrument of agriculture, which should abridge the labour of the husbandman. The books of our faith, with the voluminous commentaries of the fathers, being originally written, in what are now called, the dead languages, the knowledge of those languages was then necessary, for the accomplishment of the fashionable scholar. The moderns, of New England, have ceased to interest themselves in the disputes, whether a civil oath may be administered to an unregenerate man; or, whether souls, existing merely in the contemplation of Deity, are capable of actual transgression. Fashion has given a new direction to the pursuits of the learned. They no longer soar into the regions of infinite space; but endeavour, by the aid of natural and moral philosophy, to amend the manners and better the condition of man: and the college, at Cambridge, may be assimilated to an old beau, with his pocket holes under his arm pits, the skirts of his coat to his ancles, and three gross of buttons on his breeches; looking with contempt on the more easy, useful garb of the present day, for deviating from what was fashionable in his youth.

But, inquired my father, is there not some valuable knowledge contained in those Greek books? All that is useful in them, replied our visitor, is already translated into English; and more of the sense and spirit may be imbibed, from translations, than most scholars would be able to extract, from the originals, if they even availed themselves of such an acquaintance with that language, as is usually acquired, at college.

Well, replied my father, do you call them dead languages. It appears to me now, that confining a lad of lively genius to the study of them, for five or six of the most precious years of his youth, is like the ingenious cruelty of those tyrants, I have heard of, who chained the living and the dead together. If Updike went to college, I should wish he would learn, not *hard words,* but *useful things.*

You spake of governours of colleges, continued our visitor. Let me observe, as an apology, for the concern they may be supposed to have, in this errour, that they are moral, worthy men, who have passed the same dull routine of education, and whose knowledge is necessarily confined to these defunct languages. They must teach their pupils what they know, not what they do not know. That measure, which was measured unto them, they mete out, most liberally, unto others.

Should not the legislature, as the fathers of the people, interfere, inquired my father? We will not talk politics, at this time, replied our visitor.

My father was now determined that I should not go to college. He concealed this conversation from me, and I was left to be proud of my Greek. The little advantage, this deceased language has since been to me, has often caused me sorely to regret the mispense of time, in acquiring it. The French make it no part of their academical studies. Voltaire, D'Alembert, and Diderot, when they completed their education, were probably ignorant of the *cognata tempora*[2] of a Greek verb.

It was resolved that I should labour on my father's farm; but alas! a taste for Greek had quite eradicated a love for labour. Poring so intensely on Homer and Virgil had so completely filled my brain with the heathen mythology, that I imagined a Hamadryade in every sapling, a Naiad in every puddle; and expected to hear the sobbings of the infant Fauns, as I turned the furrow. I gave Greek names to all our farming tools; and cheered the cattle with hexameter verse. My father's hired men, after a tedious day's labour in the woods, inspecting our stores, for refreshment, instead of the customary bread and cheese and brandy, found Homer's Iliad, Virgil Delphini and Schrevelius's Lexicon,[3] in the basket.

After I had worked on the farm some months, having killed a fat heifer of my father's, upon which the family depended for their winter's beef, covered it with green boughs, and laid it in the shade to putrify, in order to raise a swarm of bees, after the manner of Virgil; which process, notwithstanding I followed closely the directions in the georgics,[4] some how or other, failed, my father consented to my mother's request, that I should renew my career of learning.

Chapter VII.

Delightful task! to rear the tender thought,
To teach the young idea how to shoot,
To pour the fresh instruction o'er the mind,
To breathe th' enliv'ning spirit, and to fix
The gen'rous purpose in the glowing breast.[1]

Thomson's Seasons.

Argument.

The Author keepeth a country School: The Anticipations, Pleasures and Profits of a Pedagogue.

By our minister's recommendation, I was engaged to keep a school, in a neighbouring town, so soon as our fall's work was over.

How my heart dilated with the prospect, in the tedious interval, previous to my entering upon my school. How often have I stood suspended over my dung fork, and anticipated my scholars, seated in awful silence around me, my arm chair and birchen sceptre of authority. There was an echo in my father's sheep pasture. More than once have I repaired there alone, and exclaimed with a loud voice, is MASTER Updike Underhill at home? I would speak with MASTER Underhill, for the pleasure of hearing how my title sounded. Dost thou smile, indignant reader, pause and recollect if these sensations have not been familiar to thee, at sometime in thy life. If thou answerest disdainfully—no—then I aver thou hast never been a corporal in the militia, or a sophimore at college.

At times, I however entertained less pleasing, but more rational contemplations on my prospects. As I had been once unmercifully whipt, for detecting my master in a false concord,[2] I resolved to be mild in my government, to avoid all manual correction, and doubted not by these means to secure the love and respect of my pupils.

In the interim of school hours, and in those peaceful intervals, when my pupils were engaged in study, I hoped to indulge myself with my favourite Greek. I expected to be overwhelmed with the gratitude of their parents, for pouring the fresh instruction over the minds of their children, and teaching their young ideas how to shoot. I anticipated independence from my salary, which was to be equal to four dollars, hard money, per month, and my boarding; and expected to find amusement and pleasure among the circles of the young, and to derive information and delight from the classic converse of the minister.

In due time my ambition was gratified, and I placed at the head of a school, consisting of about sixty scholars. Excepting three or four overgrown boys of eighteen, the generality of them were under the age of seven years. Perhaps a more ragged, ill bred, ignorant set, never were collected, for the punishment of a poor pedagogue. To study in school was impossible. Instead of the silence I anticipated, there was an incessant clamour. Predominant among the jarring sounds were, Sir, may I read? May I spell? Master, may I go out? Will master mend my pen? What with the pouting of the small children, sent to school, not to learn, but to keep them out of "harm's way," and the gruff surly complaints of the larger ones, I was nearly distracted. Homer's *poluphlosboio thalasses,* roaring sea, was a whisper to it. My resolution, to avoid beating of them, made me invent small punishments, which often have a salutary impression, on delicate minds; but they were insensible to shame. The putting of a paper fool's cap on one, and ordering another under my great chair, only excited mirth in the school; which the very delinquents themselves often increased, by loud peals of laughter. Going, one frosty morning, into my school, I found one of the larger boys sitting by the fire in my arm chair. I gently requested him to remove. He replied that he would, when he had warmed himself; "father finds wood, and not you." To have my throne usurped, in the face of the whole school, shook my government to the centre. I immediately snatched my two foot rule, and laid it pretty smartly across his back. He quitted the chair, muttering that he would tell father. I found his threats of more consequence than I apprehended. The same afternoon, a tall, rawboned man called me to the door; immediately collering me with one hand, and holding a cart whip over my head with the other; with fury in his face, he vowed he would whip the skin from my bones, if ever I struck Jotham again: ay, he would do it that very moment, if he was not afraid I would take the law of him. This was the only instance of the overwhelming gratitude of parents I received. The next day, it was reported all over town, what a cruel man the master was. "Poor Jotham came into school, half frozen and near fainting; master had been sitting a whole hour by the warm fire; he only begged him to let him warm himself a little, when the master rose in a rage, and cut open his head with the tongs, and his life was despaired of."

Fatigued with the vexations of my school, I one evening repaired to the tavern, and mixed with some of the young men of the town. Their conversation I could not relish; mine they could not comprehend. The subject of race horses being introduced, I ventured to descant upon Xanthus, the immortal courser of Achilles. They had never heard of 'squire Achilles, or his horse; but they offered to bet two to one, that Bajazet, the Old Roan, or the deacon's mare, Pumpkin and Milk, would beat him, and challenged me to appoint time and place.

Nor was I more acceptable among the young women. Being invited to spend an evening, after a quilting, I thought this a happy opportunity to introduce Andromache, the wife of the great Hector, at her loom; and Penelope, the faithful wife of Ulysses, weaving her seven years web. This was received with a stupid stare, until I mentioned the long time the queen of Ulysses was weaving; when a smart young woman observed, that she supposed Miss Penelope's yarn was rotted in whitening, that made her so long: and then told a tedious story of a piece of cotton and linen she had herself woven, under the same circumstances. She had no sooner finished, than, to enforce my observations, I recited above forty lines of Greek, from the Odyssey, and then began a dissertation on the *cæsura*. In the midst of my harrangue, a florid faced young man, at the further end of the room, with two large prominent foreteeth, remarkably white, began to sing,

"Fire upon the mountains, run boys, run;"

And immediately the whole company rushed forward, to see who should get a chance in the reel of six.

I was about retiring, fatigued and disgusted, when it was hinted to me, that I might wait on Miss Mima home; but as I could recollect no word in the Greek, which would construe into *bundling*,[3] or any of Homer's heroes, who *got the bag*,[4] I declined. In the Latin, it is true, that Æneas and Dido, in the cave, seem something like a precedent. It was reported all over the town, the next day, that master was a *papish*,[5] as he had talked French two hours.

Disappointed of recreation, among the young, my next object was the minister. Here I expected pleasure and profit. He had spent many years in preaching, for the edification of private families, and was settled in the town, in a fit of enthusiasm; when the people drove away a clergyman, respectable for his years and learning. This he was pleased to call an awakening. He lectured me, at the first onset, for not attending the conference and night meetings; talked much of gifts, and decried human learning, as carnal and devilish, and well he might, he certainly was under no obligations to it; for a new singing master coming into town, the young people, by their master's advice, were for introducing Dr. Watts's version of the Psalms.[6] Although I argued with the minister an hour, he remains firmly convinced, to this day, that the version of Sternhold and Hopkins[7] is the same in language, letter, and metre, with those Psalms King David chaunted, in the city of Jerusalem.

As for the independence I had founded, on my wages, it vanished, like the rest of my scholastic prospects. I had contracted some debts. My request for present payment, was received with astonishment. I found, I was not to expect it, until the next autumn, and then not in cash, but produce; to become my own collector, and pick up my dues, half a peck of corn or rye in a place.

I was almost distracted, and yearned for the expiration of my contract, when an unexpected period was put to my distress. News was brought, that, by the carelessness of the boys, the school house was burnt down. The common cry now was, that I ought, in justice, to pay for it; as to my want of proper government the carelessness of the boys ought to be imputed. The beating of Jotham was forgotten, and a thousand stories of my want of proper spirit circulated. These reports, and even the loss of a valuable *Gradus ad Parnassum*,[8] did not damp my joy. I am sometimes led to believe, that my emancipation from real slavery in Algiers, did not afford me sincerer joy, than I experienced at that moment.

I returned to my father, who received me with kindness. My mother heard the story of my discomfitures with transport; as, she said, she had no doubt that her dream, about my falling into the hands of savages, was now out.

Chapter VIII.

Search then the ruling passion.[1]

Pope.

Argument.

A sure Mode of discovering the Bent of a young Man's Genius.

I abode at home the remainder of the winter. It was determined that I should pursue one of the learned professions. My father, with parental pride and partiality, conceiving my aversion to labour, my inattention to farming business, and the tricks I had played him, the preceding season, as the sure indications of genius. He now told the story of the putrified heifer, with triumph; as he had read, in the news papers, that playing with paper kites was the foundation of Doctor Franklin's fame; that John Locke, who dissected the human mind, and discovered the circulation of the soul, had, in the full exercise of his understanding, played at duck and drake,[2] on the Thames, with his gold watch, while he gravely returned the pebble stone, which he held in his other hand, into his fob; and, that the learned Sir Isaac Newton made soap bladders with the funk[3] of a tobacco pipe, and was, ever after, so enamoured with his sooty junk, as to make use of the delicate finger of a young lady, he courted, as a pipe stopper.

I was allowed the choice of my profession, to discover the bent of my genius. By the advice of a friend, my father put into my hands, what he was told were some of the prime books, in the sev-

eral sciences. In divinity, I read ten funeral, five election, three or-
dination, and seventeen farewell sermons, Bunyan's Holy War, the
Life of Colonel Gardner, and the Religious Courtship.[4] In law, the
Statutes of New Hampshire and Burn's Justice abridged.[5] In physic,
Buchan's Family Physician, Culpepper's Midwifery, and Turner's
Surgery.[6] The agreeable manner in which this last author relates his
own wonderful cures, the lives of his patients, and his remarkable
dexterity, in extracting a pound of candles, from the arm of a
wounded soldier; the spirited horse, the neat little saddle bags, and
tipped bridle, of our own doctor, determined me in favour of
physic. My father did not oppose my choice. He only dryly observed, that he did not know what pretensions our family had to
practise physic, as he could not learn that we had ever been remarkable for killing any but Indians.

CHAPTER IX.

He, from thick films, shall purge the visual ray,
And on the sightless eye ball pour the day.[1]

POPE.

ARGUMENT.

The Author commences the Study of Physic, with a celebrated Physician and Occulist: A Philosophical Detail of the Operation of Couching for the Gutta Serena, by his Preceptor, upon a young Man, born Blind.

The next spring, I entered upon my studies, with a physician, not more justly celebrated for his knowledge of the materia medica,[2] than for his peculiar dexterity and success, in couching for the gutta serena,[3] and restoring persons, even born blind, to sight. The account of a cure he performed, after I had been with him about a year, may not be unacceptable to the lovers of natural research. The subject was a young man, of twenty two years of age, of a sweet disposition, amiable manners, and oppulent connexions. He was born stone blind. His blindness was in some measure compensated, by the attention of his friends; and the encreased power of his other organs of perception. His brothers and sisters enriched his mind, by reading to him, in succession, two hours every day, from the best authors. His sense of feeling was astonishingly delicate, and his hearing, if possible, more acute. His senses of taste and smelling, were not so remarkable. After the customary salutation, of shaking hands, with a stranger, he would know a person, by the touch of the same hand, several years after, though absent in the interim. He could read a book or news paper, newly printed, tolerably well, by tracing, with the tip of his finger, the indents of the types. He acquired a knowledge of the letters of the alphabet early, from the prominent letters on the gingerbread alphabets of the baker. He was master of music, and had contrived a board, perforated with many gimblet holes; and, with the assistance of a little bag of wooden pegs, shaped at top, according to his directions, he could prick almost any tune, upon its being sung to him. When in a large company, who sat silent, he could distinguish how many persons were present, by noting, with his ear, their different manner of breathing. By the rarity or density of the air, not perceivable by those in company, he could distinguish high ground from low; and by the motion of the summer's breeze, too small to move the loftiest leaf, he would pronounce, whether he was in a wood or open country.

He was an unfeigned believer, in the salutary truths of christianity. He had imbibed its benevolent spirit. When he spoke of religion, his language was love to God, and good will to man. He was no zealot, but, when he talked of the wonders of creation, he was animated with a glow of enthusiasm. You observed, the other day, as we were walking on this plain, my friend, addressing himself to me, as I was intimate in the family, that you knew a certain person, by his gait, when at so great a distance, that you could not discern his features. From this you took occasion to observe, that you saw the master hand of the great Creator, in the obvious difference that was between man and man: not only the grosser difference between the Indian, the African, the Esquimeaux, and the white man; but that which distinguishes and defines accurately, men of the same nation, and even children of the same parents. You observed, that as all the children of the great family of the earth, were compounded of similar members, features, and lineaments, how wonderfully it displayed the skill of the Almighty Artist, to model such an infinite variety of beings, and distinctly diversify them, from the same materials. You added, that the incident, you had noticed, gave fresh instance of admiration; for you was now convinced that, if even all men had been formed of so near resemblance, as not to be discerned from each other, when at rest; yet, when in motion, from their gait, air, and manner, they might readily be distinguished. While you spoke, I could perceive, that you pitied me, as being blind to a wonderful operation of creative power. I too, in my turn, could triumph. Blind as I am, I have discovered a still minuter, but as certain a distinction, between the children of men, which has escaped the touch of your eyes. Bring me five men, perfect strangers to me; pair the nails of the same finger, so as to be even with the fingers' ends, let me touch, with the tip of my finger, the nails thus prepared. Tell me each person's name, as he passes in contact before me, bring the same persons to me one month afterwards, with their nails paired, in the same manner, and I will call every one by his right name. For, be assured, my friend, that artist, who has denied to me that thing called light, hath opened the eyes of my mind, to know that there is not a greater difference between the African and the European, than what I could discover, between the finger nails of all the men of this world. This experiment he afterwards tried, with uniform success. It was amusing, in a gayer hour, to hear him argue the superiority of the touch to the sight. Certainly, the feeling is a nobler sense, than that you call sight. I infer it from the care nature has taken of the former, and her disregard to the latter. The eyes are comparatively poor, puny, weak organs. A small blow, a mote, or a straw may reduce those, who see with them, to a situation as pitiable as mine; while feeling is diffused over the whole body. Cut off my arm, and a sense of feeling remains. Completely dismember me, and, while I live, I possess it. It is coexistent with life itself.

The senses of smelling and taste are but modifications of this noble sense, distinguished, through the inaccuracy of men, by other names. The flavour of the most delicious morsel is felt by the tongue; and, when we smell the aromatic, it is the effluvia of the rose, which comes in contact with the olfactory nerves. You, that enjoy sight, inadvertently confess its inferiority. My brother, honing his penknife, the other day, passed it over his thumb nail, to discover if the edge was smooth. I heard him, and inquired, why he did not touch it with his eyes, as he did other objects. He confessed that he could not discover the gaps, by the sight. Here, the superiority of the most inaccurate feat of the feeling, was manifest. To conclude, he would archly add: in marriage, the most important concern in life, how many miserable, of both sexes, are left to deplore, in tears, their dependence on this treacherous thing, called sight. From this danger, I am happily secured, continued he, smiling and pressing the hand of his cousin, who sat beside him; a beautiful blooming young woman, of eighteen, who had been bred with him, from childhood, and whose affection for him, was such that she was willing, notwithstanding his blindness, to take him as a partner for life. They expected shortly to be married. Notwithstanding his accuracy and veracity upon subjects, he could comprehend; there were many, on which he was miserably confused. He called sight the touch of the eyes. He had no adequate idea of colours. White, he supposed, was like the feeling of down; and scarlet he resembled to the sound of martial music. By passing his hands over the porcelain, earthern, or plaister of Paris images, he could readily conceive of their being representations of men or animals. But he could have no idea of pictures. I presented him a large picture of his grand father, painted with oil colours on canvass; told him whose resemblance it was. He passed his hand over the smooth surface and mused. He repeated this; exclaimed it was wonderful; looked melancholy; but never asked for the picture again.

Upon this young man, my preceptor operated successfully. I was present during the whole process, though few were admitted. Upon the introduction of the couching instrument, and the removal of the film from the retina, he appeared confused. When the operation was completed, and he was permitted to look around him, he was violently agitated. The irritability of the ophthalmic muscles faintly expressed the perturbation of his mind. After two and twenty years of total darkness, to be thus awakened to a new world of sensation and light; to have such a flood of day poured on his benighted eye ball, overwhelmed him. The infant sight was too weak, for the shock, and he fainted. The doctor immediately intercepted the light with the proper bandages, and, by the application of volatiles,[4] he was revived. The next day, the dressings were re-moved. He had fortified his mind, and was more calm. At first, he appeared to have lost more than he had gained, by being restored to vision. When blind, he could walk tolerably well, in places familiar to him. From sight, he collected no ideas of distance. Green was a colour peculiarly agreeable to the new born sight. Being led to the window, he was charmed with a tree in full verdure, and extended his arms to touch it, though at ten rods distance. To distinguish objects within reach, he would close his eyes, feel of them with his hands, and then look earnestly upon them.

According to a preconcerted plan, the third day, his bandages were removed, in the presence of his parents, brothers, sisters, friends, and of the amiable, lovely girl, to whom he was shortly to be married. By his request, a profound silence was to be observed, while he endeavoured to discover the person of her, who was the object of his dearest affection. It was an interesting scene. The company obeyed his injunction. Not a finger moved, or a breath aspi-rated. The bandage was then removed; and, when he had recovered from the confusion of the instant effusion of light, he passed his eye hastily over the whole group. His sensations were novel and inter-esting. It was a moment of importance. For aught he knew, he might find the bosom partner of his future life, the twin soul of his affec-tion, in the fat scullion wench, of his father's kitchen; or in the per-son of the toothless, palsied, decriped nurse, who held the bason of gruel at his elbow.

In passing his eye a second time over the circle, his attention was arrested, by his beloved cousin. The agitations of her lovely fea-tures, and the evanescent blush on her cheek, would have at once betrayed her, to a more experienced eye. He passed his eye to the next person, and immediately returned it to her. It was a moment big with expectation. Many a finger was raised to the lips of the spectators, and many a look, expressive of the silence she should preserve, was cast towards her. But the conflict was too violent for her delicate frame. He looked more intensely; she burst into tears, and spoke. At the well known voice he closed his eyes, rushed towards her, and clasped her in his arms. I envied them their feelings; but I thought then, and do now, that the sensations of my preceptor, the skilful humane operator, were more enviable. The man who could restore life and usefulness, to the darling of his friends, and scatter light in the paths of an amiable young pair, must have known a joy never surpassed; except, with reverence be it spoken, by the satisfaction of our benevolent Saviour, when, by his miraculous power, he opened the eyes of the actually blind, made the dumb to sing, and the lame and impotent leap for joy.

Chapter X.

Was Milton blind, who pierc'd the gloom profound
Of lowest Hades, thro' seven fold night
Of shade, with shade compact, saw the arch fiend
From murky caves, and fathomless abyss,
Collect in close divan, his fierce compeers:
Or, with the mental eye, thro' awful clouds,
And darkness thick, unveil'd the throne of him,
Whose vengeful thunder smote the rebel fiend?
Was *Sanderson*,[1] who to the seeing crowd
Of wond'ring pupils taught, sightless himself,
The wond'rous structure of the human eye?

AUTHOR'S Manuscript Poems.

ARGUMENT.

Anecdotes of the celebrated Doctor Moyes.[2]

Mentioning the subject of the last chapter, to the celebrated Doctor Moyes, who, though blind, delivered a lecture upon optics, and delineated the properties of light and shade, to the Bostonians, in the year one thousand seven hundred and eighty five; he exhibited a more astonishing illustration of the power of the touch. A highly polished plane of steel was presented to him, with a stroke of an etching tool, so minutely engraved upon it, that it was invisible to the naked eye, and only discoverable with a powerful magnifying glass; with his fingers he discovered the extent, and measured the length of the line.

This gentleman lost his sight, at three years of age. He informed me, that being overturned, in a stage coach, one dark rainy evening, in England, when the carriage, and four horses, were thrown into a ditch, the passengers and driver, with two eyes a piece, were obliged to apply to him, who had none, for assistance, in extricating the horses. As for me, said he, after I had recovered from the astonishment of the fall, and discovered that I had escaped unhurt, I was quite at home in the dark ditch. The inversion of the order of things was amusing. I, that was obliged to be led like a child, in the glaring sun, was now directing eight persons, to pull here, and haul there, with all the dexterity and activity of a man of war's boatswain.

Chapter XI.

None are so surely caught, when they are catch'd,
As Wit turn'd Fool: Folly, in Wisdom hatch'd,
Hath Wisdom's warrant, and the help of school;
And Wit's own grace, to grace a learned Fool.[1]

SHAKESPEARE.

Argument.

The Author spouteth Greek, in a Sea Port: Its Reception among the Polite: He attempteth an Ode, in the Stile of the Ancients.

I passed my time very agreeably, with my preceptor; though I could not help being astonished, that a man of his acknowledged learning, should not, sometimes, quote Greek. Of my acquirements, in that language, I was still proud. I attributed the indifference, with which it was received in the town, where I had kept school, to the rusticity and ignorance of the people. As I now moved in the circles of polished life, I ventured, sometimes, when the young ladies had such monstrous colds, as that they could not, by the earnest persuasions of the company, be prevailed on to sing; when it had been frequently observed, that it was quaker meeting,[2] to spout a few lines from the Iliad. It is true, they did not interrupt me with,

"Fire upon the mountains, run boys, run;"

But the most sonorous lines of the divine blind bard were received with cold approbation of politeness. One young lady, alone, seemed pleased. She would frequently ask me, to repeat those lines of Wabash poetry. Though once, in the sublime passage of the hero Ulysses, hanging fifty young maidens, with his own hands, in the Odyssey, I heard the term, pedant, pronounced with peculiar emphasis, by a beau, at my back. If I had taken the hint, and passed my Greek upon my companions, for Indian, they would have heard me with rapture. I have since known that worthy, indefatigable missionary to the Indians, the Reverend Mr. K———,[3] the modern Elliot,[4] entertain the same companies, for whole evenings, with speeches in the aboriginal of America, as unintelligible to them, as my insulted Greek.

I was so pleased with the young lady, who approved the Greek heroics, that I determined to make my first essay, in metre, in an ode, addressed to her, by name. I accordingly mustered all the high sounding epithets of the immortal Grecian bard, and scattered them with profusion, through my ode. I praised her golden locks, and assimilated her to the ox eyed[5] Juno; sent her a correct copy, and dispersed a number of others, among her friends. I afterwards found, that what I intended as the sublimest panegyric, was received as cutting insult. The golden tresses, and the ox eyed epithet, the most favourite passages, in my poem, were very unfortunate; as the young lady was remarkable, for very prominent eyes, which resembled what, in horses, are called wall eyes. Her hair was, what is vulgarly called, carroty. Its unfashionable colour she endeavoured, in vain, to conceal, by the daily use of a leaden comb.

CHAPTER XII.

Honour's a sacred tie, the law of kings,
The noble mind's distinguished perfection,
Which aids and strengthens virtue, where it meets her,
And imitates her actions, where she's not.[1]

ADDISON.

ARGUMENT.

The Author in imminent Danger of his Life in a Duel.

The very next morning, after I had presented my ode, and before I
had heard of its reception, a young gentleman, very genteelly dressed,
entered our drug room, where I was compounding a cathartic, with
my spatula; and, with a very stately air, inquired for Mr. Updike
Underhill. Upon being informed that I was the person, with two of
the most profound bows, I had ever seen, he advanced towards me,
and with slow and solemn emphasis, said, then sir, I have the honour to present you with a billet, from my friend, Mr. Jasper T——.
Two more bows, as stately and low as the former. I took the letter,
which was as big as a governmental packet; and, in the midst of a
large folio sheet, read the following letter, from Mr. Jasper T——,
a professed admirer of the young lady, to whom I had addressed my
ode, after the manner of the Greeks.

DEAR SIR,
  Them there very extraordinary pare of varses, you did yourself the
onner to address to a young lada of my partecting acquaintance calls

loudly for explination. I shall be happy to do myself the onner of wasting a few charges of powder with you on the morro morning precisely at one half hour before sun rosa at the lower end of —— wharff.

Dear Sir, I am with grate parsonal esteem your sincere friend, ardent admirer well wisher and umble servant to command,

JASPER T——

Please to be punctual to the hour seconds if you incline.

July 24th, 1782.
Thursday A. M. ante merry dying.

Though I was engaged to watch that night, with one of my preceptor's customers; yet, as Mr. Jasper T——, seemed so friendly and civil, I could not find it in my heart, to refuse him, and replied that I would, with pleasure, wait upon the gentleman. Sir, resumed the bearer, you are a man of honour, every inch of you, and I am your most obedient, most obsequious, and most humble servant: and then, making two profound bows, in the shop, and one more at the door, he retired. He was no sooner departed, than I sat down, to reperuse this elegant and very extraordinary billet. I had no particular acquaintance with Mr. Jasper T——, and why he should write to me, at all, puzzled me. The first part of the letter, I doubted not, contained an approbation of my ode, and a request to be indulged with an explanation of some of its peculiar beauties. I began to recollect illustrations and parodies, from some favourite passages in the Iliad. But, what we were to do, in wasting a few charges of powder, was utterly inexplicable. At one time, indeed, I thought it an invitation to shoot partridges, and bethought myself of scouring a long barrelled gun, which had descended as an heir loom in our family; and had, perhaps, killed Indians, on Long Island, in the hands of my brave ancestor, Captain John Underhill. Then again, I reflected, that the lower end of a wharf, in a populous town, was not the most probable place, to spring a covey of partridges. But what puzzled me most, was his punctual attention to hours, and even seconds. My doubts were all cleared, by the entrance of a fellow student, to whom I communicated the letter. He was born in Carolina, and understood the whole business. It is a challenge, said he. A challenge! exclaimed I. For what? Why only, repeated he cooly, to fight a duel, with Mr. Jasper T——, with sword and pistol. Pho! replied I, you banter. Do look at the conclusion of the letter. Will you make me believe that any man, in his senses, would conclude, with all these expressions of esteem and friendship, an invitation to give him an opportunity of cutting my throat, or blowing my brains out? You have been bred in yankee land, replied my fellow student. Men of honour are above the common rules of propriety and common sense. This letter, which is a challenge, bating some little inaccuracies of grammar and spelling, in substance, I assure you, would not disgrace a man of the highest honour; and, if Mr. Jasper T—— acts as much the man of honour, on the wharf, as he has on paper, he will preserve the same stile of good breeding and politeness there also. While, with one hand, he, with a deadly longe, passes his sword through your lungs, he will take his hat off, with the other, and bow gracefully to your corps. Lord deliver me from such politeness, exclaimed I. It seems to me, by your account of things, that the principal difference between a man of honour, and a vulgar murderer, is that the latter will kill you in a rage, while the former will write you complaisant letters, and smile in your face, and bow gracefully, while he cuts your throat. Honour, or no honour, I am plaguy sorry I accepted his invitation. Come, continued my fellow student, you consider this little affair too seriously. I must indoctrinate you. There is no more danger, in these town duels, than in pounding our great mortar. Why, I fought three duels myself in Carolina, before I was seventeen years old; and one was for an affront offered to the negro wench, who suckled me: and I declare I had rather fight ten more, than pass once, in a stage waggon, over Horse Neck. I see your antagonist has offered you to bring a second. I will go with you. When you arrive on the ground, we seconds shall mark out your position, to stand in, and to be sure, as in case of blood shed, we shall come into difficulty, we shall place you at a pretty respectable distance. You will then turn a copper for the first fire; but I should advise you to grant it to him. This will give him a vast idea of your firmness, and contempt of danger. Your antagonist, with banishment from his country, and the gallows staring him in the face, will be sure not to hit you, on his own account. The ball will pass, at least, ten rods over your head. You must then discharge your pistol, in the air, and offer him to fire again; as, in the language of the duellist, you will have given him his life, so it will be highly inconsistent, in him, to again attempt yours. We seconds shall immediately interfere, and pronounce you both men of honour. The matter in controversy will be passed over. You will shake hands, commence warm friends, and the ladies will adore you. Oh! Updike, you are a lucky fellow. I cannot think, said I, why Mr. Jasper T——, should have such bloody designs against me. I never intended to affront the young lady. Lisp not a word of that, replied my instructer, as you value your reputation on 'change.[2] When he has fired over your head, you may confess what you please, with honour; but however inoffensive you may have been, if you make such a confession before, you are a man of no honour. You will be posted, in the coffee house, for a coward. Notwithstanding the comfortable address of my friend, the thoughts of a premature death, or being crippled for life, distressed me. Nor was the fear of killing my antagonist, and of what my poor parents would suffer, from my being exposed to infamous punishment, less alarming. I passed some hours of dreadful anxiety; when I was relieved from my distress, in a way I little apprehended. My challenger, who had lived some years in town, as a merchant's clerk, viewing me as a raw lad, from the country, that would never dare accept his challenge, when this messenger returned, was petrified with astonishment. When assured that I had accepted his challenge, as a man of courage and honour, his heart died within him. His friend had no sooner gone to prepare the pistols, than by communicating the business, as a great secret, to two or three female friends, the intended duel was noised about town. The justices, selectmen, and grand jurors, convened. Warrants were issued, and constables dispatched into all quarters. I was apprehended, in the sick man's chamber, where I was watching, by the high sheriff, two deputies, three constables, and eleven stout assistants; carried, in the dead of the night, before the magistrates, where I met my antagonist, guarded by a platoon of the militia, with a colonel at their head. We were directed to shake hands, make friends, and pronounce, on our honours, that we would drop an affair, which we had, neither of us, any heart to pursue. My acceptance of the challenge, however unintentional, established my reputation, among the bucks and belles. The former pronounced me a man of spunk and spirit; and the latter were proud of my arm in an evening rural walk on the paved street. None dared to call me pedant; and, I verily believe that, if I had spouted a whole Iliad, in the ball room, no one would have ventured to interrupt me: for I had proved myself a MAN OF HONOUR.

Updike Underhill taking leave of the learned Lady.

Chapter XIII.

The flower of learning, and the bloom of wit.[1]

YOUNG.

Argument.

The Author is happy, in the Acquaintance of a Learned Lady.

In the circle of my acquaintance, there was a young lady, of not the most promising person, and, of rather a vinegar aspect, who was just approximating towards thirty years of age. Though, by avoiding married parties, mingling with very young company, dressing airily; shivering in lawn and sarcenet,[2] at meeting, in December; affecting a girlish lisp, blush, and giggle, she was still endeavouring to ward off that invidious appellation of old maid. Upon good grounds, I am led to believe, that the charity of the tea table had added to her years; because, from a long acquaintance with her, I could never induce her to remember any event, however trivial, which happened before Lexington battle. The girls, of my age, respected me, as a man of spirit; but I was more fond of being esteemed, as a man of learning. This young lady loved literature, and lamented to me her ignorance of the Greek. I gave her a decided preference to her rivals. She borrowed books of me, and read them with astonishing rapidity. From my own little library, and from those of my friends, I procured above sixty volumes for her; among which were Locke on Human Understanding, Stackhouse's Body of Divinity,[3] and Glass's works, not on cookery, but the benignant

works of John Glass, the father of Sandiman, and the Sandimanians;[4] in which collection I did not however omit Pope's Homer, and
Dryden's Virgil: and, to my astonishment, though I knew that her
afternoons were devoted to the structure of caps and bonnets, she
perused those sixty volumes completely, and returned them to me,
in less than a month. There was one thing peculiarly pleasing to
me, as a man of letters; that she never made dog leaves, or soiled the
books; a slovenly practice, of which even great scholars are some
times guilty. I would, at times, endeavour to draw her into a conversation, upon the author she had recently perused. She would
blush, look down, and say that it did not become a young girl, like
her, to talk upon such subjects, with a gentleman of my sense. The
compliment it contained ever rendered the apology irresistable.
One day, she asked me to lend her a dictionary. I immediately procured for her the great Doctor Johnson's, in two volumes folio.
About three days afterwards, she offered to return them. Knowing
that a dictionary was a work, to which reference was often necessary; and, thinking it might be of some service to even a lady of her
learning, I pressed her to keep it longer. When she replied, with the
prettiest lisp imaginable, that they were indeed very pretty story
books; but, since I had lent them to her, she had read them all
through twice; and then inquired, with the same gentle lisp, if I
could not lend her a book, called Rolling Belly Lettres.[5] I was in absolute astonishment. Virgil's traveller, treading on the snake in the
grass,[6] was comparatively in perfect composure. I took a folio under
each arm, and skipped out of the house, as lightly as if I had had
nothing heavier, than a late antifederal election sermon to carry.
This learned young lady was amazingly affronted, at my abrupt departure; but, when the cause of it was explained to her, some
months after, she endeavoured to persuade a journeyman tailor,
who courted her niece, to challenge me to fight a duel, who actually
penned a challenge, upon one of his master's pasteboard patterns;
and, I verily believe, would have sent it, by his second, if he had not
been informed, that my character was established, as a man of honour.

CHAPTER XIV.

A Babylonish dialect,
Which learned pedants much affect.[1]

HUDIBRAS.

ARGUMENT.

*The Author quitteth the Study of Gallantry, for that of Physic: He eu-
logiseth the Greek Tongue, and complimenteth the Professors of Cambridge, Yale, and Dartmouth; and giveth a gentle Hint to careless
Readers.*

Disgusted with the frivolity of the young, and the deceit of the an-
tiquated, I now applied myself sedulously to my studies. Cullen,
Munroe, Boerhaave, and Hunter,[2] were my constant companions.
As I progressed in valuable science, my admiration of the Greek
declined. I now found, that Machaon and Podalirious, the surgeons
of Homer, were mere quacks; ignorant of even the application of
plaisters, or the eighteen tailed bandage: and, in botany, inferiour to
the Indian Powwows; and that the green ointment, of my learned
friend, Doctor Kitteridge,[3] would have immortalized a bone setter,
in the Grecian era, and translated him, with Esculapius, to a seat
among the gods. In justice to that venerable language, and to the
learned professors of Cambridge, Yale, and Dartmouth, I will candidly confess, that my knowledge of it, was now, in the first year of
my apprenticeship, of some service to me, in now and then finding
the root of the labels cyphered on our gallipots. I shall mention a
little incident, which happened about this time, as it contains a les-

son, valuable to the reader, if he has penetration enough to discover it, and candour enough to apply it to himself. Though I applied myself closely to my books; yet, as hours of relaxation were recommended, by my preceptor, I sometimes indulged in the dance, and in sleighing rides. The latter being proposed, at a time when I was without the means of paying my club, I had retired, with discontent, to my chamber; where I accidentally cast my eyes upon a little old fashioned duodecimo bible, with silver clasps, in the corner of my trunk, a present from my mother, at parting; who had recommended the frequent perusal of it, as my guide in difficulty, and consolation in distress. Young people, in perplexity, always think of home. The bible reproached me. To remove the uneasy sensation, and for the want of something more agreeable to do, I took up the neglected book. No sooner had I unclasped it, than a guinea dropt from the leaves, which had been deposited there, by the generous care of my affectionate mother; and, by my inexcusable inattention, had lain there undiscovered, for more than two years. I hastily snatched the brilliant prize, joined my young companions, and resolved that, in gratitude, I would read a chapter in the bible, every remaining day of my life. This resolution I then persevered in, a whole fortnight. As I am on this subject, I will observe, though no zealot, I have since, in the hours of misery and poverty, with which the reader shall be acquainted, in the sequel, drawn treasures of support and consolation, from that blest book, more precious than the gems of Golconda, or the gold of Ophir.

CHAPTER XV.

Well skill'd
In every virtuous plant and healing herb,
That spreads her verdant leaf to th' morning ray.[1]

MILTON'S COMUS.

ARGUMENT.

The Author panegyrizes his Preceptor.

In June, one thousand seven hundred and eighty five, I completed my studies. My enlightened, generous preceptor, presented me with a Dispensatory,[2] Cullen's First Lines,[3] and an elegant shagreen case of pocket surgical instruments. As it is possible that some friend of his may peruse this work, suffer me to pay him a little tribute of gratitude. He was an unaffected gentleman, and a man of liberal science. In him were united, the acute chymist, the accurate botanist, the skilful operator, and profound physician. He possessed all the essence, without the parade of learning. In the most simple language, he would trace the latent disease, to its diagnostic; and, from his lips, subjects the most abstruse, were rendered familiar to the unlettered man. Excepting when he was with his pupils, or men of science, I never heard him use a technical term. He observed once, that the bold truths of Paracelsus[4] delighted him; but, it partook so much of the speech of our country practitioners, that he was disgusted with the pomposity of Theophrastus Bombastus. He was both an instructor and parent to his pupils. An instructor in all the depth of science he possessed, and a tender parent in directing them, in the paths of virtue and usefulness. May he long live, to bless his country with the healing art; and, may he be hereafter blest himself, in that world, which will open new sources of intelligence, to his inquiring mind.

Chapter XVI.

The lady Baussiere rode on.[1]

Tristram Shandy.

Argument.

Doctor Underhill visiteth Boston, and maketh no Remarks.

Having collected some small dues for professional services, rendered certain merchants and lawyers' clerks, I concluded to make a short tour, to Boston, for the purpose of purchasing a few medical authors and drugs. I carried letters of introduction, from my preceptor, to the late Dr. Joseph Gardner,[2] and other gentlemen of the faculty. The wit and wine of this worthy man still relish on recollection. The remarks I made upon this hospitable, busy, national, town born people; my observations upon their manners, habits, local virtues, customs, and prejudices; the elocution of their principal clergymen; with anecdotes of publick characters, I deal not in private foibles; and a comparitive view of their manners, at the beginning, and near the close of the eighteenth century, are pronounced, by the partiality of some friends, to be original, and to those who know the town, highly interesting. If this homespun history of private life, shall be approved, these remarks will be published by themselves in a future edition[3] of this work. I quitted Boston, with great reluctance, having seventeen invitations to dinner, besides tea parties, on my hands.

CHAPTER XVII.

A hornet's sting,
And all the wonders of an insect's wing.[1]

MRS. BARBAULD.

ARGUMENT.

*The Author inspects the Museum at Harvard College: Account of the
Wonderful Curiosities, Natural and Artificial, he saw there.*

On my return, I passed through Cambridge; and, by the peculiar
politeness and urbanity of the then librarian, I inspected the college museum. Here, to my surprise, I found the curiosities of all
countries, but our own. When I inquired for the natural curiosities
of New England, with specimens of the rude arts, arms, and antiquities of the original possessors of our soil, I was shewn, for the former, an overgrown gourd shell, which held, I do not recollect how
many gallons; some of the shavings of the cannon, cast under the
inspection of Colonel M——; a stuffed wild duck, and the curious
fungus of a turnip: and, for the latter, a miniature birch canoe, containing two or three rag aboriginals with paddles, cut from a shin-
gle. This last article, I confess, would not disgrace the baby house of
a child, if he was not above seven years of age. To be more serious,
I felt then for the reputation of the first seminary of our land. Sup-

pose a Raynal or Buffon[2] should visit us; repair to the museum of the university, eagerly inquiring after the natural productions and original antiquities of our country, what must be the sensations of the respectable rulers of the college, to be obliged to produce, to them, these wretched, bauble specimens.

Chapter XVIII.

Asclepiades boasted that he had articled with fortune, not to be a physician.[1]

Rabelais.

Argument.

The Author mounteth his Nag, and setteth out, full Speed, to seek Practice, Fame, and Fortune, as a Country Practitioner.

In the autumn of one thousand seven hundred and eighty five, I returned to my parents, who received me with rapture. My father had reared, for me, a likely pie bald mare. Our saddler equipped me with horse furniture, not forgetting the little saddle bags, which I richly replenished with drugs, purchased at Boston. With a few books, and my surgeon's instruments, in my portmanteau, and a few dollars in my pocket, I sat out, with a light heart, to seek practice, fame, and fortune, as a country practitioner.

My primary object was to obtain a place of settlement. This I imagined an easy task, from my own acquirements, and the celebrity of my preceptor. My first stop was at a new township, though tolerably well stocked with a hardy laborious set of inhabitants. Five physicians of eminence had, within a few years, attempted a settlement in this place. The first fell a sacrifice to strong liquor; the second put his trust in horses, and was ruined, by the loss of a valuable sire; the third quarrelled with the midwife, and was obliged to remove; the fourth having prescribed, rather unluckily, for a young woman of his acquaintance, grievously afflicted with a tympany,[2] went to the Ohio; and the last, being a prudent man, who sold his books and instruments for wild land, and raised his own crop of medicine, was actually in the way of making a great fortune; as, in only ten years practice, he left, at his decease, an estate, both real and personal, which was appraised at one hundred pounds, lawful money. This account was not likely to engage the attention of a young man, upon whose education twice the sum had been expended.

In the next town, I was assured I might do well, as a physician, if I would keep a grog shop, or let myself, as a labourer, in the hay season, and keep a school in the winter. The first part of the proposition, I heard with patience; but, at the bare mention of a school, I fled the town abruptly. In the neighbouring town, they did not want a physician, as an experienced itinerant doctor visited the place, every March, when the people had most leisure to be sick and take physic. He practiced with great success, especially in slow consumptions, charged very low, and took his pay in any thing and every thing. Besides, he carried a mould with him, to run pewter spoons, and was equally good at mending a kettle and a constitution.

CHAPTER XIX.

Here phials, in nice discipline are set,
There gallipots are rang'd in alphabet.
In this place, magazines of pills you spy;
In that, like forage, herbs in bundles lie;
While lifted pestles, brandish'd in the air,
Descend in peals, and civil wars declare.[1]

GARTH.

ARGUMENT.

The Author encountereth Folly, Ignorance, Impudence, Imbecility, and Quacks: The Characters of a Learned, a Cheap, a Safe, and a Musical Doctor.

At length, I fixed my residence in a town, where four physicians were already in full practice, of such contrariety in theory, that I never knew any two of them agree in any practice, but in abusing me, and decrying my skill. It was however four months before I had any practice, except the extracting of a tooth, from a corn fed girl, who spun at my lodgings, who used to look wistfully at me, and ask, if the doctorer did not think the tooth ache a sign of love? and say she felt dreadfully all over; and the application of a young virgin, in the neighbourhood, who wished to be favoured with a private lecture upon the virtues of the savin bush.[2] I verily believe I might have remained there to this day unemployed, if my landlord, a tavern keeper, finding my payment for board rather tardy, had not, by sometimes sending his boy, in a violent haste, to call me out of meeting, and always vowing I was cute at the trade, at length drawn the attention of the people towards me.

I had now some opportunity of increasing my information, by inspecting the practice of my seniors. The principal physician had been regularly educated. As I had been likewise, he affected to pay me some attention, on purpose to mortify those three quacks, who, he said, had picked up their knowledge, as they did their medicine, by the way side. He was a very formal man, in manners and practice. He viewed fresh air highly noxious, in all diseases. I once visited a patient of his, in dog days, whose parched tongue and acrid skin denoted a violent fever. I was almost suffocated, upon entering the room. The windows were closed, and the cracks stuffed with tow; the curtains were drawn close round the patient's bed, which was covered with a rug, and three comfortable blankets; a large fire was made in the room; the door listed,[3] and the key hole stopped; while the Doctor gravely administered irritating stimulants to allay the fever. He carried a favourite practical author, in his bags, and after finding the patient's case, in the index, pulled out a pair of money seales, and, with the utmost nicety, weighed off the prescribed dose, to the decimal of a drachm. He told me, as a great secret, that about thirteen years and one day past, he had nearly destroyed a patient, by administering half a drachm of pill cochia[4] more than was prescribed in the books. He was called the learned doctor.

The practice of the second town physician was directly opposite. He prescribed large doses of the most powerful drugs. If he had been inclined to weigh his medicine, I believe it would have been with gross weight, rather than troy.[5] He was an untaught disciple of the English Ratcliffe,[6] careless, daring, and often successful. He was admirable in nervous cases, rose cancers,[7] and white swellings.[8] Upon the first symptoms of these stubborn disorders, he would drive them, and the subjects of them, to a state of quiescence. He was called the cheap doctor; because he always speedily cured or— killed.

The third physician dealt altogether in simples. The only compound he ever gave, or took, was buttered flip,[9] for a cough. It was said, that, if he did no good, he never did any harm. He was called the safe doctor.

The fourth physician was not celebrated for being learned, safe, or cheap; but he had more practice than all the other three together, for he was a musical* man, and well gifted in prayer.

* Do not let guitars and fiddles possess thy brain, gentle reader. Musical, as here used, is synonymous with entertaining or facetious.

Chapter XX.

Around bright trophies lay,
Probes, saws, incision knives, and tools to slay.[1]

GARTH.

Argument.

Sketch of an Hereditary Doctor, and a Literary Quack: Critical Operation in Surgery.

There was another gentleman in town, who had some pretensions to the character of a physician: even the same pretensions with the crowned heads of Europe, to their wisdom, power, and greatness. He derived it from his birth; for he was the seventh son of a seventh son, and his mother was a doctress. He did not indeed bear the name or rank, but I remember him with the learned; as he was sometimes called to visit a patient, at that critical, interesting period, when the other physicians had given him over; but his ordinary practice lay wholly among sheep, horses, and cattle. He also could boast of astonishing success, and was as proud and opinionated as the best of them; and, for aught I know, it was as instructive to hear him talk of his ring-bones, wind galls, and spavins,[2] as to hear our first physician descant upon his paroxysms and peripneumony.[3]

Being sent for, one day, to attend a man whose leg was said to be broken, by a fall from a frame at a raising, I found, upon my arrival at the patient's, that a brother of the faculty, from the vicinity, had arrived before me, and completed the operation. He was celebrated for his skill in desperate cases; and universally allowed to be a man of learning. He had prescribed a gill of burnt brandy, with a pepper pod in it, to keep up the patient's spirits, under the operation, and took another himself, to keep his hand steady. He splintered the fractured limb, with the bone of two pair of old fashioned stays, he had caused to be ript to pieces and bound round the leg, with all the garters in the neighbourhood. He bowed gracefully, as I entered, and regretted extremely that he had not my assistance in setting the bones; and with a loud voice, and the most unparalleled assurance, began to lay the case before me, and amplify the operation he had performed. Sir, said he, when I came to view the patient, I had little hopes of saving his life. I found the two lesser bones of the leg, the musa and the tristis shivered into a thousand splinters. While the larger bone, the ambobus, had happily escaped unhurt. Perceiving I could scarce refrain from laughing, and was about to speak; sir, said he, winking upon me, I perceive you are one of us men of science, and I wish you to suspend your opinion, until a private consultation; lest our conversation may alarm the patient too much, for you know, as the learned Galen observes,

> Omne quod exit in *Hun,* seu Græcum, sive Latinum
> Esse genus neutrum, sic invariabile nomen.[4]

By the way, nurse, these learned languages are apt to make the professors of them very thirsty. While the toddy was making, he proceeded. When I pondered this perilous, piteous, pertinacious, pestiferous, petrifying case, I immediately thought of the directions of the learned doctors Hudibras and Mc'Fingal,[5] not forgetting, as the wound was on the leg, the great Crookshank's church history.[6] When we had drunk our liquor, of which he took four fifths, by his direction a new mug was made a little stronger, and we retired to our consultation.

I am much obliged to you, said he, for not discovering my ignorance, to these people; though, it is ten to one, if I had not rather convinced the blockheads of yours, if you had attempted it. A regular bred physician, sometime since, attempted this. He declared, over the sick man's bed, that I was ignorant, and presuming. I replied that he was a quack; and offered to leave our pretensions to knowledge, to the company, which consisted of a midwife, two experienced nurses, and some others, not so eminent for learning. He quoted Cullen and Chesselden;[7] and I Tully[8] and Virgil. Until at length, when I had nearly exhausted my stock of cant phrases, and he was gaining the attention of our judges, I luckily bethought me of Lilly's Grammar. I began Propria quæ maribus;[9] and before I had got twenty lines, the opinion of the audience was apparently in my favour. They judged naturally enough, that I was the most learned man, because the most unintelligible. This raised the doctor's ire so much that from disputing me, he began to berate them for a parcel of fools, sots, and old women, to put their lives in the hands of such an ignoramus as me. This quickly decided the contest in my favour. The old nurses raised their voices, the midwife her broom stick, and the whole train of mob caped judges, their skinny fists, and we drove him out of the house in triumph. Our victory was so complete, that, in the military stile, we did not allow him to remain on the field to bury his dead.

But it is time to tell you who I am. Sir, I drink your health. In brief, sir, I am the son of a respectable clergyman, received a college education, entered into merchandize, failed, and, by a train of misfortunes, was obliged to commence doctor, for sustenance. I settled myself in this back country. At first I was applied to chiefly, in desperate cases where no reputation is lost, if the patient dies, and much gained, if he recovers. I have performed some surprising cures; but how I cannot tell you, except it was by allowing my patients small beer, or any thing else they hankered after, which I have heard was sometimes efficacious, in the crisis of a fever. But talking of drink, sir, I wish your health. I believe I have never injured any persons, by my prescriptions, as a powdered, burnt crust, chalk, and juice of beets and carrots are my most powerful medicines. We can be of mutual service to each other; nurse, another mug. We doctors find this a very difficult case. As I have borne down these country quacks, by superiour effrontery, I can recommend you to full practice. I will call you to consult with me, in difficult cases for, as I was saying, sir, I wish your good health, mine are all difficult cases; and you, in return, shall lend me books, and give me such instructions as will enable me to do good, as well as get fame and bread. The proposal was reasonable. I closed with it. He emptied the third mug, and we returned to our patient. When the dressings were removed, I discovered that there was not the slightest fracture of the fibula or tibia; but only a slight contusion on the patula, which would perhaps not have alarmed any other person, but our patient, who was a rich old bachelor. I recommended an emollient, which my learned brother acquiesced in, saying, with his usual air, that it was the very application he intended, having applied the garters and whalebone, merely to concoct the tristis, the musa and the ambobus firmly together.

A young girl, at the door, shewed him a wound on her elbow, which she had received in struggling about red ears at a husking;[10] which he gravely pronounced to be a fistula in ano. This gentleman is really a man of abilities; has since made valuable acquirements in the knowledge of the human machine, and the materia medica. If he could be led to substitute the aquatic draughts of Doctor Sangrado, as a succedaneum for the diffusible stimuli of Brown,[11] he would become useful in the faculty, and yet see happy days.

The doctor kept his word. He read my books, received my instructions, and recommended me to his patients. But, as I copied my preceptor, in the simplicity of my language I never attempted to excite the fear of my patients, to magnify my skill; and could not reduce three fractured bones in a limb, which contained but two. My advice was little attended to, except when backed with that of my pupil, accompanied with frequent quotations from Lilly. He obtained all the credit of our success; and the people generally supposed me a young man of moderate talents, whom the learned doctor might make something of, in a course of years.

Chapter XXI.

For man's relief the healing art was given;
A wise physician is the boon of heaven.[1]

POPE.

ARGUMENT.

A Medical Consultation.

A merry incident gave a perfect insight into the practice of the several physicians I have just eulogized. A drunken jockey, having fallen from his horse, at a public review, was taken up senseless, and extended upon the long table of the tavern. He soon recovered his breath, and groaned most piteously. As his head struck the ground first, it was apprehended by some, unacquainted with its solidity, that he had fractured his skull. The faculty hastened, from all quarters, to his assistance. The learned, scrupulous physician, after requesting that the doors and windows might be shut, approached the patient; and, with a stately air, declined giving his opinion, as he had unfortunately left at home his Pringle[2] on contusions.

The cheap doctor immediately pronounced the wound a compound fracture, prescribed half a dose of crude opium, and called for the trepanning instruments.

The safe doctor proposed brown paper, dipped in rum and cobwebs, to staunch the blood. The popular physician, the musical doctor, told us a jovial story; and then suddenly relaxing his features, observed, that he viewed the groaning wretch as a monument of justice: that he, who spent his days in tormenting horses, should now, by the agency of the same animal, be brought to death's door, an event, which he thought ought to be set home upon our minds by prayer.

While my new pupil, pressing through the crowd, begged that he might state the case to the company; and, with an audible voice, winking upon me, began. The learned doctor Nominativo Hoc Caput, in his treatise on brains, observes that, the seat of the soul may be known, from the affections of the man. The residence of a wise man's soul is in his ears; a glutton's, in his palate; a gallant's, in his lips; an old maid's, in her tongue; a dancer's, in his toes; a drunk-ard's, in his throat. By the way, landlord, give us a button of sling. When we learned wish to know if a wound endangers life, we con-sequently inquire into the affections of the patient, and see if the wound injures the seat of his soul. If that escapes, however deep and ghastly the wound, we pronounce life in no danger. A horse jockey's soul—gentlemen, I wish your healths, is in his heel, under the left spur. When I was pursuing my studies, in the hospitals in England, I once saw seventeen horse jockies, some of whom were noblemen, killed by the fall of a scaffold in Newmarket, and all wounded in the heel. Twenty others, with their arms, backs, and necks broken, survived. I saw one noble jockey, with his nominativo caret, which is Greek for a nobleman's head, split entirely open. His brains ran down his face, like the white of a broken egg; but, as his heel was unhurt, he survived; and his judgment in horses is said not to be the least impaired. Come, pull off the patient's boot, while I drink his better health. Charmed with the harrangue, some of the spectators were about following his directions, when the other doctors interfered. They had heard him, with disdainful impa-tience, and now each raised his voice, to support his particular opin-ion, backed by his adherents. Bring the brown paper—compound fracture—cobwebs I say—hand the trepanning instruments—give us some tod, and pull off the boot, echoed from all quarters. The landlord forbad quarrelling in his house. The whole company rushed out, to form a ring on the green, for the medical professors;

and they to a consultation of fisty cuffs. The practitioner in sheep, horses, and cattle, poured a dose of urine and molasses down the patient's throat; who soon so happily recovered as to pursue his vocation, swop horses three times, play twenty rubbers of all fours,[3] and get dead drunk again before sunset.

Chapter XXII.

To kinder skies, where gentler manners reign, We turn.[1]

Goldsmith's Traveller.

Argument.

Disappointed in the North, the Author seeketh Treasure in the South.

As my practice increased, my drugs decreased. At the expiration of eighteen months, I found my phials, gallipots, and purse, empty; and my day book full of items. To present a doctor's bill, under seven years, or until my patients died, in which I was not nigh so fortunate as my brother functioners, was complete ruin to my future practice. To draw upon my father, who had already done for me beyond his ability, was still worse. I had often heard the southern states spoken of, as the high road to fortune. I was told that the inhabitants were immensely opulent, paid high fees with profusion, and were extremely partial to the characteristic industry of their New England brethren. By the advice of our attorney, I lodged my accompt books in his office, with a general power to collect. He advanced me a sum sufficient to pay my travelling expenses; and, with my books and surgeon's instruments, I sat out, in the stage, for the southward; condemning the illiberality and ignorance of our own people, which prevented the due encouragement of genius, and made them the prey of quacks; intending, after a few years of successful practice, to return in my own carriage, and close a life of reputation and independence, in my native state.

Chapter XXIII.

One not vers'd in schools,
But strong in sense, and wise without the rules.[1]

Pope.

Argument.

Anecdotes of Doctor Benjamin Franklin, whom the Author visits in Philadelphia.

I carried a request to the late Doctor Benjamin Franklin, then president of the state of Pennsylvania, for certain papers, I was to deliver further southward. I anticipated much pleasure, from the interview with this truly great man: To see one, who, from small beginnings, by the sole exertion of native genius, and indefatigable industry, had raised himself to the pinnacle of politics and letters. A man, who, from an humble printer's boy, had elevated himself to be the desirable companion of the great ones of the earth: who, from trundling a wheelbarrow in bye lanes, had been advanced to pass in splendour, through the courts of kings; and, from hawking vile ballads, to the contracting and signing treaties, which gave peace and independence to three millions of his fellow citizens, was a sight interesting in the extreme.

I found the doctor surrounded by company, most of whom were young people. He received me with the attention due to a young stranger. He dispatched a person for the papers I wanted; asked me politely to be seated; inquired after the family I sprang from; and told me a pleasing anecdote of my brave ancestor, Captain Underhill. I found, in the doctor, all that simplicity of language, which is remarkable in the fragment of his life, published since his decease; and which was conspicuous in my medical preceptor. I have since been in a room a few hours with Governour Jay, of New York;[2] have heard of the late Governour Livingston, of New Jersey;[3] and am now confirmed in the opinion, I have suggested, that men of genuine merit, as they possess the essence, need not the parade of great knowledge. A rich man is often plain in his attire, and the man, who has abundant treasures of learning, simple in his manners and stile.

The doctor, in early life, was economical from principle; in his latter days, perhaps from habit. Poor Richard held the purse strings of the president of Pennsylvania. Permit me to illustrate this observation, by an anecdote. Soon after I was introduced, an airy, thoughtless relation, from a New England state, entered the room. It seems he was on a party of pleasure, and had been so much involved in it, for three weeks, as not to have paid his respects to his venerable relative. The purpose of his present visit was, to solicit the loan of a small sum of money, to enable him to pay his bills, and transport himself home. He preluded his request, with a detail of embarrassments, which might have befallen the most circumspect. He said that he had loaded a vessel for B——, and as he did not deal on credit, had purchased beyond his current cash, and could not readily procure a draft upon home. The doctor, inquiring how much he wanted, he replied, with some hesitation, fifty dollars. The benevolent old gentleman went to his escritoir, and counted him out an hundred. He received them with many promises of punctual payment, and hastily took up the writing implements, to draught a note of hand, for the cash. The doctor, who saw into the nature of the borrower's embarrassments, better than he was aware; and was possessed with the improbability of ever recovering his cash again, stepped across the room, laying his hand gently upon his cousin's arm, said, stop cousin, we will save the paper; a quarter of a sheet is not of great value, but it is worth saving: conveying, at once, a liberal gift and gentle reprimand for the borrower's prevarication and extravagance. Since I am talking of Franklin, the reader may be as unwilling to leave him as I was. Allow me to relate another anec-

A Medical Consultation.

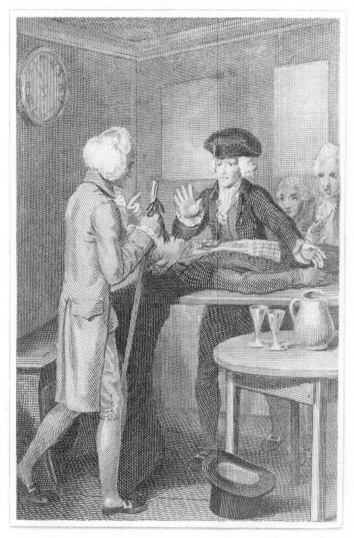

dote. I do not recollect how the conversation was introduced; but a young person in company, mentioned his surprize, that the possession of great riches should ever be attended with such anxiety and solicitude; and instanced Mr. R—— M——,[4] who, he said, though in possession of unbounded wealth, yet was as busy and more anxious, than the most assiduous clerk in his counting house. The doctor took an apple from a fruit basket, and presented it to a little child, who could just totter about the room. The child could scarce grasp it in his hand. He then gave it another, which occupied the other hand. Then choosing a third, remarkable for its size and beauty, he presented that also. The child, after many ineffectual attempts to hold the three, dropped the last on the carpet, and burst into tears. See there, said the philosopher; there is a little man, with more riches than he can enjoy.

Chapter XXIV.

St. Stephen's day, that holy morn,
　　As he to church trudg'd by, sir,
He heard the beagles, heard the horn,
　　And saw poor puss scud by, sir,

His book he shut, his flock forsook,
　　And threw aside his gown, sir,
And strode his mare to chase the hare,
　　And tally ho the hound, sir.

SPORTING SONG.

ARGUMENT.

Religious Exercises in a Southern State.

In one of the states, southward of Philadelphia, I was invited, on a Sunday, to go to church. I will not say which, as I am loth to offend; and our fashionable fellow citizens of the south arm of the union may not think divine service any credit to them. My friend apologized for inviting me to so hum drum an amusement, by assuring me, that immediately after service, there was to be a famous match run for a purse of a thousand dollars, besides private bets, between 'Squire L's imported horse, Slammerkin, and Colonel F's bay mare, Jenny Driver. When we arrived at the church, we found a brilliant collection of well dressed people, anxiously waiting the arrival of the parson, who, it seems, had a small branch of the river M——— to pass; and, we afterwards learned, was detained by the absence of his negro boy, who was to ferry him over. Soon after, our impatience was relieved, by the arrival of the parson, in his canonicals: a young man, not of the most mortified countenance, who, with a switch, called supple jack,[1] in his hand, belaboured the back and head of the faulty slave, all the way from the water to the church door; accompanying every stroke, with suitable language. He entered the church, and we followed. He ascended the reading desk, and, with his face glowing with the exercise of his supple jack, began the service with, I said I will take heed unto my ways, that I sin not with my tongue. I will keep my tongue as it were with a bridle, when I am before the wicked.[2] When I mused the fire burned within me, and I spake with my tongue, &c. &c. He preached an animated discourse, of eleven minutes, upon the practical duties of religion, from these words, remember the sabbath day, to keep it holy; and read the fourth commandment, in the communion. The whole congregation prayed fervently, that their hearts might be inclined to keep this holy law. The blessing was pronounced; and parson and people hastened to the horse race. I found the parson as much respected on the turf, as upon the hassoc.[3] He was one of the judges of the race; descanted, in the language of the turf, upon the points of the two rival horses, and the sleeve of his cassoc was heavy laden, with the principal bets. The confidence of his parishioners was not ill founded; for they assured me, upon oath and honour, that he was a gentleman, of as much uprightness as his grace the archbishop of Canterbury. Ay, they would sport him for a sermon or a song, against any parson in the union.

The whole of this extraordinary scene was novel to me. Besides, a certain staple of New England I had with me, called conscience, made my situation, in even the passive part I bore in it, so awkward and uneasy, that I could not refrain from observing to my friend my surprise at the parson's conduct, in chastising his servant immediately before divine service. My friend was so happily influenced by the habits of these liberal, enlightened people, that he could not even comprehend the tendency of my remark. He supposed it levelled at the impropriety, not of the minister, but the man; not at the act, but the severity of the chastisement; and observed, with warmth, that the parson served the villain right, and, that if he had been his slave, he would have killed the black rascal, if he was sure he should have to pay an hundred guineas to the public treasury for him. I will note here, that the reader is requested, whenever he meets with quotations of speeches, in the above scenes, excepting those during divine service, that he will please, that is, if his habits of life will permit, to interlard those quotations with about as many oaths, as they contain monosylables. He may rest assured, that it will render the scene abundantly more natural. It is true, I might have inserted them myself, and supported thus doing, by illustrations and parodies from grave authors; but I never swear profanely myself, and I think it almost as bad to oblige my readers to purchase the imprecations of others. I give this hint of the introduction of oaths, for the benefit of my readers to the southward of Philadelphia; who, however they may enjoy a scene, which reflects such honour upon their country, when seasoned with these palatable expletives, without them perhaps would esteem it as tasteless and vapid, as a game at cards or billiards, without bets; or boiled veal or turkey, without ham.

Chapter XXV.

Hope springs eternal in the human breast,
Man never is—but always to be blest.[1]

Pope.

Argument.

Success of the Doctor's southern Expedition: He is in Distress: Contemplates a School: Prefers a Surgeon's Birth, on board a Ship, bound to Africa, Via London.

I found the southern states not more engaging, to a young practitioner, than the northern. In the sea ports of both, the business was engrossed by men of established practice and eminence. In the interiour country, the people could not distinguish, or encourage merit. The gains were small, and tardily collected; and, in both wings of the union, and I believe every where else, fortune and fame are generally to be acquired in the learned professions, solely, by a patient, undeviating application to local business.

If dissipation could have afforded pleasure, to a mind yearning after professional fame and independence, I might, so long as my money lasted, have been happy, at the southward. I was often invited to the turf; and, might have had the honour of being intoxicated frequently, with the most respectable characters. An association with the well educated of the other sex was not so readily attained. There was a haughty reserve, in the manners of the young ladies. Every attempt at familiarity, in a young stranger, habituated to the social, but respectful intercourse, customary in the northern states, excited alarm. With my New England ideas, I could not help viewing, in the anxious efforts of their parents and relatives, to repel every approach to innocent and even chastened intercourse, a strong suspicion of that virtue, they were solicitous to protect.

Depressed by the gloomy view of my prospects; and determined never to face my parents again, under circumstances, which would be burthensome to them, I attempted to obtain practice in the town of F———, in Virginia, but in vain. The very decorum, prudence, and economy, which would have enhanced my character at home, were here construed into poverty of spirit. To obtain medical practice, it was expedient, to sport, bet, drink, swear, &c. with my patients. My purse forbad the former; my habits of life the latter. My cash wasted, and I was near suffering. I was obliged to dispose of my books, for present subsistance; and, in that country, books were not the prime articles of commerce. To avoid starving, I again contemplated keeping a school. In that country, knowledge was viewed as a handicraft trade. The school masters, before the war, had been usually collected from unfortunate European youth, of some school learning, sold for their passage into America. So that to purchase a school master and a negro was almost synonimous. Mr. J———n,[2] and some other citizens of the world, who had been cast among them, had by their writings, influence, and example, brought the knowledge of letters into some repute, since the revolution; but, I believe, those excellent men have yet to lament the general inefficacy of their liberal efforts. This statement, and my own prior experience in school keeping, would have determined me rather to have prefered labouring, with the slaves on their plantations, than sustaining the slavery and contempt of a school.

When reduced to my last dollar; and beginning to suffer, from the embarrassments of debt, I was invited, by a sea captain, who knew my friends, to accept the birth of surgeon, in his ship. Every new pursuit has its flattering prospects. I was encouraged by handsome wages, and a privilege in the ship, to carry an adventure; for the purchase of which, the owners were to advance me, on account of my pay. I was to be companion to the captain, and have a fine chance of seeing the world. To quit my home, for all parts of the

union I considered as home; to tempt the perilous ocean, and encounter the severities of a sea faring life, the diseases of torrid
climes, and perhaps a total separation from my friends and parents,
was melancholy; but the desire to see the world, to acquire practical knowledge, in my profession, to obtain property, added to the
necessity of immediate subsistance, and the horrours of a jail, determined me to accept his offer. I accordingly entered surgeon,
on board the ship Freedom, Captain Sidney Russell commander,
freighted with tobacco, bound to London, and thence to the coast
of Africa. I had little to do in my passage to London. My destination, as a surgeon, being principally in the voyage from that city to
the African coast, and thence to the West Indies; and, if I had not
suffered from a previous nausea or sea sickness, the novelty of the
scene would have rendered me tolerably happy. In the perturbation of my thoughts, I had omitted writing to my parents of the
places of my destination. This careless omission afterwards, caused
them and me much trouble. We arrived safely in the Downs.[3]

CHAPTER XXVI.

Now mark a spot or two,
That so much beauty would do well to purge;
And shew this queen of cities, that so fair,
May yet be foul, so witty, yet not wise.[1]

COWPER.

ARGUMENT.

London.

The ship being sold, and another purchased, while the latter was sitting out, at Plymouth, for her voyage to Africa. I was ordered, by the captain, to London, to procure our medicine chest, and case of surgical instruments. Here a field of boundless remark opened itself to me.

Men of unbounded affluence, in plain attire, living within the rules of the most rigid economy; crowds of no substance, strutting in embroidery and lace; people, whose little smoky fire of coals was rendered cheerless by excise, and their daily draught of beer embittered by taxes; who administer to the luxury of pensioners and place men, in every comfort, convenience, or even necessary of life they partake; who are entangled by innumerable penal laws, to the breach of which, banishment and the gallows are almost universally annexed; a motley race, in whose mongrel veins runs the blood of all nations, speaking with pointed contempt of the fat burgo master of Amsterdam, the cheerful French peasant, the hardy tiller of the Swiss cantons, and the independent farmer of America; rotting in dungeons, languishing wretched lives in fœtid jails, and boasting of the GLORIOUS FREEDOM OF ENGLISHMEN: hereditary senators, ignorant and inattentive to the welfare of their country, and unacquainted with the geography of its foreign possessions; and politicians, in coffee houses, without one foot of soil, or one guinea in their pockets, vaunting, with national pride, of our victories, our colonies, our minister, our magna charta, and our constitution! I could not refrain from adopting the language of Doctor Young, and exclaiming in parody,

> How poor, how rich, how abject, how august,
> How complicate, how wonderful are Britons!
> How passing wonder they who made them such,
> Who center'd in their make such strange extremes
> Of different nations, marvelously mix'd,
> Connexion exquisite of distant climes,
> As men, trod worms, as Englishmen, high gods.[2]

Chapter XXVII.

Thus has he, and many more of the same breed, that, I know, the drossy age doats on, only got the tune of the time and outward habit of encounter; a kind of yesty collection, which carries through and through the most fond and winnowed opinions; if you blow them to their trial, the bubbles are out.[1]

SHAKESPEARE.

Argument.

The Author passeth by the Lions in the Tower, and the other Insignia of British Royalty, and seeth a greater Curiosity, called Thomas Paine, Author of the Rights of Man: Description of his Person, Habit, and Manners: In this Chapter due meed is rendered to a great American Historical Painter, and a prose Monody over our lack of the Fine Arts.

Omitting the lions in the tower, the regalia in the jewel office, and the other insignia of British royalty, of which Englishmen are so justly proud, I shall content myself, with mentioning the most singular curiosity, I saw in London. It was the celebrated Thomas Paine, author of Common Sense, the Rights of Man, and other writings, whose tendency is to overturn ancient opinions of government and religion.

I met this interesting personage, at the lodgings of the son of a late patriotic American governour;[2] whose genius, in the fine art of historical painting, whose sortie at Gibralter, whose flowing drapery, faithful and bold expression, in the portraits of our beloved president, and other leaders, both military and political, in our glorious revolution; when the love of the fine arts shall be disseminated in our land, will leave posterity to regret and admire the imbecility of contemporary patronage.

Thomas Paine resembled the great apostle to the Gentiles, not more in his zeal and subtlety of argument, than in personal appearance; for, like that fervid apostle, his bodily presence was both mean and contemptible. When I saw him, he was dressed in a snuff coloured coat, olive velvet vest, drab breeches, coarse hose. His shoe buckles of the size of half a dollar. A bob tailed wig covered that head, which worked such mickle woe to courts and kings. If I should attempt to describe it, it would be in the same stile and principle, with which the veteran soldier bepraiseth an old standard: the more tattered, the more glorious. It is probable that this was the same identical wig, under the shadow of whose curls, he wrote Common Sense in America, many years before. He was a spare man, rather under size; subject to the extreme of low, and highly exhilirated spirits; often sat reserved in company; seldom mingled in common chit chat. But when a man of sense and elocution was present, and the company numerous, he delighted in advancing the most unaccountable, and often the most whimsical, paradoxes; which he defended in his own plausible manner. If encouraged by success, or the applause of the company, his countenance was animated, with an expression of feature, which, on ordinary occasions, one would look for in vain, in a man so much celebrated for acuteness of thought; but if interrupted by extraneous observation, by the inattention of his auditory, or in an irritable moment, even by the accidental fall of the poker, he would retire into himself, and no persuasions could induce him to proceed upon the most favourite topic.

CHAPTER XXVIII.

He could distinguish and divide,
A hair 'twixt south and south west side;
He'd undertake to prove by force
Of argument, a man's no horse;
He'd prove a buzzard is no fowl,
And that a LORD MAY BE AN OWL.[1]

HUDIBRAS.

ARGUMENT.

Curious Argument, between Thomas Paine and the noted Peter Pindar:[2] Peter setteth a Wit Noose, and catcheth Thomas, in one of his own Logic Traps.

I heard Thomas Paine once assert, in the presence of Mr. Wolcott, better known, in this country, by the facetious name of Peter Pindar, that the minority, in all deliberative bodies, ought, in all cases, to govern the majority. Peter smiled. You must grant me, said *Uncommon Sense*, that the proportion of men of sense, to the ignorant among mankind, is at least as twenty, thirty, or even forty nine, to an hundred. The majority of mankind are consequently most prone to errour; and, if we would atchieve right, the minority ought, in all cases, to govern. Peter continued to smile archly. If we look to experience, continued Paine, for there are no conclusions I more prize than those drawn, not from speculation, but plain matter of fact, we shall find an examination into the debates of all deliberative bodies, in our favour. To proceed no farther than your country, Mr. Wolcott, I love to look at home. Suppose the resolutions of the houses of lords and commons had been determined by this salutary rule; why, the sensible minority would have governed. George Washington would have been a private citizen; and the United States of America mere colonies, dependent on the British crown. As a patriotic Englishman, will you not confess, that this would have been better than to have these United States independent, with the illustrious Washington at their head, by their wisdom confounding the juggling efforts of your ministry to embroil them; and to have the comfortable prospect before you, that from the extent of their territory, their maritime resource, their natural encrease, the asylum they offer to emigrants, in the course of two centuries, Scotland and Ireland, if the United States have not too much real pride to attempt it, may be reduced to the same dependence upon them, as your West India islands now have upon you: and even England, haughty England, thrown in as a make weight, in the future treaty between them and the French nation. Peter, who had listened with great seeming attention, now mildly replied. I will not say but that your arguments are cogent, though not entirely convincing. As it is a subject rather out of my line, I will, for form sake, hold the negative of your proposition, and leave it to the good company, which is right. Agreed, said Paine, who saw himself surrounded by his admirers. Well, gentlemen, said Peter, with all the gravity of a speaker of the house of commons; you, that are of the opinion that the minority, in all deliberative bodies, ought, in all cases, to govern the majority, please to rise in the affirmative. Paine immediately stood up himself, and, as he had foreseen, we all rose in his favour. Then I rise in the negative, cried Peter. I am the wise minority, who ought, in all cases, to govern your ignorant majority; and, consequently, upon your own principles, I carry the vote. Let it be recorded.

This unexpected manœuvre raised a hearty laugh. Paine retired from the presence of triumphant wit, mortified with being foiled at his own weapons.

Chapter XXIX.

Fierce Roberspierre strides o'er the crimson'd scene,
And howls for lamp posts and the guillotine;
While wretched Paine, to 'scape the bloody strife,
Damns his mean soul to save his meaner life.

Author's *Manuscript Poems.*

Argument.

Reasonable Conjectures upon the Motives, which induced Thomas Paine to write that little Book, called the Age of Reason.

In the frequent interviews I had with this celebrated republican apostle, I never heard him express the least doubt of, or cast the smallest reflection upon revealed religion. He spake of the glowing expressions of the Jewish prophets with fervour; and had quoted liberally from the scriptures, in his Common Sense. How he came to write that unreasonable little pamphlet, called the Age of Reason, I am at a loss to conjecture. The probable opinion attributes it to his passion for paradox; that this small morsel of infidelity was offered as a sacrifice to save his life from the devouring cruelty of Roberspierre, that Moloch of the French nation. It probably had its desired effect; for annihilating revealed religion could not but afford a diabolical pleasure, to that ferocious wretch and his inhuman associates, who could not expect a sanction for their cruelties, while the least vestige of any thing sacred remained among men.

When the reign of the terrorists ceased, an apology was expected; and, even by the pious, yet catholic American, would have

been received. To the offended religion of his country no propitia-
tory sacrifice was made. This missionary of vice has proceeded
proselyting. He has added second parts, and made other, and auda-
cious adjuncts to deism. No might nor greatness escapes him. He
has vilified a great prophet, the saviour of the Gentiles; he has
railed at Washington, a saviour of his country. A tasteful, though ir-
religious scholar might tolerate a chastised scepticism, if exhibited
by an acute Hume, or an eloquent Bolingbroke.[1] But one cannot re-
press the irritability of the fiery Hotspur,[2] when one beholds the
pillars of morality shaken by the rude shock of this modern vandal.
The reader should learn, that his paltry system is only an outrage of
wine;* and that it is in the ale house, he most vigorously assaults the
authority of the prophets, and laughs most loudly at the gospel,
when in his cups.

I have preserved an epigram of Peter Pindar's, written, originally, in a
blank leaf of a copy of Paine's Age of Reason, and not inserted in any
of his works.

Epigram

Tommy Paine wrote this book to prove that the bible
Was an old woman's dream of fancies most idle;
That Solomon's proverbs were made by low livers,
That prophets were fellows, who sang semiquavers;
That religion and miracles all were a jest,
And the *Devil in torment* a tale of the priest.
Tho' Beelzebub's absence from hell I'll maintain,
Yet we all must allow that the DEVIL'S IN PAINE.[4]

---

*Mr. Johnson, a respectable bookseller in St. Paul's church yard, London,[3] has asserted
that Mr. Paine's tongue used to flow most freely against revealed religion, when he was most
intoxicated with "ale, or viler liquors."

Chapter XXX.

Man hard of heart to man! of horrid things:
Most horrid! mid stupendous highly strange!
    Hear it not ye stars!
And thou pale moon! turn paler at the sound:
Man is to man the sorest surest ill![1]

Argument.

The Author sails for the Coast of Africa: Manner of purchasing Negro Slaves.

On the eighteenth of July, one thousand seven hundred and eighty eight, I received orders, from my captain, to join the ship in the Downs. I accordingly took passage in a post chaise; and, after a rapid journey of seventy four miles, arrived, the same afternoon at Deal; and the next morning entered as surgeon, on board the ship Sympathy, of three hundred tons, and thirty eight men, Captain Sydney Russell commander; bound to the coast of Africa, thence to Barbadoes, and to South Carolina with a cargo of slaves.

We were favoured with a clear sky and pleasant gales; and, after a short and agreeable voyage, we touched at Porto Santo, one of the Madeira isles; where we watered and supplied ourselves with fresh provisions in abundance, to which the captain added, at my request, a quantity of Madeira, malmsey,[2] and tent wines,[3] for the sick. We had a fine run, from the Madeiras to the Canary isles. The morning after we sailed, I was highly gratified with a full view of the island

and peak of Teneriff; which made its appearance the day before, rising above the ocean, at one hundred miles distance. We anchored off Fuertuventura[4] one of the Canaries, in a good bottom. I went on shore, with the mate, to procure green vegetables; as I ever esteemed them the specific for that dreadful sea disorder, the scurvy. Before we had reached the Madeiras, though I had stored our medicine chest with the best antiscorbutics, and we had a plenty of dried vegetables on board, yet the scurvy had began to infect us. A plentiful distribution of green vegetables, after our arrival at Porto Santo, soon expelled it from the crew. At Fuertuventura, I was delighted with the wild notes of the Canary bird, far surpassing the most excellent of those I had seen in cages, in the United States.

I was anxious to visit the Cape de Verd islands; but, our course being too far east, we ran down to the little island of Goree,[5] to which the contentions of the English and French crowns have annexed its only importance. The French officers received us with politeness, and were extremely anxious for news, from their parent country. Soon after, we dropt anchor off Loango city, upon a small well peopled island, near the coast of Congo[6] or lower Guinea, in possession of the Portuguese. Our captain carried his papers on shore, and, the next day, weighed anchor and stood in for the continent. All hands were now employed to unlade the ship, and the cargo was deposited in a Portuguese factory, at a place called Cacongo,[7] near the mouth of the river *Zaire*. The day after our arrival at Cacongo, several Portuguese and Negro merchants, hardly distinguishable however, by their manners, employments, or complexions, came to confer with the captain, about the purchase of our cargo of slaves. They contracted to deliver him two hundred and fifty head of slaves, in fifteen days' time. To hear these men converse upon the purchase of human beings, with the same indifference, and nearly in the same language, as if they were contracting for so many head of cattle or swine, shocked me exceedingly. But, when I suffered my imagination to rove to the habitation of these victims to this infamous, cruel commerce, and fancied that I saw the peaceful husbandman dragged from his native farm; the fond husband torn from the embraces of his beloved wife; the mother, from her babes; the tender child, from the arms of its parents and all the tender, endearing ties of natural and social affection rended by the hand of avaricious violence, my heart sunk within me. I execrated myself, for even the involuntary part I bore in this execrable traffic: I thought of my native land and blushed. When the captain kindly inquired of me how many slaves I thought my privilege in the ship entitled me to transport, for my adventure, I rejected my privilege, with horrour; and declared I would sooner suffer servitude than purchase a slave. This observation was received in the great cabin with repeated bursts of laughter, and excited many a stroke of coarse ridicule. Captain Russell observed, that he would not insist upon my using my privilege, if I had so much of the yankee about me. Here is my clerk, Ned Randolph, will jump at the chance; though the rogue has been rather unlucky in the trade. Out of five and twenty negroes he purchased, he never carried but one alive to port; and that poor devil was broken winded, and he was obliged to sell him for half price in Antigua.

Punctual to the day of the delivery, the contractors appeared, and brought with them about one hundred and fifty negroes, men, women, and children. The men were fastened together, in pairs, by a bar of iron, with a collar to receive the neck at each extremity; a long pole passing over their shoulder, and between each two, bound by a staple and ring, through which the pole was thrust, and thus twenty, and sometimes thirty, were connected together; while their conductors incessantly applied the scourge to those, who loitered, or sought to strangle themselves, by lifting their feet from the ground in despair, which sometimes had been successfully attempted. The women and children were bound with cords, and driven forward by the whip. When they arrived at the factory, the men were unloosed from the poles; but still chained in pairs, and turned into strong cells, built for the purpose. The dumb sorrow of some, the frenzy of others, the sobbings and tears of the children, and shrieks of the women, when they were presented to our captain, so affected me that I was hastening from this scene of barbarity, on board the ship; when I was called by the mate, and discovered, to my surprize and horrour, that, by my station in the ship, I had a principal and active part of this inhuman transaction imposed upon me. As surgeon, it was my duty to inspect the bodies of the slaves, to see, as the captain expressed himself, that our owners were not shammed off with unsound flesh. In this inspection, I was assisted by Randolph the clerk, and two stout sailors. It was transacted with all that unfeeling insolence, which wanton barbarity can inflict upon defenceless wretchedness. The man, the affrighted child, the modest matron, and the timid virgin were alike exposed to this severe scrutiny, to humanity and common decency equally insulting.

I cannot reflect on this transaction yet without shuddering. I have deplored my conduct with tears of anguish; and, I pray a merciful God, the common parent of the great family of the universe, who hath made of one flesh and one blood all nations of the earth, that the miseries, the insults, and cruel woundings, I afterwards received, when a slave myself, may expiate for the inhumanity, I was necessitated to exercise, towards these MY BRETHREN OF THE HUMAN RACE.

Chapter XXXI.

Can thus
The image of God in man created, once
So goodly and erect, though faulty since,
To such unsightly suffering be debased
Under inhuman pains?[1]

Milton.

Argument.

Treatment of the Slaves, on board the Ship.

Of one hundred and fifty Africans we rejected seventeen, as not merchantable. While I was doubting which to lament most, those, who were about being precipitated into all the miseries of an American slavery, or those, whom we had rejected, as too wretched for slaves; Captain Russell was congratulating the slave contractors, upon the immense good luck they had, in not suffering more by this lot of human creatures. I understood that, what from wounds received by some of these miserable creatures, at their capture, or in their violent struggles for liberty, or attempts at suicide; with the fatigue of a long journey, partly over the burning sands of a sultry climate, it was usual to estimate the loss, in the passage to the sea shore, at twenty five per cent.

No sooner was the purchase completed, than these wretched Africans were transported in herds aboard the ship, and immediately precipitated between decks, where a strong chain, attached to a staple in the lower deck, was rivetted to the bar, before described; and then the men were chained in pairs, and also hand cuffed, and two sailors with cutlasses guarded every twenty: while the women and children were tied together in pairs with ropes, and obliged to supply the men with provisions, and the slush bucket; or, if the young women were released, it was only to gratify the brutal lust of the sailors: for though I cannot say I ever was witness to an actual rape, yet the frequent shrieks of these forlorn females in the births of the seamen, left me little charity to doubt of the repeated commission of that degrading crime. The eve after we had received the slaves on board, all hands were piped on deck, and ordered to assist in manufacturing and knotting cat o'nine tails, the application of which, I was informed, was always necessary to bring the slaves to their appetite. The night after they came on board was spent by these wretched people, in sobbings, groans, tears, and the most heart rending bursts of sorrow and despair. The next morning all was still. Surprised by this unexpected silence, I almost hoped that providence, in pity to these her miserable children, had permitted some kindly suffocation to put a period to their anguish. It was neither novel nor unexpected to the ship's crew. It is only the dumb fit come on, cried every one. We will cure them. After breakfast, the whole ship's crew went between decks, and carried with them the provisions for the slaves, which they one and all refused to eat. A more affecting group of misery was never seen. These injured Africans, prefering death to slavery, or perhaps buoyed above the fear of dissolution, by their religion, which taught them to look with an eye of faith to a country beyond the grave; where they should again meet those friends and relatives, from whose endearments they had been torn; and where no fiend should torment, or christian thirst for gold, had, wanting other means, resolved to starve themselves, and every eye lowered the fixed resolve of this deadly intent. In vain were the men beaten. They refused to taste one mouthful; and, I believe, would have died under the operation, if the ingenious cruelty of the clerk, Randolph, had not suggested the plan of whipping the women and children in sight of the men;

assuring the men they should be tormented until all had eaten. What the torments, exercised on the bodies of these brave Africans, failed to produce, the feelings of nature effected. The Negro, who could undauntedly expire under the anguish of the lash, could not view the agonies of his wife, child, or his mother; and, though repeatedly encouraged by these female sufferers, unmoved by their torments, to persevere unto death; yet, though the *man* dared to die, the *father* relented, and in a few hours they all eat their provisions, *mingled with their tears.*

Our slave dealers being unable to fulfil their contract, unless we tarried three weeks longer, our captain concluded to remove to some other market. We accordingly weighed anchor, and steered for Benin, and anchored in the river Formosa, where we took in one hundred and fifteen more slaves. The same process in the purchase was pursued here; and, though I frequently assured the captain, as a physician, that it was impracticable to stow fifty more persons between decks, without endangering health and life, the whole hundred and fifteen were thrust, with the rest, between decks. The stagnant confined air of this infernal hole, rendered more deleterious by the stench of the fæces, and violent perspiration of such a crowd, occasioned putrid diseases; and, even while in the mouth of the Formosa, it was usual to throw one or two Negro corpses over every day. It was in vain I remonstrated to the captain. In vain I enforced the necessity of more commodious births, and a more free influx of air for the slaves. In vain I represented, that these miserable people had been used to the vegetable diet, and pure air of a country life. That at home they were remarkable for cleanliness of person, the very rites of their religion consisting, almost entirely, in frequent ablutions. The captain was, by this time, prejudiced against me. He observed that he did not doubt my skill, and would be bound by my advice, as to the health of those on board his ship, when he found I was actuated by the interest of the owners; but, he feared, that I was now moved by some *yankee nonsense about humanity.*

Randolph, the clerk, blamed me in plain terms. He said he had made seven African voyages, and with as good surgeons as I was; and that it was their common practice, when an infectious disorder prevailed, among the slaves, to make critical search for all those, who had the slightest symptoms of it, or whose habits of body inclined them to it; to tie them up and cast them over the ship side together, and thus, at one dash, to purify the ship. *What signifies, added he, the lives of the black devils; they love to die. You cannot please them better, than by chucking them into the water.*

When we stood out to sea, the rolling of the vessel brought on the sea sickness, which encreased the filth; the weather being rough, we were obliged to close some of the ports, which ventilated the space between decks; and death raged dreadfully among the slaves. Above two thirds were diseased. It was affecting to observe the ghastly smile on the countenance of the dying African, as if rejoicing to escape the cruelty of his oppressors. I noticed one man, who gathered all his strength, and, in one last effort, spoke with great emphasis, and expired. I understood, by the linguist, that, with his dying breath, he invited his wife, and a boy and girl to follow him quickly, and slaken their thirst with him at the cool streams of the fountain of their Great Father, beyond the reach of the wild white beasts. The captain was now alarmed for the success of his voyage; and, upon my urging the necessity of landing the slaves, he ordered the ship about, and we anchored near an uninhabited part of the gold coast. I conjecture not far from Cape St. Paul.

Tents were erected on the shore, and the sick landed. Under my direction, they recovered surprisingly. It was affecting to see the effect gentle usage had upon these hitherto sullen, obstinate people. As I had the sole direction of the hospital, they looked on me as the source of this sudden transition from the filth and rigour of the ship, to the cleanliness and kindness of the shore. Their gratitude was excessive. When they recovered so far as to walk out, happy was he, who could, by picking a few berries, gathering the wild fruits of the country, or doing any menial services, manifest his affection for me. Our linguist has told me, he has often heard them, behind the bushes, praying to their God for my prosperity, and asking him with earnestness, why he put my good *black* soul into a *white* body. In twelve days all the convalescents were returned to the ship, except five, who staid with me on shore, and were to be taken on board the next day.

Chapter XXXII.

Chains are the portion of revolted man;
Stripes and a dungeon.[1]

Cowper.

Argument.

The Author taken Captive by the Algerines.

Near the close of the fourteenth of November, one thousand seven
hundred and eighty eight, as the sun was sinking behind the mountains of Fundia, I sat at the door of my tent, and perceived our ship,
which lay at one mile's distance, getting under way, apparently in
great haste. The jolly boat, about ten minutes before, had made
towards the shore; but was recalled by a musket shot from the ship.
Alarmed by this unexpected manœuvre, I ran to the top of a small
hill, back of the hospital, and plainly discovered a square rigged
vessel in the offing, endeavouring to lock our ship within the land;
but a land breeze springing up from the north east, which did not
extend to the strange vessel, and our ship putting out all her light
sails, being well provided with ring sail, scudding sails, water sails,
and driver, I could perceive she out sailed her. It was soon so dark
that I lost sight of both, and I passed a night of extreme anxiety,
which was increased by, what I conjectured to be, the flashes of
guns in the *south west*; though at too great distance for me to hear
the reports.

The next morning no vessels were to be seen on the coast, and the ensuing day was spent in a state of dreadful suspense. Although I had provisions enough with me for some weeks, and was sheltered by our tents, yet to be separated from my friends and country, perhaps forever, and to fall into the hands of the barbarous people, which infested this coast, was truly alarming. The five Africans, who were with me, could not conceal their joy, at the departure of the ship. By signs they manifested their affection towards me; and, when I signified to them that the vessel was gone not to return, they clapped their hands, and pointing inland, signified a desire to convey me to their native country, where they were sure I should be happy. By their consultation, I could see that they were totally ignorant of the way. On the third day towards evening, to my great joy, I saw a sail approaching the shore, at the prospect of which my African associates manifested every sign of horrour. I immediately concluded that no great blame would arise, from my not detaining five men, in the absence of the ship; and I intimated to them that they might conceal themselves in the brush and escape. Four quitted me; but one, who made me comprehend, that he had a beloved son among the slaves, refused to go, prefering the company of his child, and *slavery* itself, to *freedom* and the land of his nativity. I retired to rest, pleased with the imagination of soon rejoining my friends, and proceeding to my native country. On the morning of the fourth day, as I was sleeping in my tent with the affectionate negro at my feet, I was suddenly awakened, by the blowing of conch shells, and the sound of uncouth voices. I arose to dress myself, when the tent was overset, and I received a blow from the back of a sabre, which levelled me to the earth; and was immediately seized and bound by several men of sallow and fierce demeanour, in strange habits, who spake a language I could not comprehend. With the negro, tents, baggage, and provisions, I was carried to the boat, which, being loaded, was immediately pushed off from the shore, and rowed towards a vessel, which I now, for the first time, noticed, and had no doubt but it was the same, which was in pursuit of the Sympathy. She was rigged differently from any I had ever seen, having two masts, a large square main sail, another of equal size, seized by the middle of a main yard to her fore mast, and, what the sailors call, a shoulder of mutton sail abast; which, with top sails and two banks of oars, impelled her through the water with amazing velocity: though, from the clumsiness of her rigging, an American seaman would never have pronounced her a good sea boat. On her main mast head was a broad black pennant, with a half moon, or rather crescent, and a drawn sabre, in white and red, emblazoned in the middle. The sides of the vessel were manned as we approached, and a tackle being let down, the hook was attached to the cord, which bound me, and I was hoisted on board in the twinkling of an eye. Then, being unbound, I was carried upon the quarter deck, where a man, who appeared to be the captain, glittering in silks, pearl, and gold, set cross legged upon a velvet cushing to receive me. He was nearly encircled by a band of men, with monstrous tufts of hair on their upper lips, dressed in habits of the same mode with their leader's, but of coarser contexture, with drawn scimitars in their hands, and by his side a man of lighter complexion, who, by the captain's command, inquired of me, in good English, if I was an Englishman. I replied I was an American, a citizen of the United States. This was no sooner interpreted to the captain than, at a disdainful nod of his head, I was again seized, hand cuffed, and thrust into a dirty hole in the fore castle, where I lay twenty four hours, without straw to sleep on, or any thing to eat or drink. The treatment we gave the unhappy Africans, on board the Sympathy, now came full into my mind; and, what was the more mortifying, I discovered that the negro who was, captured with me, was at liberty, and fared as well as the sailors on board the vessel. I had not however been confined more than one half hour, when the interpreter came to examine me privately respecting the destination of the ship, to which he suspected I belonged; was anxious to know if she had her full cargo of slaves; what was her force; whether she had English papers on board; and if she did not intend to stop at some other African port. From him I learned that I was captured by an Algerine Rover, Hamed Hali Saad captain; and should be carried into slavery at Algiers. After I had lain twenty four hours in this loathsome place, covered with vermin, parched with thirst, and fainting with hunger, I was startled at a light, let through the hatchway, which opened softly, and a hand presented me a cloth, dripping with cold water, in which a small quantity of boiled rice was wrapped. The door closed again softly, and I was left to enjoy my good fortune in the dark. If Abraham had indeed sent Lazarus to the rich man, in torment,[2] it appears to me, he could not have received a greater pleasure, from the cool water on his tongue, than I experienced in sucking the moisture from this cloth. The next day, the same kindly hand appeared again, with the same refreshment. I begged to see my benefactor. The door opened further, and I saw a countenance in tears. It was the face of the grateful African, who was taken with me. I was oppressed with gratitude. Is this, exclaimed I, one of those men, whom we are taught to vilify as beneath the human species, who brings me sustenance, perhaps at the risk of his life, who shares his morsel with one of those barbarous men, who had recently torn him from all he held dear, and whose base companions are now transporting his darling son to a grievous slavery? Grant me, I ejaculated, once more to taste the freedom of my native country, and every moment of my life shall be dedicated to preaching against this detestable commerce. I will fly to our fellow citizens in the southern states; I will, on my knees, conjure them, in the name of humanity, to abolish a trafic, which causes it to bleed in every pore. If they are deaf to the pleadings of nature, I will conjure them, for the sake of consistency, to cease to deprive their fellow creatures of freedom, which their writers, their orators, representatives, senators, and even their constitutions of government, have declared to be the unalienable birth right of man. My sable friend had no occasion to visit me a third time; for I was taken from my confinement, and, after being stripped of the few clothes, and the little property I chanced to have about me, a log was fastened to my leg by a chain, and I was permitted to walk the fore castle of the vessel, with the African and several Spanish and Portuguese prisoners. The treatment of the slaves, who plied the oars, the management of the vessel, the order which was observed among this ferocious race, and some notices of our voyage, might afford observations, which would be highly gratifying to my readers, if the limits of this work would permit. I will just observe however that the regularity and frequency of their devotion was astonishing to me, who had been taught to consider this people as the most blasphemous infidels. In the days after I was captured, the Rover passed up the straits of Gibralter, and I heard the garrison evening gun fired from that formidable rock; and the next morning hove in sight of the city of Algiers.

END OF VOLUME FIRST

VOLUME II

Chapter I.

There dwell the most forlorn of human kind
Immured, though unaccused, condemned, untried,
Cruelly spared, and hopeless of escape.[1]

Cowper.

Argument.

The Author is carried into Algiers: Is brought before the Dey: Description of his Person, Court and Guards: Manner of selecting the Tenth Prisoner.

We saluted the castle with seven guns, which was returned with three, and then entered within the immense pier, which forms the port. The prisoners, thirty in number, were conveyed to the castle, where we were received with great parade by the Dey's troops or cologlies,[2] and guarded to a heavy strong tower of the castle. The Portuguese prisoners, to which nation the Algerines have the most violent antipathy, were immediately, with every mark of contempt, spurned into a dark dungeon beneath the foundations of the tower, though there were several merchants of eminence, and one young nobleman, in the number. The Spaniards, whom the Dey's subjects equally detest, and fear more, were confined with me in a grated room, on the second story. We received, the same evening, rations similar to what, we understood, were issued to the garrison. The next day, we were all led to a cleaning house, where we were cleaned from vermin, our hair cut short, and our beards close shaved; thence taken to a bath, and, after being well bathed, we were clothed in coarse linen drawers, a strait waistcoat of the same without sleeves, and a kind of tunic or loose coat over the whole, which, with a pair of leather slippers, and a blue cotton cap, equipped us, as we were informed, to appear in the presence of the Dey, who was to select the tenth prisoner from us in person. The next morning, the dragomen or interpreters, were very busy in impressing upon us the most profound respect for the Dey's person and power, and teaching us the obeisance necessary to be made in our approaches to this august potentate. Soon after, we were paraded; and Captain Hamed presented each of us with a paper, written in a base kind of Arabic, describing, as I was informed, our persons, names, country, and conditions in life; so far as our captors could collect from our several examinations. Upon the back of each paper was a mark or number. The same mark was painted upon a flat oval piece of wood, somewhat like a painter's palette, and suspended by a small brass chain to our necks, hanging upon our breasts. The guards then formed a hollow square. We were blind folded until we passed the fortifications, and then suffered to view the city, and the immense rabble, which surrounded us, until we came to the palace of the Dey. Here, after much military parade, the gates were thrown open, and we entered a spacious court yard, at the upper end of which the Dey was seated, upon an eminence, covered with the richest carpeting fringed with gold. A circular canopy of Persian silk was raised over his head, from which were suspended curtains of the richest embroidery, drawn into festoons by silk cords and tassels, enriched with pearls. Over the eminence, upon the right and left, were canopies, which almost vied in riches with the former, under which stood the Mufti,[3] his numerous Hadgi's,[4] and his principal officers, civil and military; and on each side about seven hundred foot guards were drawn up in the form of a half moon.

The present Dey, Vizier Hassen Bashaw,[5] is about forty years of age, five feet ten inches in height, inclining to corpulency, with a countenance rather comely than commanding; an eye which betrays sagacity, rather than inspires awe: the latter is sufficiently inspired by the fierce appearance of his guards, the splendour of his attendants, the grandeur of his court, and the magnificence of his attire. He was arrayed in a sumptuous Turkish habit. His feet were shod with buskins, bound upon his legs with diamond buttons in loops of pearl; round his waist was a broad sash, glittering with jewels, to which was suspended a broad scimitar, the hilt of which dazzled the eye with brilliants of the first water, and the sheath of which was of the finest velvet, studded with gems and the purest gold. In his scarf was stuck a poignard and pair of pistols of exquisite workmanship. These pistols and poignard were said to have been a present from the late unfortunate Louis the sixteenth. The former was of pure gold, and the value of the work was said to exceed that of the precious mettle two hundred times. Upon the Dey's head was a turban with the point erect, which is peculiar to the royal family. A large diamond crescent shone conspicuous in the front, on the back of which a socket received the quills of two large ostrich feathers, which waved in graceful majesty over his head. The prisoners were directed by turns to approach the foot of the eminence. When within thirty paces, we were made to throw ourselves upon the earth and creep towards the Dey, licking the dust as a token of reverence and submission. As each captive approached, he was commanded to rise, pull off his slippers, and stand with his face bowed to the ground, and his arms crossed over his breast. The chieux or secretary[6] then took the paper he carried and read the same. To some the Dey put questions by his drogoman, others were dismissed by a slight nod of his head. After some consultation among the chief men, an officer came to where the prisoners were paraded, and called for three by the number, which was marked on their breasts. The Dey's prerogative gives him the right to select the tenth of all prisoners; and, as the service or ransom of them constitutes one part of his revenue, his policy is to choose those, whose friends or wealth would be most likely to enrich his coffers. At this time, he selected two wealthy Portuguese merchants, and a young nobleman of the same nation, called Don Juan Combri. Immediately after this selection, we were carried to a strong house, or rather prison, in the city, and there guarded by an officer and some of the crew of the Rover, that had taken us. The remainder of us being considered as private property, another selection was made by the captain and owners of the Rover; and all such, as could probably pay their ransom in a short time, were removed into a place of safety and suffered only a close confinement. The remnant of my companions being only eleven, consisted of the Negro slave, five Portuguese, two Spanish sailors, an Italian fiddler, a Dutchman from the Cape of Good Hope, and his Hottentot servant. As we could proffer no probability of ransom we were reserved for another fate.

Chapter II.

Despoiled of all the honours of the free,
The beaming dignities of man eclipsed,
Degraded to a beast, and basely sold
In open shambles, like the stalled ox.

AUTHOR'S Manuscript Poems.

Argument.

The Slave Market.

On the next market day, we were stripped of the dress, in which we appeared at court. A napkin was wrapped round our loins, and a coarse cloak thrown over our shoulders. We were then exposed for sale in the market place, which was a spacious square, inclosed by ranges of low shops, in different sections of which were exposed the various articles intended for sale. One section was gay with flowers; another exposed all the fruits of the season. Grapes, dates, pomegranates, and oranges lay in tempting baskets. A third was devoted to sallads and pot herbs; a fourth to milk and cream. Between every section was a small room, where those, who come to market, might occasionally refresh themselves with a pipe of tobacco, a cud of opium, a glass of sherbet, or other cooling liquors. Sherbet is composed of lemons, oranges, sugar, and water. It is what we, in New England, call beverage. In the centre of the market, an oblong square was railed in, where the dealers in beasts and slaves exposed their commodities for sale. Here were camels, mules, asses, goats, hares, dromedaries, women and men, and all other creatures, whether for appetite or use; and I observed that the purchasers turned from one article to the other, with equal indifference. The women slaves were concealed in a latticed shop, but the men were exposed in open view in a stall, situated between those appropriated to the asses and to the kumrah, a wretched looking, though serviceable animal in that country, propagated by a jack upon a cow.[1] I now discovered the reason of the alteration in our dress; for, as the people here, no more than in New England, love to buy a pig in the poke, our loose coats were easily thrown open, and the purchaser had an opportunity of examining into the state of our bodies. It was astonishing to observe, how critically they examined my muscles, to see if I was naturally strong; moved my limbs in various directions, to detect any latent lameness or injury in the parts; and struck suddenly before my eyes, to judge by my winking, if I was clear sighted. Though I could not understand their language, I doubt not, they spoke of my activity, strength, age, &c. in the same manner, as we at home talk in the swop of a horse. One old man was very critical in his examination of me. He made me walk, run, lie down, and lift a weight of about sixty pounds. He went out, and soon returned with another man. They conferred together, and the second was more critical in his examination than the first. He obliged me to run a few rods, and then laid his hand suddenly to my heart, to see, as I conjecture, if my wind was good. By the old man I was purchased. What the price given for me was, I cannot tell. An officer of the market attested the contract, and I was obliged by the master of the shop, who sold me upon commissions, for the benefit of the concerned in the Rover, to lie down in the street, take the foot of my new master, and place it upon my neck; making to him, what the lawyers call, attornment.[2] I was then seized by two slaves, and led to the house of my new master.

Perhaps the free citizen of the United States may, in the warmth of his patriotism, accuse me of a tameness of spirit, in submitting to such gross disgrace. I will not justify myself. Perhaps I ought to have asserted the dignity of our nation, in despite of bastinadoes, chains, or even death itself. Charles the twelfth of Sweden has however been stigmatized by the historian, as a madman, for opposing the insulting Turk, when a prisoner, though assisted by nearly two hundred brave men.[3] If any of my dear countrymen censure my want of due spirit, I have only to wish him in my situation at Algiers, that he may avail himself of a noble opportunity of suffering gloriously for his country.

Chapter III.

True, I talk of dreams,
Which are the children of an idle brain,
Begot of nothing but vain fantasy,
Which is as thin of substance as the air,
And more inconstant than the wind;
Who woos
Even now the frozen bosom of the north,
And, being anger'd, puffs away from thence,
Turning his face to the dew dropping south.[1]

Shakespeare.

Argument.

The Author Dreameth whilst Awake.

The higher his rank in society, the further is man removed from nature. Grandeur draws a circle round the great, and often excludes from them the finer feelings of the heart. The wretched are all of one family; and ever regard each other as brethren. Among the slaves of my new master, I was received with pity, and treated with tenderness, bordering upon fraternal affection. They could not indeed speak my language, and I was ignorant of theirs; but, by dividing the scanty meal, composing my couch of straw, and alleviating my more rugged labours, they spake that universal language of benevolence, which needs no linguist to interpret.

It is true, I did not meet, among my fellow slaves, the rich and the noble, as the dramatist and the novelist had taught me to expect.

To betray a weakness I will confess that, sometime after I was captured, I often suffered fancy to cheat me of my "weary moments," by portraying those scenes, which had often amused me in my closet, and delighted me on the stage. Sometimes, I even contemplated with pleasure the company and converse of my fellow slaves. I expected to find them men of rank at least, if not of learning. I fancied my master's cook an English lord; his valet an Italian duke; his groom a knight of Malta; and even his foot boy some little lively French marquis. I fancied my future master's head gardener, taking me one side, professing the warmest friendship, and telling me in confidence that he was a Spanish Don with forty noble names; that he had fallen in love with my master's fair daughter, whose mother was a christian slave; that the young lady was equally charmed with him; that she was to rob her father of a rich casket of jewels, there being no dishonour in stealing from an infidel; jump into his arms in boy's clothes that very night, and escape by a vessel, already provided, to his native country. I saw in imagination all this accomplished. I saw the lady descend the rope ladder; heard the old man and his servants pursue; saw the lady carried off breathless in the arms of her knight; arrive safe in Spain; was present at the lady's baptism into the catholic church, and at her marriage with her noble deliverer. I was myself almost stifled with the caresses of the noble family, for the part I had borne in this perilous adventure; and in fine married to Donna some body, the Don's beautiful sister; returned into my own country, loaded with beauty and riches; and perhaps was aroused from my reverie by a poor fellow slave, whose extreme ignorance had almost blunted the sensibility of his own wretchedness.

Indeed, so sweet were the delusions of my own fancy, I am loth to destroy the innocent gratification, which the readers of novels and plays enjoy from the works of a Behn and a Colman;[2] but the sober character of the historian compels me to assure my readers that, whatever may have happened in the sixteenth century, I never saw during my captivity, a man of any rank, family, or fortune among the menial slaves. The Dey, as I have already observed, selecting his tenth prisoner from those, who would most probably afford the richest ransom, those concerned in the captures are influenced by the same motive. All, who may be expected to be ransomed, are deprived of their liberty, it is true; but fed, clothed, and never put to manual labour, except as a punishment for some actual crime, or attempting to recover their liberty. The menial slaves are generally composed of the dregs of those nations, with whom they are at war; but, though my fellow slaves were grossly illiterate, I must do them the justice to say, they had learned well the kinder virtues: those virtues, which schools and colleges often fail to teach, which, as Aristotle well observes, are like a flame of fire. Light them up in whatever climate you will, they burn and shine ever the same.

CHAPTER IV.

One day (may that returning day be night,
The stain the curse of each succeeding year!)
For something or for nothing, in his pride
He struck me. While I tell it do I live!!![1]

Young's Revenge.

ARGUMENT.

Account of my Master Abdel Melic: description of his House, Wife, Country House, and severe Treatment of his Slaves.

The name of my master was Abdel Melic. He had been formerly an officer in the Dey's troops, and, it was said, had rendered the Dey's father some important service in an insurrection, and was therefore highly respected; though at that time he had no publick employment. He was an austere man; his natural severity being probably encreased by his employment as a military officer. I never saw the face of any other person in his family, except the male slaves. The houses of the Algerines are nearly all upon the same model; consisting of a building towards the street of one or two stories, which is occupied by the master and male domestics, and which is connected by a gallery upon the ground, if the house is of one story; if of two, the entrance is above stairs, to a building of nearly the same size behind, which has no windows or lattices at the side, but only looking into a garden, which is always surrounded by a high wall. In these back apartments the women are lodged, both wives and slaves. My master had a wife, the daughter of a principal officer in the Dey's court, and, to my surprise, had only one. I found it to be a vulgar errour, that the Algerines had generally more. It is true they are allowed four by their law; but they generally find, as in our country, one lady sufficient for all the comforts of connubial life; and never take another, except family alliance or barrenness renders it eligible or necessary. The more I became acquainted with their customs, the more was I struck with their great resemblance to the patriarchical manners, described in holy writ. Concubinage is allowed; but few respectable people practise it, except for the sake of heirs. With the Algerines the barrenness of a RACHEL is sometimes compensated to the husband, by the fertility of a BILHAH.[2] After I had lived in this town house about three weeks, during which time I was clothed after the fashion of the country, my master moved, with his whole family, to a country house on the river Saffran.[3] Our journey, which was about twelve miles, was performed in the evening. Two carriages, resembling our travelling waggons, contained the women. Only the bodies of them were latticed, and furnished with curtains to cover them in the day time, which were rolled up in the evening. Two slaves preceded the carriages. Abdel Melic followed on horseback, and I accompanied a baggage waggon in the rear. When we arrived at the country house, the garden gates were thrown open, and the carriages with the women entered. The men were introduced to the front apartments. I found here several more slaves, equally ignorant and equally attentive and kind towards me, as those I had seen in the town. The next day, we were all set to work in digging for the foundation of a new wall, which was to enlarge our master's gardens. The weather was sultry. The soil below the surface was almost a quicksand. I, unused to hard labour, found my strength soon exhausted. My fellow slaves, compassionating my distress, were anxious, by changing places with me, to render my share of the labour less toilsome. As we had our stint for the whole party staked out to us every morning, it was in the power of my kind fellow labourers to favour me much. Often would they request me, by signs, to repose myself in the shade, while they encouraged each other to perform my share of the task. After a while, our master came to inspect the work; and, conceiving that it did not progress as fast as he wished, he put an overseer over us, who, finding me not so active as the rest, first threatened and then struck me with his whip. This was the first disgraceful blow I had ever received. Judge you, my gallant, freeborn fellow citizens, you, who rejoice daily in our federal strength and independence, what were my sensations. I threw down my spade with disdain, and retired from my work, lowering indignation upon my insulting oppressor. Upon his lifting his whip to strike me again, I flew at him, collared him, and threw him on his back. Then, setting my foot on his breast, I called upon my fellow slaves to assist me to bind the wretch, and to make one glorious effort for our freedom. But I called in vain. They could not comprehend my language; and, if they could, I spoke to slaves, astonished at my presumption, and dreading the consequences for me and themselves. After their first astonishment, they ran and took me gently off from the overseer, and raised him with the greatest respect. No sooner was he upon his feet than, mad with rage, he took up a mattoc;[4] and, with a violent blow upon my head, levelled me to the ground. I lay senseless, and was awakened from my stupor by the severe lashes of his whip, with which the dastardly wretch continued to beat me, until his strength failed. I was then left to the care of my fellow slaves, who could only wash my wounds with their tears. Complaint was immediately made to my master, and I was sent to work in a stone quarry about two miles from the house. At first, I rejoiced in escaping the malice of this merciless overseer, but soon found I had made no advantageous exchange. I was surrounded by the most miserable objects. My fellow labourers had been put to this place, as a punishment for domestic crimes, or for their superiour strength, and all were obliged to labour equally hard. To break hard rocks with heavy mauls, to transport large stones upon our backs up the craggy sides of the quarry, were our common labours; and to drink water, which would have been delicious, if cold, and to eat black barley bread and onions, our daily fare; while the few hours, allotted to rest upon our flinty beds, were disturbed by the tormenting insects, or on my part by the more tormenting dreams of the dainties of my father's house. There is a spring under a rock upon my father's farm, which we called the cold spring, from which we used to supply our family with water, and prided ourselves in presenting it as a refreshing beverage, in summer, to our visitors. How often, after working beyond my strength, on a sultry African day, in that horrid quarry, have I dreamed of dipping my cup in that cold spring, and fancied the waters eluding my taste as I raised it to my lips. Being presented with a tumbler filled from this spring, after my return, in a large circle of friends, the agonies I had suffered came so forcibly into my recollection, that I could not drink the water, but had the weakness to melt into tears.

How naturally did the emaciated prodigal, in the scripture, think upon the bread in his father's house. Bountiful Father of the Universe, how are the common blessings of thy providence despised. When I ate of the bread of my father's house, and drank of his refreshing spring, no grateful return was made to him or thee. It was amidst the parched sands and flinty rocks of Africa that thou taughtest me, that the bread was indeed pleasant, and the water sweet. Let those of our fellow citizens, who set at nought the rich blessings of our federal union, go like me to a land of slavery, and they will then learn how to appreciate the value of our free government.

Chapter V.

A christian is the highest stile of man.
And is there, who the blessed cross wipes off,
As a foul blot from his dishonour'd brow?
If angels tremble, 'tis at such a sight:
The wretch they quit, desponding of their charge,
More struck with grief or wonder, who can tell?[1]

YOUNG.

Argument.

The Author is encountered by a Renegado:[2] Struggles between Faith, the World, the Flesh, and the Devil.

As I was drooping under my daily task, I saw a young man habited in the Turkish dress, whose clear skin and florid cheek convinced me he was not a native of the country; whose mild air and manners betrayed nothing of the ferocity of the renegado. The stile of his turban pronounced him a Mahometan; but the look of pity, he cast towards the christian slaves, was entirely inconsistent with the pious hauteur of the mussulman; for christian dog is expressed as strongly by the features as the tongue of him, they call a true believer. He arrested my attention. For a moment I suspended my labour. At the same moment, an unmerciful lash, from the whip of the slave driver, recalled my attention to my work, and excited his, who was the cause of my neglect. At his approach, the slave driver quitted me. The stranger accosted me, and in good English commiserated my distresses, which, he said, he should deplore the more, if they were remediless. When a man is degraded to the most abject slavery, lost to his friends, neglected by his country, and can anticipate no rest but in the grave, is not his situation remediless, I replied? Renounce the Christian, and embrace the Mahometan faith; you are no longer a slave, and the delights of life await you, retorted he. You see me. I am an Englishman. For three years after my captivity, like you, I groaned under the lash of the slave driver; I ate the scanty morsel of bitterness, moistened with my tears. Borne down by the complicated ills of hunger and severe labour, I was carried to the infirmary for slaves, to breathe my last, where I was visited by a Mollah or Mahometan priest. He pitied the misfortunes of a wretch, who, he said, had suffered a cruel existence, in this life, and had no rational hopes of exchanging it for a better, in the world to come. He opened the great truths of the mussulman faith. By his assistance I recovered my health, and was received among the faithful. Embraced and protected by the rich and powerful, I have now a house in the city, a country residence on the Saffran, two beautiful wives, a train of domestics; and a respectable place in the Dey's customs defrays the expense. Come, added he, let me send my friend, the Mollah, to you. He will remove your scruples, and, in a few days, you will be as free and happy as I am. I looked at him with astonishment. I had ever viewed the character of an apostate as odious and detestable. I turned from him with abhorrence, and for once embraced my burthen with pleasure. Indeed I pity you, said he. I sorrow for your distresses, and pity your prejudices. I pity you too, replied I, the tears standing in my eyes. My body is in slavery, but my mind is free. Your body is at liberty, but your soul is in the most abject slavery, in the gall of bitterness and bond of iniquity. You have sold your God for filthy lucre; and "what shall it profit you, if you gain the whole world and lose your own soul, or what shall a man give in exchange for his soul."[3] I respect your prejudices, said the stranger, because I have been subject to them myself. I was born in Birmingham in England, and educated a rigid dissenter. No man is more subject to prejudice than an Englishman, and no sectary more obstinately attached to his tenets than the dissenter. But I have conversed with the Mollah, and I am

convinced of the errours of my education. Converse with him likewise. If he does not convince you, you may glory in the christian
faith; as that faith will be then founded on rational preference, and
not merely on your ignorance of any other religious system. Sug-
gest the least desire to converse with the Mollah, and an order from
the Mufti will come to your master. You will be clothed and fed at
the public expense; be lodged one month in the college of the
priest; and not returned to your labours, until the priest shall declare you incorrigible. He then left me. The heat increased, and my
strength wasted. The prospect of some alleviation from labour, and
perhaps a curiosity to hear what could be said in favour of so de-
testably ridiculous a system, as the Mahometan imposture,[4] induced me, when I saw the Englishman again, to signify my consent
to converse with the Mollah.

Chapter VI.

Hear I, or dream I hear that distant strain,
Sweet to the soul and tasting strong of Heaven,
Soft wasted on celestial pity's plume!![1]

Anon.

Argument.

*The Author is carried to the sacred College of the Mussulman Priest:
The Mortifications and Austerities of the Mahometan Recluse. The
Mussulman mode of Proselyting.*

The next day, an order came from the Mufti to my master, who received the order, touched his forehead with the tefta[2] respectfully, and directed me to be instantly delivered to the Mollah. I was carried to the college, a large gloomy building, on the outside; but, within the walls, it was an earthly paradise. The stately rooms, refreshing baths, cooling fountains, luxuriant gardens, ample larders, rich carpets, downy sofas, and silken mattresses, offered with profusion all those soft excitements to indolent pleasure, which the most refined voluptuary could desire. I have often observed that, in all countries, except New England, those, whose profession it is to decry the luxuries and vanities of this world some how or other, contrive to possess the greatest portion of them.

Immediately upon my entering these sacred walls, I was carried to a warm bath, into which I was immediately plunged; while my attendants, as if emulous to cleanse me from all the filth of errour, rubbed me so hard with their hands and flesh brushes, that I verily thought they would have flayed me. While I was relaxed with the tepid, I was suddenly plunged into a contiguous cold bath. I confess I apprehended dangerous consequences, from so sudden a check of such violent perspiration; but I arose from the cold bath highly invigorated.* I was then anointed in all parts, which had been exposed to the sun with a preparation of a gum, called the balm of Mecca.[5] This application excited a very uneasy sensation, similar to the stroke of the water pepper, to which "the liberal shepherds give a grosser name."[6] In twenty four hours, the sun browned cuticle peeled off, and left my face, hands, legs, and neck as fair as a child's of six months old. This balm the Algerine ladies procure at a great expense, and use it as a cosmetic to heighten their beauty.

After I had been clothed in the drawers, slippers, loose coat, and shirt of the country, if shirt it could be called, which neck had none; with a decoction of the herb henna, my hands and feet were tinged yellow: which colour, they said, denoted purity of intention. I was lodged and fed well, and suffered to amuse myself, and recover my sanity of body and mind. On the eleventh day, as I was reclining on the margin of a retired fountain, reflecting on my dear native country, I was joined by the Mollah. He was a man of about thirty years of age, of the most pleasing countenance and engaging deportment. He was born at Antioch, and educated a christian of the Greek church. He was designed by his parents for a preferment in that church, when he was captured by the Algerines, and almost immediately, conformed to the mussulman faith; and was in high esteem in the sacred college of the priests. As he spoke latin and some modern languages fluently, was well versed in the bible and christian doctrines, he was often employed in proselyting the European slaves, and prided himself in his frequent success.

---

* The Indian of North America surprised the European physician, by a process founded on similar principles.[3] The patient, in the most violent fever, was confined in a low hut, built of turf and flat stones, which had been previously heated by fire. When the profusest perspiration was thus excited, the patient was carried, and often, with Indian fortitude, ran to the next stream, and plunged frequently through the ice into the coldest water. This process, which Bœrhaave and Sydenham[4] would have pronounced delotery, ever produced pristine health and vigour, when prescribed by the Indian physician or Powwow.

He accosted me with the sweetest modulation of voice; kindly inquired after my welfare; begged to know if my lodging, dress, and fare, were agreeable; assuring me that, if I wished to alter either, in such a manner as to bring them nearer to the fare and modes of my native country, and would give my directions, they should be obeyed. He requested me to appoint a time, when we might converse upon the great subject of religion. He observed that he wished me free from bodily indisposition, and that the powers of my mind would recover their activity. He said, the holy faith, he offered to my embraces, disdained the use of other powers than rational argument; that he left to the church of Rome, and its merciless inquisitors, all the honour and profit of conversion by faggots, dungeons, and racks. He made some further inquiry, as to my usage in the college, and retired. I had been so long accustomed to the insolence of domestic tyranny; so often groaned under the whip and burthen; so often been buffetted, spurned and spit upon, that I had steeled my mind against the force and terrour, I anticipated from the Mollah; but was totally unprepared for such apparent candour and gentleness. Though I viewed his conduct as insidious, yet he no sooner retired than, overcome by his suavity of manners, for the first time I trembled for my faith, and burst into tears.

CHAPTER VII.

But pardon, gentles all,
The flat, unraised spirit, that hath dared,
On this unworthy scaffold, to bring forth
So great an object.[1]

SHAKESPEARE.

ARGUMENT.

The Author confereth with a Mollah or Mahometan Priest: Defendeth the Verity of the Christian Creed, and resigns his Body to Slavery, to preserve the Freedom of his Mind.

Upon the margin of a refreshing fountain, shadowed by the fragrant branches of the orange, date, and pomegranate, for five successive days I maintained the sacred truths of our holy religion, against the insidious attack of the mussulman priest. To be more perspicuous, I have condensed our conversation, and, to avoid useless repetition, have assumed the manner of a dialogue.

Mollah. Born in New England, my friend, you are a christian purified by Calvin. Born in the Campania of Rome, you had been a papist. Nursed by the Hindoos, you would have entered the pagoda with reverence, and worshipped the soul of your ancestor in a duck. Educated on the bank of the Wolga[2] the Delai Lama had been your god. In China, you would have worshipped Tien,[3] and perfumed Confucius, as you bowed in adoration before the tablets of your ancestors. Cradled with the Parsees of Indostan, you had adored fire,[4] and trembled with pious awe, as you presented your rice and your ghee to the adorable cock and dog.

A wise man adheres not to his religion, because it was that of his ancestors. He will examine the creeds of other nations, compare them with his own, and hold fast that, which is right.

Author. You speak well. I will bring my religion to the test. Compare it with the—the—

Mollah. Speak out boldly. No advantage shall be taken. You would say, with the Mahometan imposture. To determine which of two revealed religions is best, two inquiries are alone necessary. First, which of them has the highest proof of its divine origin, and which inculcates the purest morals: that is, of which have we the greatest certainty that it came from God, and which is calculated to do most good to mankind.

Author. True. As to the first point, our bible was written by men divinely inspired.

Mollah. Our alcoran[5] was written by the finger of the Deity himself. But who told you, your bible was written by men divinely inspired.

Author. We have received it from our ancestors, and we have as good evidence for the truths it contains, as we have in profane history for any historical fact.

Mollah. And so have we for the alcoran. Our sacred and profane writers all prove the existence of such a prophet as Mahomet, that he received the sacred volume from the hand of Gabriel, and the traditions of our ancestors confirm our faith.

Author. We know, the christian religion is true, from its small beginnings and wonderful increase. None but Deity himself could have enabled a few illiterate fishermen to spread a religion over the world, and perpetuate it to posterity.

Mollah. Your argument I allow to be forcible, but grant us also the use of it. Mahomet was an illiterate camel driver. Could he, who could not read nor write, have published a book, which for its excellence has astonished the world? Would the learned of Medina and Mecca have become his disciples? Could Omar and Abubeker,[6] his successours, equally illiterate, have become the admiration of the world? If you argue from the astonishing spread of your faith, view our prophet, born five hundred and sixty nine years, and dating the promulgation of his doctrine six hundred and twenty years after the birth of your prophet. See the extensive countries of Persia, Arabia, Syria, Egypt, all rejoicing in its benign influence. See our holy faith pouring its divine rays of light into Russia, and Tartary. See it received by enlightened Greece, raising its crescent through the vast Turkish empire, and the African states. See Palestine, and Jerusalem the birth place of your prophet, filled with the disciples of ours. See Asia and Africa, and a great part of Europe acknowledging the unity of God, and the mission of his prophet. In a word, view the world. See two mahometans of a religion, which arose six hundred and twenty years after yours, to one christian, computing those of all denominations, and then give your argument of the miraculous spread of religion its due weight.

My blood boiled to hear this infidel vaunt himself thus triumphantly against my faith; and, if it had not been for a prudence, which in hours of zeal I have since had cause to lament, I should have taken vengeance of him upon the spot. I restrained my anger, and observed, our religion is supported by miracles.

Mollah. So is ours; which is the more remarkable, as our great prophet declared, he was not sent into the world to work miracles, but to preach the unity of the first cause, the resurrection of the dead, the bliss of paradise, and the torments of the damned. Yet his whole life was a miracle. He was no sooner born than, with a voice, like the thundering of Hermon,[7] he pronounced the adorable creed to his mother and nurses: *I profess that there is only one God, and that I am his apostle.* He was circumcised from all eternity; and, at the same hour, a voice of four mighty angels was heard proclaiming from the four corners of the holy house. The first saying, proclaim the truth is risen, and all lies shall return into hell. The second uttering, now is born an apostle of your own nation, and the Omnipotent is with him. The words of the third were, a book full of illustrious light is sent to you from God; and the fourth voice was heard to say, O Mahomet, we have sent thee to be a prophet, apostle, and guide to the world.

When the sent of God was about three years old, the blessed child retired into a cave, at the basis of mount Uriel; when the archangel Gabriel, covering his face with his wings, in awful respect approached him saying, Bismillahi Rrahmani Rrhahimi;[8] in the name of the one Almighty, Compassionate, and Merciful, I am sent to pluck from thy heart the root of evil; for thy prayers have shaken the pillars of eternal decree. The infant prophet said, the will of thy Lord and mine be done. The archangel, then opened his bosom with a lancet of adamant, and, taking out his heart, squeezed from it the black drop of original sin; and, having restored the heart, sunk gently into the bosom of the Houri.

Do you wish for more miracles? Hear how the prophet, in the dark night, passed the seven heavens upon the sacred mule; of the mighty angel he saw, of such astonishing magnitude, that it was twelve thousand days journey in the space between his eye brows; of the years he spent in perusing the book of destiny; and how he returned, so speedily that, the mattress was not cold, and he recovered the pitcher at his bed side, which he had overset at his departure, so that not one drop of water was lost. Contrast these with those of your prophet. He then vented a volume of reproach horrible to hear, and too blasphemous to defile my paper.

Author. Our religion was disseminated in peace; yours was promulgated by the sword.

Mollah. My friend, you surely have not read the writings of your own historians. The history of the christian church is a detail of bloody massacre: from the institution of the christian thundering legion, under Constantine the great, to the expulsion of the Moors out of Spain by the ferocious inquisition, or the dragooning of the Hugonots from France, under Louis the great. The mussulmen never yet forced a man to adopt their faith. When Abubeker, the caliph, took a christian city, he forbore to enter a principal church, as he should pray in the temple of God; and, where he prayed, the building would be established as a mosque by the piety of the faithful. The companions and successours of the apostle conquered cities and kingdoms, like other nations. They gave civil laws to the conquered, according to the laws of nations; but they never forced the conscience of any man. It is true, they then and we now, when a slave pronounces the ineffable creed, immediately knock off his fetters and receive him as a brother; because we read in the book of Zuni that the souls of true believers are bound up in one fragrant bundle of eternal love. We leave it to the christians of the West Indies, and christians of your southern plantations, to baptize the unfortunate African into your faith, and then use your brother christians as brutes of the desert.

Here I was so abashed for my country, I could not answer him.

Author. But you hold a sensual paradise.

Mollah. So the doctors of your church tell you; but a sensual heaven is no more imputable to us than to you. When the Most Holy condescends to reveal himself to man in human language, it must be in terms commensurate with our conception. The enjoyment of the Houri, those immortal virgins, who will attend the beatified believer; the splendid pavilions of the heavens, are all but types and significations of holy joys too sublime for man in flesh to conceive of. In your bible, I read, your prophet refers to the time, when he should drink new wine in his father's kingdom. Now would it be candid in me to hastily brand the heaven of your prophet as sensual, and to represent your faithful in bliss as a club of wine bibbers?

Author. But you will allow the preeminence of the morality of the sacred scriptures.

Mollah. Your scriptures contain many excellent rules of life. You are there taught to be kindly affectionate one towards another; but they recommend the use of wine, and do not forbid gaming. The alcoran, by forbidding in express terms the use of either, cuts from its follower the two principal sources of disquiet and misery. Read then this spotless book. There you will learn to love those of our faith, and not hate those of any other. You will learn the necessity of being virtuous here, that you may be happy and not miserable hereafter. You will learn resignation to the will of the Holy One; because you will know, that all the events of your life were, in the embryo of time, forged on the anvils of Divine Wisdom. In a word, you will learn the unity of God, which, notwithstanding the cavil of your divines, your prophet, like ours, came into the world to establish, and every man of reason must believe. You need not renounce your prophet. Him we respect as a great apostle of God; but Mahomet is the seal of the prophets. Turn then, my friend, from slavery to the delights of life. Throw off the shackles of education from your soul, and be welcome to the joys of the true believer. Lift your finger to the immensity of space, and confess that there is one God, and that Mahomet is his apostle.

I have thus given a few sketches of the manner of this artful priest. After five days conversation, disgusted with his fables, abashed by his assurance, and almost confounded by his sophistry, I resumed my slave's attire, and sought safety in my former servitude.

Chapter VIII.

Et cest lingue, nest sorsque un term similitudinarie, et est a tant a dire, *Hotchpot.*[1]

Coke on Littleton, *Lib.* iii. *Sec.* 268.

Argument.

The Language of the Algerines.

The very day, I was dismissed from the college of the priests, I was returned to my master, and the next morning sent again to labour in the quarry. To my surprise, no harsh reflections were made upon, what these true believers must have stiled, my obstinate prejudice against the true faith; for I am sensible that my master was so good a mussulman as to have rejoiced in my conversion, though it might affect his purse. I experienced the extremest contumely and severity; but I was never branded as a heretic. I had by this time acquired some knowledge of their language, if language it could be called, which bad defiance to modes and tenses, appearing to be the shreds and clippings of all the tongues, dead and living, ever spoken since the creation. It is well known on the sea coasts of the Mediterranean by the name of Lingua Franca. Probably it had its rise in the awkward endeavours of the natives to converse with strangers from all parts of the world, and the vulgar people, calling all foreigners *Franks,* supplied its *name.* I the more readily acquired this jargon, as it contained many Latin derivatives. If I have conjectured the principle, upon which the *Lingua Franca* was originally formed, it is applied through all stages of its existence: every person having good right to introduce words and phrases from his vernacular tongue, and which, with some alteration in accent, are readily adopted.*

This medley of sounds is generally spoken, but the people of the higher rank pride themselves in speaking pure Arabic. My conference with the Mollah was effected in Latin, which the priest pronounced very differently from the learned president and professors of Harvard college, but delivered himself with fluency and elegance.

---

* I well recollect, being once at a loss to name a composition of boiled barley, rice and treacle, I called for the HASTY PUDDING[2] and MOLASSES. The phrase was immediately adopted, and HASCHI PUDAH MOLASCHI is now a synonima with the ancient name: and, I doubt not, if a dictionary of the Lingua Franca shall ever be compiled, the name of the staple cookery of New England will have a conspicuous place.

Chapter IX.

With aspect sweet, as heavenly messenger
On deeds of mercy sent, a form appears.
Unfading chaplets bloom upon her brow,
Eternal smiles play o'er her winning face,
And frequent promise opes her flattering lips.
'Tis HOPE, who from the dayless dungeon
Points the desponding wretch to scenes of bliss,
And ever and anon she draws the veil
Of blank futurity, and shews him where,
Far, far beyond the oppressor's cruel grasp,
His malice and his chains, he shares again
The kindred mirth and feast under the roof
Paternal, or beside his social fire
Presses the lovely partner of his heart,
While the dear pledges of their mutual love
Gambol around in sportive innocence.
   Anon th' illusive phantom mocks his sight,
And leaves the frantic wretch to die
In pristine darkness, fetters and despair!!

AUTHOR'S *Manuscript Poems.*

ARGUMENT.

The Author plans an Escape.

I found many more slaves at work in the stone quarry, than when I quitted it; and the labours and hard fare seemed, if possible, to be augmented. The ease and comfort, with which I lived for some

weeks past, had vitiated my appetite, softened my hands, and relaxed my whole frame, so that my coarse fare and rugged labours
seemed more insupportable. I nauseated our homely food, and the
skin peeled from my hands and shoulders. I made what inquiries I
could, as to the interiour geography of the country, and comforted
myself with the hope of escape; conceiving it, under my desperate circumstances, possible to penetrate unobserved the interiour
country, by the eastern boundaries of the kingdom of Morocco,
and then pass on south west, until I struck the river Sanaga,[1] and
coursing that to its mouth I knew would bring me to some of the
European settlements near Goree or Cape Verd. Preparatory to my
intended escape I had procured an old goat's skin, which to make
into something like a knapsack, I deprived myself of many hours of
necessary sleep; and of many a scanty meal to fill it with provisions.
By the use of my Lingua Franca and a little Arabic, I hoped to obtain the assistance of the slaves and lower orders of the people,
through whom I might journey. The only insurmountable difficulty
in my projects was to elude the vigilance of our overseers. By a kind
of roll call the slaves were numbered every night and morning, and
at meal times: but, very fortunately, a probable opportunity of escaping unnoticed soon offered. It was announced to the slaves that
in three days time there would be a day of rest, a holiday, when they
would be allowed to recreate themselves in the fields. This intelligence diffused general joy. I received it with rapture. I doubled
my diligence in my preparations; and, in the afternoon previous
to this fortunate day, I contrived to place my little stock of provisions under a rock at a small distance from the quarry. At sunset we
were all admitted to bathe, and I retired to my repose with bright
hopes of freedom in my heart, which were succeeded by the most
pleasing dreams of my native land. That Beneficent Being, who
brightens the slumbers of the wretched with rays of bliss, can alone
express my raptures, when, in the visions of that night, I stepped
lightly over a father's threshhold; was surrounded by congratulating friends and faithful domestics; was pressed by the embraces of a
father; and with holy joy felt a mother's tears moisten my cheek.

Early in the dawn of the morning, I was awakened by the congratulations of my fellows, who immediately collected in small groups, planning out the intended amusements of the day. Scarce had they portioned the little space alloted to ease, according their various inclinations, when an express order came from our master that we should go under the immediate direction of our overseers, to a plain, about five miles distance, to be present at a publick spectacle. This was a grievous disappointment to them, and more especially to me. I buoyed up my spirits however with the hopes that, in the hurry and crowd, I might find means to escape, which, although I knew I could not return for my knapsack, I was resolved to attempt, having a little millet and two onions in my pocket.

Chapter X.

O beasts of pity void! to oppress the weak,
To point your vengeance at the friendless head.[1]

ANON.

Argument.

The Author present at a Public Spectacle.

We were soon paraded and marched to the plain, to be amused with the promised spectacle, which, notwithstanding it might probably frustrate my attempts for freedom, I anticipated with a pleasing curiosity. When we arrived at the plain, we found, surrounding a spot, fenced in with a slight railing, a large concourse of people, among whom I could discern many groups of men, whose habits and sorrow indented faces shewed them to be of the same miserable order with us. In the midst of this spot there was a frame erected, somewhat resembling the stage of our pillories; on the centre of which a pole or strong stake was erected, sharpened at the end and pointed with steel. While I was perplexing myself with the design of this apparatus, military music was heard at a distance; and soon after a strong party of guards approached the scaffold, and soon mounted upon the stage a miserable wretch, with all the agonies of despair in his countenance, who I learned from his sentence, proclaimed by a public crier, was to be impaled alive for attempting to escape from bondage. The consciousness that I had been, one moment before, meditating the same act, for which this wretch was to suffer so cruelly, added to my feelings for a fellow creature, excited so strong a sympathy for the devoted wretch, that I was near fainting.

I will not wound the sensibility of my tail of this fiend like punishment. Suffice it to say that, after they had stripped the sufferer naked, except a cloth around the loins, they inserted the iron pointed stake into the lower termination of the vertebræ, and thence forced it up near his back bone, until it appeared between his shoulders; with devilish ingenuity contriving to avoid the vital parts. The stake was then raised into the air, and the suffering wretch exposed to the view of the assembly, writhing in all the contortions of insupportable agony. How long he lived, I cannot tell, I never gave but one look at him: one was enough to appal a New England heart. I laid my head on the rails, until we retired. It was now obvious, it was designed by our master, that this horrid spectacle should operate upon us as a terrifying example. It had its full effect on me. I thought no more of attempting an escape; but, during our return, was miserably tormented least my knapsack and provisions should be found and adduced against me, as evidence of my intent to desert. Happily for me, I recovered them the next day, and no suspicions of my design were entertained.

Chapter XI.

If perchance thy home
Salute thee with a father's honoured name,
Go, call thy sons, instruct them what a debt
They owe their ancestors and make them swear
To pay it, by transmitting down entire
Those sacred rights, to which themselves were born.[1]

AKENSIDE.

Argument.

The Author feels that he is indeed a Slave.

I now found that I was indeed a slave. My body had been en-
thralled, but the dignity of a free mind remained; and the same insulted pride, which had impelled me to spurn the villain slave
driver, who first struck me a disgraceful blow, had often excited a
surly look of contempt upon my master, and the vile instruments of
his oppression; but the terrour of the late execution, with the un-
abating fatigue of my body, had so depressed my fortitude, that I
trembled at the look of the overseer, and was meanly anxious to
conciliate his favour, by attempting personal exertions beyond my
ability. The trite story of the insurgent army of the slaves of ancient Rome, being routed by the mere menaces and whips of their
masters, which I ever sceptically received, I now credit. A slave myself, I have learned to appreciate the blessings of freedom. May my
countrymen ever preserve and transmit to their posterity that liberty, which they have bled to obtain; and always bear it deeply en-

graven upon their memories, that, when men are once reduced to slavery, they can never resolve, much more achieve, any thing, that is manly, virtuous, or great.

Depression of spirits, consequent upon my blasted hope of escape, coarse fare, and constant fatigue reduced me to a mere skeleton: while over exertion brought on an hæmoptysis or expectoration of blood, and menaced an approaching hectic;[2] and soon after, fainting under my burthen, I was taken up and conveyed in a horse litter to the infirmary for slaves, in the city of Algiers.

Chapter XII.

Oft have I prov'd the labours of thy love,
And the warm effort of thy gentle heart,
Anxious to please.[1]

Blair's Grave.

Argument.

The Infirmary.

Here I was lodged comfortably, and had all the attention paid me, which good nurses and ignorant physicians could render. The former were men, who had made a vow of poverty, and whose profession was to attend the couches of the sick; the latter were more ignorant than those of my own country, who had amused me in the gayer days of life. They had no theory nor any systematic practice; but it was immaterial to me. I had cast my last anxious thoughts upon my dear native land, had blessed my affectionate parents, and was resigned to die.

One day as I was sunk upon my bed, after a violent fit of coughing, I was awakened from a doze, by a familiar voice, which accosted me in Latin. I opened my eyes and saw at my side, the Mollah, who attempted to destroy my faith. It immediately struck me that his purpose was to tempt me to apostatize in my last moments. The religion of my country was all I had left of the many blessings, I once enjoyed, in common with my fellow citizens. This rendered it doubly dear to me. Not that I was insensible of the excellence and verity of my faith; no. If I had been exposed to severer agonies than

I suffered, and had been flattered with all the riches and honours, these infidels could bestow, I trust I should never have foregone that faith, which assured me for the miseries, I sustained in a cruel separation from my parents, friends, and intolerable slavery, a rich compensation in that future world, where I should rejoin my beloved friends, and where sorrow, misery, or slavery, should never come. I judged uncandidly of the priest. He accosted me with the same gentleness, as when at the college, commiserated my deplorable situation, and, upon my expressing an aversion to talk upon religion, he assured me that he disdained taking any advantage of my weakness; nor would attempt to deprive me of the consolation of my faith, when he feared I had no time left to ground me in a better. He recommended me to the particular care of the religious, who attended the sick in the hospital; and, having learned in our former conferences that I was educated a physician, he influenced his friend the director of the infirmary to purchase me, if I regained my health, and told him I would be serviceable, as a minor assistant. If any man could have effected a change of my religion, it was this priest. I was charmed with the man, though I abominated his faith. His very smile exhilerated my spirits and infused health; and, when he repeated his visits, and communicated his plan of alleviating my distresses, the very idea, of being freed from the oppressions of Abdel Melic, made an exchange of slavery appear desirable. I was again attached to life, and requested him to procure a small quantity of the quinquina or jesuits bark.[2] This excellent specific was unknown in the infirmary; but, as the Algerines are all fatalists, it is immaterial to the patient, who is his physician, and what he prescribes. By his kindness the bark was procured, and I made a decoction, as near to Huxham's, as the ingredients I could procure would admit,[3] which I infused in wine; no brandy being allowed, even for the sick. In a few weeks, the diagnostics were favourable, and I recovered my pristine health; and, soon after, the director of the hospital purchased me of my late master, and I was appointed to the care of the medicine room, with permission to go into the city for fresh supplies.

Chapter XIII.

Hail Esculapians, hail, ye Coan race,
Thro' earth and sea, thro' chaos' boundless space;
Whether in Asia's pamper'd courts ye shine,
Or Afric's deadly realms beneath the line.

PATENT ADDRESS.

ARGUMENT.

The Author's Practice as a Surgeon and Physician, in the City of Algiers.

My circumstances were now so greatly ameliorated that, if I could have been assured of returning to my native country in a few years, I should have esteemed them eligible. To observe the customs, habits, and manners of a people, of whom so much is said and so little known at home; and especially to notice the medical practice of a nation, whose ancestors have been spoken of with respect, in the annals of the healing art, was highly interesting.

After a marked and assiduous attention of some months to the duties of my office, I acquired the confidence of my superiours so far, that I was sometimes sent abroad in the city to examine a patient, who had applied for admission into the infirmary; and sometimes the physicians themselves would condescend to consult me. Though they affected to despise my skill, I had often the gratification of observing that they administered my prescriptions with success.

In surgery they were arrant bunglers. Indeed, their pretensions to knowledge in this branch were so small that my superiour adroitness scarce occasioned envy. Applications, vulgarly common in the United States, were there viewed with admiration. The actual cautery was their only method of staunching an external hemorrhage. The first amputation, I operated, drew all the principal physicians around me. Nothing could equal their surprise, at the application of the spring tourniquet, which I had assisted a workman to make for the occasion, except the taking up of the arteries. My friend the Mollah came to congratulate me on my success, and spread my reputation wherever he visited. A poor creature was brought to the hospital with a depressed fracture upon the os frontis,[1] sunk into a lethargy, and died. I proposed trepanning, but found those useful instruments unknown in this country. By the care of the director, I had a set made under my direction; but, after having performed upon a dead, I never could persuade the Algerine faculty to permit me to operate upon a living subject. What was more amusing, they pretended to improve the aid of philosophy against me, and talked of the weight of a column of air pressing upon the dura mater, which, they said, would cause instant death. Of all follies the foppery of learning is the most insupportable. Professional ignorance and obstinacy were not all I had to contend with. Religious prejudice was a constant impediment to my success. The bigotry of the Mahometan differs essentially from that of the Roman catholic. The former is a passive, the latter an active principle. The papist will burn infidels and heretics; the Mussulman never torments the unbeliever, but is more tenaciously attached to his own creed, makes his faith a principle in life, and never suffers doubt to disturb, or reason to overthrow it. I verily believe that, if the alcoran had declared, that the earth was an immense plain and stood still, while the sun performed its revolution round it, a whole host of Gallileos, with a Newton at their head, could not have shaken their opinion, though aided by all the demonstrative powers of experimental philosophy.

I was invited by one of the faculty to inspect the eyes of a child, which had lost its sight about three years; I proposed couching, and operated on the right eye with success. This child was the only son

of an opulent Algerine, who, being informed that an infidel had restored his son to sight, refused to let me operate on the other,
protesting that, if he had known that the operator was an unbeliever, his son should have remained blind, until he opened his eyes
upon the Houri of paradise. He sent me however a present of
money, and offered to make my fortune, if I would abjure the christian faith and embrace Ismaelism,[2] which, he said, he believed,
I should one day do: as he thought that God never would have
decreed that I should restore his son to sight, if he had not also decreed that I should be a true believer.

Chapter XIV.

Ryghte thenne there settenne onne a garyshe seatte,
A statlie dame lyche to an aunciant mayde;
Grete nationes and hygh kynges lowe at her feette,
Obeyseence mayde, as if of herre afrayede,
As overe theme her yronne rodde she swayde.

Hyghte custome was the loftie tyrantes namme,
Habyte bye somme yelypt, the worldlinges godde,
Panym and faythsman bowe before the dame,
Ne lawe butte yeldethe to her sovrenne nodde,
Reasonne her soemanne couchenne at her rodde.

FRAGMENT OF ANCIENT POETRY.

Argument.

Visits a sick Lady.

My reputation increased, and I was called the learned slave; and, soon after, sent for to visit a sick lady. This was very agreeable to me; for, during my whole captivity, I had never yet seen the face of a woman; even the female children being carefully concealed, at least from the sight of the vulgar. I now anticipated much satisfaction from this visit, and hoped that, through the confidence, with which a tender and successful physician seldom fails to inspire his patient, I should be able to acquire much useful information upon subjects of domestic concern, impervious to travellers. Preparatory to this visit, I had received a new and better suit of clothes than I

had worn, as a present from the father of the young lady. A gilt waggon came to the gate of the hospital, which I entered with our principal physician, and was drawn by mules to a country house, about
five miles from the city, where I was received by Hadgi Mulladin,
the father of my patient, with great civility. Real gentlemen are the
same in all countries. He treated us with fruit and sherbet; and,
smiling upon me, after he had presented a bowl of sherbet to the
principal physician, he handed me another bowl, which to my surprise I found filled with an excellent Greek wine, and archly inquired of me how I liked the *sherbet.* Hadgi Mulladin had travelled
in his youth, and was supposed to have imbibed the libertine principles of the christian, as it respected wine. This was the only instance, which came to my knowledge, of any professed Mussulman
indulging himself with wine or any strong liquor; and it was not
unnoticed by the principal physician, who afterwards gravely told
me that Hadgi Mulladin would be undoubtedly damned for drinking wine; would be condemned to perpetual thirst in the next
world, while the black spirit would present him with red hot cups
of scalding wine. Exhilirated by the wine and the comparitively
free manners of this Algerine, I was anxious to see my patient. I was
soon gratified. Being introduced into a large room, I was left alone
nigh an hour. A side door was then opened, and two eunuchs came
forward with much solemnity and made signs for me to retire to the
farthest part of the room, as if I had been infested with some ma-
lignant disorder. They were, in about ten minutes, followed by four
more of the same sex, bearing a species of couch, close covered
with double curtains of silk, which they set down in the midst of
the room; and every one drew a broad scimitar from his belt, flour-
ishing it in the air, inclined it over his shoulder, and stood guard at
every corner of the couch. While I was wondering at this parade,
the two first eunuchs retired and soon returned; the one bearing an
ewer or bason of water, the other a low marble stand, and some
napkins in a China dish. I was then directed to wash my feet; and,
another bason being produced, it was signified that I must wash my
hands, which I did three times. A large thick muslin veil was then
thrown over my head, I was led towards the couch, and was pre-

sented with a pulse glass,[1] being a long glass tube graduated and terminated below with a hollow bulb, and filled with some liquid, which rose and fell like spirits in the thermometer. This instrument was inserted through the curtains, and the bulb applied to the pulse of my patient, and the other extremity put under my veil. By this I was to form my opinion of her disorder, and prescribe a remedy; for I was not allowed to ask any questions or even to speak to, much more see the lady, who was soon reconveyed to her apartment. The two first eunuchs now marched in the rear, and closed and fastened the doors carefully after them. After waiting alone two hours or more, I was called to give my advice; and never was I more puzzled. To confess ignorance would have ruined my reputation, and reputation was then life itself. The temptations to quackery were powerful and overcame me. I boldly pronounced her disease to be an intermittent fever, prescribed venesection, and exhibited some common febrifuge, with directions to throw in the bark,[2] when the fever ceased. My prescriptions were attended with admirable success; and, if I had conformed to their faith, beyond a doubt, I might have acquired immense riches. But I was a slave, and all my gains were the property of my master. I must do him the justice to say that, he permitted me to keep any particular presents, that were made to me. Frequent applications were made to the director for my advice and assistance to the diseased; and, though he received generally my fee, yet it was sufficiently gratifying to me to be permitted to walk abroad, to amuse myself, and obtain information of this extraordinary people, as much of which, as the prescribed limits of this little work will admit, I shall now lay before my readers.

Chapter XV.

O'er trackless seas beneath the starless sky,
Or when thick clouds obscure the lamp of day,
The seaman, by the faithful needle led,
Dauntle's pursue his devious destin'd course.
Thus, on the boundless waste of ancient time,
Still let the faithful pen unerring point
The polar truth.

Author's Manuscript Poems.

Argument.

Sketch of the History of the Algerines.

Much antiquarian lore might here be displayed, in determining whether the state of Algiers was part of the ancient Mauritinia Massilia,[1] or within the boundaries of the republic of Carthage; and pages of fruitless research might be wasted, in precisely ascertaining the era, when that portion of the sea coast of Africa, now generally known by the name of the Barbary* Shore, was subdued by the Romans, or conquered by the Vandals.

---

* Bruce, an Englishman,[2] who travelled to collect fairy tales for the amusement of London cits, observes that this territory was called *Barbaria* by the Greeks and Romans from *Beber,* signifying a shepherd; and even the accurate compiler of the American edition of Guthrie's Geography[3] has quoted the observation in a marginal note. We cannot expect that geographers should be philologists anymore than that every printer should be a Webster. How the Greeks or Romans came by the word *Beber,* I leave Mr. Bruce to elucidate. The former had the term *barbaros,* a barbarian, which they indiscriminately applied to all foreigners;

The history of nations, like the biography of man, only assumes an interesting importance, when its subject is matured into vigour. To trace the infancy of the old world, we run into childish prattle and boyish tales. Suffice it then to say, that the mixed multitudes, which inhabited this country, were reduced to the subjection of the Greek emperours by the arms of the celebrated Belisarius,[4] and so continued, until the close of the seventh century, when they were subdued by the invincible power, and converted to the creed of the ancient caliphs, the immediate successours of the prophet Mahomet, who parcelled the country into many subordinate governments, among which was that of Algiers; which is now bounded, on the north, by the Mediterranean; on the south, by mount Atlas, so familiar to the classic reader, and the chain of hills, which extends thence to the north east; on the west, by the kingdom of Morocco;* and, on the east, by the state of Tunis. The state of Algiers is about five hundred miles in length, upon the coast of the Mediterranean, and from fifty to one hundred and twenty miles in breadth, and boasts about as large an extent of territory, as is contained in all the United States proper, which lay to the north of Pennsylvania including the same.

It was nine hundred years after the conquest of the caliphs, and at the beginning of the tenth century, that the Algerines, by becoming formidable to the Europeans, acquired the notice of the enlightened historian.[7] About this time, two enterprizing young men, sons of a potter, of the island of Mytelene the ancient Lesbos, called Horric[8] and Hayraddin,[9] collecting a number of desperadoes, seized upon a brigantine and commenced pirates, making indiscriminate depredations upon the vessels of all nations. They soon augmented their force to a fleet of twelve gallies, beside small craft,

---

and, when Greek literature became fashionable in Roman schools, the latter adopted the term, and *barbarus* was applied by the Romans with the same foppish contempt.

* The common geography compilers add the kingdom of Tefilet,[5] I conjecture, upon the authority of Dr. Shaw,[6] though I could never hear of any such kingdom in Africa. The face of many a country, which that learned writer describes, differs as much from the truth, as his own physiognomy from the true line of beauty.

with which they infested the sea coast of Spain and Italy, and carried their booty into the ports of Barbary, styling themselves the lords of the sea, and the enemies of all those, who sailed upon it. European nations were not then possessed of such established and formidable navies, as at the present day: even the English, who seem formed for the command of the sea, had but few ships of force. Henry the eighth built some vessels, which, from their unmanageable bulk, were rather suited for home defence than foreign enterprize; and the fleet of Elizabeth, which, in fifteen hundred and eighty eight, destroyed the Spanish Armada, was principally formed of ships, chartered by the merchants, who were the general resource of all the maratime powers. The fleet of these adventurers was therefore formidable; and, as Robertson says, soon became terrible from the straits of the Dardanelles to those of Gibralter. The prospects of ambition increase, as man ascends its summit. Horric, the elder brother, surnamed Barbarossa, as some assert, from the red colour of his beard, aspired to the attainment of sovereign power upon land; and a favourable opportunity soon offered of gratifying his pride. His frequent intercourse with the Barbary States induced an acquaintance with Eutimi, then king of Algiers,[10] who was then at war with Spain, and had made several unsuccessful attacks upon a small fort, built by that nation on the Oran.[11] In his distress, this king inconsiderately applied to Barbarossa, for assistance who readily embraced the invitation, and conducted himself like more modern allies. He first assisted this weak king against his enemy, and then sacrificed him to his own ambition; for, leaving his brother Hayraddin to command the fleet, he entered the city of Algiers, at the head of five thousand men, was received by the inhabitants, as their deliverer, assisted them against the Spaniards, and then arrested and disarmed the principal people, secretly murdered the unsuspecting Eutimi, and caused himself to be proclaimed king of Algiers. Lavish of his treasures to his adherents, and cruelly vindictive to those, he distrusted, he not only established his government, but dethroned the neighbouring king of Temecien,[12] and announced his dominions to his own. But the brave Marquis de

Comeres, the Spanish governour of Oran,[13] by the direction of the
Emperour Charles the fifth, assisted the dethroned king; and, after
defeating Barbarossa in several bloody battles, besieged him in
Temecien, the capital of that kingdom, where this ferocious adven-
turer was slain in attempting his escape, but fought his pursuers
with a brutal rage, becoming the ferocity of his life. Upon the death
of Barbarossa, his brother Hayraddin assumed the same name, and
the kingdom of Algiers. This Barbarossa is better known to the European annalist for rendering his dominions tributary to the Grand
Seignior.[14] He enlarged his power with a body of the Turkish soldiers; and, being promoted to the command of the Turkish fleet, he
spread the fame of the Ottoman power through all Europe: for
though obliged by the superiour power of the Emperour Charles
fifth to relinquish his conquest of Tunis, which he had effected by a
similar treachery, with which his brother had possessed himself of
Algiers; yet his being the acknowledged rival of Andrew Doria,[15]
the first sea commander of his age, has laurelled his brow among
those, who esteem glory to consist in carnage. This Barbarossa built
a mole[16] for the protection of the harbour of Algiers, in which, it is
said, he employed thirty thousand christian slaves, and died a natural death, and was succeeded by Hassan Aga, a renegado from Sardinia,[17] elected by the soldiers, but confirmed by the Grand Seignior,
who, taking an advantage of a violent storm, which wrecked the
navy of the Emperour Charles fifth, who had invaded his territo-
ries, drove that proud emperour from the coast, defeated the rear of
his army, and captured so many of his soldiers, that the Algerines,
it is reported, sold many of their prisoners by way of contempt, at
the price of an onion per head. Another Hassan, son to the second
Barbarossa,[18] succeeded and defeated the Spaniards, who invaded
his dominions under the command of the Count de Alcandara,[19]
killed that nobleman, and took above twelve thousand prisoners.
But his successour, Mahomet,[20] merited the most of his country,
when, by ingratiating himself with the Turkish soldiers, by incor-
porating them with his own troops, he annihilated the contests of
these fierce rivals, formed a permanent body of brave, disciplined

troops, and enabled his successour to renounce that dependence upon the Grand Seignior, to which the second Barbarossa had submitted.

In sixteen hundred and nine, the Algerines received a vast accession of strength and numbers from the emigrant Moors, whom the weak policy of Spain had driven to their dominions. Embittered by christian severity, the Moors flocked on board the Algerine vessels, and sought a desperate revenge upon all, who bore the christian name. Their fleet was said to consist, at this period, of upwards of forty ships, from two to four hundred tons burthen. Though the French with that gallantry, which distinguished them under their monarchs, undertook to avenge the cause of Europe and christianity; and, in sixteen hundred and seventeen, sent a fleet of fifty ships of war against them, who sunk the Algerine admiral and dispersed his fleet; yet this bold people were so elated, by their accession of numbers and riches, that they committed wanton and indiscriminate outrage, on the person and property of all nations, violating the treaties made by the Grand Seignior, seizing the ships of those powers, with which he was in alliance, even in his own ports; and, after plundering Scandaroon in Syria, an Ottoman city,[21] they, in sixteen hundred and twenty three, threw off their dependence on the sublime Porte.[22] In sixteen hundred and thirty seven, the Algerine rovers entered the British channel, and made so many captures that, it was conjectured, near five thousand English were made prisoners by them; and, in the same year, they dispatched Hali Pinchinin[23] with sixteen gallies to rob the rich chapel of our lady of Loretto;[24] which proving unsuccessful, they ravaged the shores of the Adriatic, and so enraged the Venetians, that they fitted out a fleet of twenty eight sail, under the command of Admiral Cappello, who, by a late treaty with the Porte, had liberty to enter any of its harbours, to destroy the Algerine gallies. Cappello was ordered by the Venetians to sink, burn, and destroy, without mercy, all the corsairs of the enemy, and he bravely and successfully executed his commission. He immediately overtook and defeated Pinchinin, disabled five of his gallies; and, this Algerine retreating to Valona[25] and landing his booty, where he erected batteries for its defence, the brave Cappello manned his boats and small craft, and captured his whole fleet. In these actions, about twelve hundred Algerines were slain; and, what was more pleasing, sixteen hundred christian galley slaves set at liberty. History affords no instance of a people, so repeatedly and suddenly recovering their losses, as the Algerines. Within a few years, we find them fitting out seventy sail of armed vessels, and making such daring and desperate attacks upon the commerce of nations, that the most haughty maritime powers of Europe were more anxious, to shelter themselves under a treaty and pay an humiliating tribute, than to attempt nobly to reduce them to reason and humanity. But, after many ineffectual attempts had been made to unite the force of Europe against them, the gallant French, by the command of Louis fourteenth, again roused themselves to chasten this intractable race. In sixteen hundred and eighty two, the Marquis du Quesne,[26] with a large fleet and several bomb ketches,[27] reached Algiers; and, with his sea mortars, bombarded it so violently that, he laid almost the whole city in ruins. Whether his orders went no further, or the vice admiral judged he had chastised them sufficiently, or whether a violent storm drove his fleet from its moorings, does not appear. But it is certain, that he left the city abruptly; and the Algerines, to revenge this insult, immediately sent their fleet to the coast of France, and took signal reparation.

The next year, Du Quesne cast anchor before Algiers with a larger fleet; and, for forty eight hours, made such deadly discharges with his cannon, and showered so many bombs over this devoted city, that the Dey sued for peace.

The French admiral with that generosity, which is peculiar to his nation, insisted, as an indispensable preliminary, that all the christian slaves should be sent on board his squadron, with Mezemorto the Dey's admiral,[28] as a hostage for the performance of this preliminary article. The Dey assembled his divan, or council of great officers, and communicated the French demands. Mezemorto immediately collected the sailors, who had manned the ramparts, and with whom he was a favourite; and, accusing the Dey of cowardice, he so inflamed them that, being joined by the soldiers, they murdered the Dey, and elected Mezemorto in his stead. This was a signal for renewed hostility, and never was there a scene of greater carnage. The French seemed to have reserved their fire for this moment, when they poured such incessant vollies of red hot shot, bombs, and carcasses into the city, that it was nearly all in flames. The streets run blood, while the politic and furious Mezemorto, dreading a change in the public mind, and conscious that another cessation of arms would be attended with his death or delivery to the French, ran furiously round the ramparts and exhorted the military to their duty; and, to make his new subjects desperate, caused all the French slaves to be murdered; and, seizing the French consul, who had been a prisoner among them, since the first declaration of war, he ordered him to be tied hand and foot, and placed over a bomb mortar and shot into the air towards the French fleet. The French were so highly enraged, the sailors could scarce be prevented from attempting to land, and destroy this barbarous race. The vice admiral contented himself with levelling their fortifications, reducing the city to rubbish, and burning their whole fleet. A fair opportunity now presented of preventing the Algerines from again molesting commerce. If the European maritime powers had by treaty engaged themselves to destroy the first armed galley of the Algerines, which appeared upon the seas, and conjointly forbidden them to repair their fortifications; this people might ere this have from necessity turned their attention to commerce; the miscreants and outcasts of other nations would have no longer found refuge among them; and this people might at this time have been as celebrated for the peaceful arts, as they are odious for the constant violation of the laws of nations and humanity. This was surely the common interest of the European powers; but to talk of their common interest is idle. The narrow politics of Europe seek an individual not a common good; for no sooner had France humbled the Algerines than England thought it more for her interest to enter into a treaty with the new Dey, and, by way of douceur, sent to Algiers a ship load of naval and military stores, to help them to rebuild their navy and strengthen their fortresses; while France,

jealous lest the affections of the monster Mezemorto, who bar-
barously murdered their fellow citizens, should be attached to their
rival the English, immediately patched up a peace with the Algerines upon the most favourable terms to the latter; and, to conclude
the farce, sent them another ship load of similar materials of superiour value to those, presented by the English. This, my readers, is
a small specimen of European policy.

The latest authentic account of any attack upon the Algerines
was on the twenty third of June, one thousand seven hundred and
seventy five; when the Spaniards sent the Count O'Reilly[29] with a
respectable fleet, twenty four thousand land forces, and a prodi-
gious train of artillery, to destroy the city. The count landed about
two thirds of his troops, about a league and an half to the eastward
of the city; but, upon marching into the country, they were opposed
by an immense army of natives. The Spaniards say, it consisted of
one hundred and fifty thousand, probably exaggerated by their apprehensions. This is certain, they had force sufficient, or superiour
skill to defeat the Spaniards, who retreated to their ships with the
loss of thirteen cannon, some howitzers, and three thousand killed,
besides prisoners; while they destroyed six thousand Algerines. No
sooner had the treaty of Paris, in one thousand seven hundred and
eighty two, completely liberated the United States from their dependence upon the British nation than that haughty, exasperated
power, anxious to shew their late colonists the value of that protection, under which their vessels had heretofore navigated the Mediterranean, excited the Algerines to capture the shipping of the
United States, who, following from necessity the policy of European nations, concluded a treaty with this piratical state on the fifth
of September, one thousand seven hundred and ninety five.[30]

Thus I have delineated a sketch of Algerine history from actual
information, obtained upon the spot, and the best European authorities. This dry detail of facts will probably be passed over by
those, who read for mere amusement, but the intelligent reader
will, in this concise memoir, trace the leading principles of this
despotic government; will account for the avarice and rapacity of a

people, who live by plunder; perceive whence it is that they are thus suffered to injure commerce and outrage humanity; and justify our executive in concluding, what some uninformed men may esteem, a humiliating, and too dearly purchased peace with these free booters.

Chapter XVI.

Not such as erst illumin'd ancient Greece,
Cities for arts and arms and freedom fam'd,
The den of despots and the wretche's grave.

AUTHOR'S *Manuscript Poems.*

ARGUMENT.

Description of the City of Algiers.

I cannot give so particular a description of this city, as I could wish, or my readers may desire. Perhaps no town contains so many places impervious to strangers. The interiour of the Dey's palace, and the female apartment of every house are secluded even from the natives. No one approaches them but their respective masters, while no stranger is permitted to inspect the fortifications; and the mosques, or churches, are scrupulously guarded from the polluted steps of the unbeliever. A poor slave, branded as an infidel, would obtain only general information from a residence in the midst of them.

Algiers is situated in the bay of that name, and built upon the sea shore, an eminence, which rises above it, and which naturally gave the distinction of the upper and lower city. Towards the sea, it is strengthened with vast fortifications, which are continued upon the mole, which secures the port from storms and assaults. I never perambulated it, but should judge that, a line drawn from the west arm of the mole, and extended by land, until it terminated on the east, comprehending the buildings, would measure about two miles. It contains one hundred and twenty mosques, two hundred and twenty public baths, and innumerable coffee houses. The mosques are large stone buildings, not lofty in proportion to their extent on the ground, and have usually erected, upon their corners, small square towers or minarets, whence the inferiour priests call the people to prayers. The baths are convenient buildings, lighted on the top, provided with cold and warm waters, which you mingle at your pleasure, in small marble cisterns, by the assistance of brass cocks. Every bather pays two rials at his entrance, for which he is accommodated with a dressing room, contiguous to the bathing cistern, towels, flesh brushes, and other conveniences, a glass of sherbet, and an assistant, if he chooses. The coffee houses or rooms are generally piazzas, with an awning over them, projecting from the front of the houses into the streets. Here the inhabitants delight to loll, to drink sherbet, sip coffee, and chew opium, or smoak tobacco, steeped in a decoction of this exhilarating drug.

I have already sketched a description of the houses, and shall only add, that the roofs are nearly flat with a small declivity to cast the rain water into spouts. Algiers is tolerably well supplied with spring water, conveyed in pipes from the back country; but the Algerines, who are immoderately attached to bathing, prefer rain water, as best adapted to that use, considering it a luxury in comparison with that, obtained from the springs or sea.

The inhabitants say, Algiers contains twenty thousand houses, one hundred and forty thousand believers, twenty two thousand Jews, and six thousand christian slaves. I suspect, Algerine vanity has exaggerated the truth; but I cannot contradict it. Immediately before the census of the inhabitants of the United States, I am told, persons, who possessed much better means of calculation, misrated the population of the principal towns most egregiously.

CHAPTER XVII.

See the deep curse of power uncontrol'd.

ANON.

ARGUMENT.

The Government of the Algerines.

It has been noticed that Hayraddin Barbarossa, in the beginning of the sixteenth century, rendered his kingdom tributary to the Grand Seignior; and that, in the year one thousand six hundred and twenty three, the Algerines threw off their dependence on the sublime Porte. Since that time, the Turkish court have made several attempts to reduce the Algerines to their subjection; and, by siding with the numerous pretenders to the regency, so common in this unstable government, they have, at times, apparently effected their design: while the Algerines, by assassinating or dethroning those princes, whose weakness or wants have induced them to submit to extraneous power, have reduced their dependence on the sublime Porte to a mere name. At present, the Grand Seignior, fearful of losing the very shadow of authority, he has over them, contents himself with receiving a tribute almost nominal; consisting chiefly of a present, towards defraying the expenses of the annual canopy, which is sent to adorn the prophet's tomb at Medina: while, on the other hand, the Algerines, dreading the Grand Seignior's interference in their popular commotions, allow the sublime Porte to confirm the election of their Dey, and to badge his name, by affixing and terminating it with those of the principal officers of the Turkish government. Hence the present Dey, whose real name is Hassan, is styled Vizier, which is also the appellation of the Grand Seignior's first minister. As Bashaw, which terminates the Dey's name, is the Turkish title of their viceroys and principal commanders, he makes war or peace, negotiates treaties, coins money, and performs every other act of absolute independence.

Nor is the Dey less independent of his own subjects. Though he obtains his office frequently by the election of a furious soldiery, and wades to the regency through the blood of his predecessor; yet he is no sooner invested with the insignia of office, than, an implicit reverence is paid to his commands, even by his ferocious electors; and, though he often summons his divan or council of great officers, yet they are merely advisory. He conducts foreign affairs, at his own good pleasure; and, as to internal, he knows no restraint, except from certain local customs, opinions, and tenets, which he himself venerates, in common with his meanest subjects. Justice is administered in his name. He even determines controversies in his own person, besides being supposed virtually present in the persons of his cadis or judges. If he inclines to interfere in the determination of a suit, upon his approach, the authority of the cadis cease, and is merged in that of the Dey. Some customs have been intimated, which restrain the Dey's despotism. These relate principally to religion, property, and females. He will not condemn a priest to death; and, although upon the decease of a subject, his landed property immediately escheats to the reigning Dey, yet he never seizes it, in the life of the possessor; and, when a man is executed for the highest crime, the females of his family are treated with respect: nay, even in an insurrection of the soldiery, when they murdered their Dey, neither they nor his successour violated the female apartments of the slain. A mere love of novelty in the soldiery, the wish to share the largesses of a new sovereign, the policy of his courtiers, the ambition or popularity of his officers or children, have not unfrequently caused the dethroning of the Dey; but the more systematic cause of his being so frequently dethroned shall be noticed in our next chapter.

Chapter XVIII.

May these add to the number, that may scald thee;
Let molten coin be thy damnation.[1]

SHAKESPEARE.

ARGUMENT.

Revenue.

The Dey's revenue is stated by writers at seven hundred thousand dollars per annum. If the limits of this work would permit, I think I could prove it under rated, from a view of his expenditures. It arises from a slight tax upon his subjects, a tribute from some Moors and tribes of Arabs, in the interiour country; a capitation tax upon the Jews; prizes taken at sea; presents from foreign powers, as the price of peace; annual subsidies from those nations, with whom he is in alliance; and customary presents, made by his courtiers on his birth day. To these may be added sums, squeezed from his Bashaws in the government of the interiour provinces, and from the Jews, as the price of his protection. With these supplies he has to support the magnificence of his court, defray the expense of foreign embassies, pay his army, supply his navy, and repair his fortifications; and, by frequent gratuities, if he is not very successful and popular, support his interest among those, who have the power to dethrone him. His proportion of the prizes, captured at sea, and the conciliatory presents, made by the commercial powers, are the principal sources of his revenue. It is obviously the policy of the Dey, by frequently enfringing his treaties, to augment his finances, by new captures or fresh premiums for his friendship. A pacific Dey is sure not to reign long; for, beside the disgust of the formidable body of sailors, who are emulous of employ, when the reigning Dey has once gone through the routine of seizing the vessels, receiving the presents, and concluding treaties with the usual foreign powers, he finds that the annual payments, secured by treaties, are insufficient for the maintenance of his necessary expenditures; and is therefore constrained frequently to declare war as a principle of self preservation. I have been told, the present Dey condescended to explain these principles to an American agent in Algiers, and grounded his capturing the American shipping upon this necessity. I must, said the Dey, be at war with some nation, and yours must have its turn. When the Dey, from a pacific disposition or dread of foreign power, is at peace with the world, the disgusted sailor and avaricious soldier join to dethrone him; having established it, as a maxim, that all treaties expire with the reigning Dey, and must be renewed with his successour. This is undoubtedly the true source whence spring those frequent and dreadful convulsions, in the regency of Algiers.

Chapter XIX.

All arm'd in proof, the fierce banditti join
In horrid phalanx, urg'd by hellish rage
To glut their vengeance in the blood of those,
That worship him, who shed his blood for all.

AUTHOR'S *Manuscript Poems.*

Argument.

The Dey's Forces.

There are but few vessels actually belonging to the Dey's navy. He has many marine officers, who rank in the sea service; but, except on great expeditions, are permitted to command the gallies of private adventurers; and it is these picaroons, that make such dreadful depredations on commerce. I can give but a slender account of his land forces. Those in established pay are said to amount to about eight thousand foot, and two thousand Moorish horse. To these may be added four thousand inhabitants of the city, who enrol themselves as soldiers, for protection in military tumults, receive no pay, but are liable to be called upon to man the fortifications in emergency, insurrection, or invasion. Perhaps there are more of this species in the provinces. The horse are cantoned in the country round the city, and do duty by detachments at the palace. Three thousand foot are stationed in the fortifications, and marshalled as the Dey's guards. The residue of the land forces are distributed among the Bashaws to overawe the provinces. But the principal reliance, in case of invasion, is the vast bodies of what may be styled militia, which the Bashaws, in case of emergency, lead from the interiour country.

Chapter XX.

Quaint fashion too was there,
Whose caprice trims
The Indian's wampum,
And the crowns of kings.

Author's *Manuscript Poems.*

Argument.

Notices of the Habits, Customs, &c. of the Algerines.

The men wear next to their bodies a linen shirt, or rather chemise, and drawers of the same texture. Over their shirt a linen or silk gown, which is girded about their loins by a sash, in the choice of which they exhibit much fancy. In this dress their legs and lower extremity of their arms are bare. As an outer garment, a loose coat of coarser materials is thrown over the whole. They wear turbans, which are long pieces of muslin or silk curiously folded, so as to form a cap comfortable and ornamental. Slippers are usually worn, though the soldiers are provided with a sort of buskin, resembling our half boots. The dress of the women, I am told, for I never had the pleasure of inspecting it very critically, resembles that of the men, except that their drawers are longer, and their out side garment is like our old fashioned riding-hoods. When the ladies walk the streets, they are muffled with bandages or handkerchiefs of muslin or silk over their faces, which conceals all but their eyes; and, if too nearly inspected, will let fall a large vail, which conceals them intirely. The men usually set cross legged upon mattresses, laid upon low seats at the sides of the room. They loll on cushions at their meals; and, after their repasts, occasionally indulge with a short slumber. I have such a laudable attachment to the customs of my own country, that I doubt whether I can judge candidly of their cookery or mode of eating. The former would be unpalatable and the latter disgusting to most Americans; for saffron is their common seasoning. They cook their provisions to rags or pap, and eat it with their fingers, though the better sort use spoons. Their diversions consist in associating in the coffee houses, in the city, and, in the country, under groves, where they smoke and chat, and drink cooling not inebriating liquors. Their more active amusements are riding and throwing the dart, at both which they are very expert. They sometimes play at chess and drafts, but never at games of chance or for money; those being expressly forbidden by the alcoran.

Chapter XXI.

Prætulerim scriptor delirus inersque videri,
Dum mea delectant mala me vel denique fallant.[1]

HOR. Epis ii.

Done into English Metre.
I'd rather wield as dull a pen
As chatty B— or bungling Ben;[2]
Tedious as Doctor P—nce, or rather
As Samuel, Increase, Cotton M—r;[3]
And keep of truth the beaten track,
And plod the old cart rut of fact,
Than write as fluent, false and vain
As cit Genet[4] or Tommy Paine.

Argument.

Marriages and Funerals.

It is the privilege of travellers to exaggerate; but I wish not to avail myself of this prescriptive right. I had rather disappoint the curiosity of my readers by conciseness, than disgust them with untruths. I have no ambition to be ranked among the Bruces and Chastelreux[5] of the age. I shall therefore endeavour rather to improve the understanding of my reader, with what I really know, than amuse him with stories, of which my circumscribed situation rendered me necessarily ignorant. I never was at an Algerine marriage; but obtained some authentic information on the subject.

That extreme caution, which separates the sexes in elder life, is also attached to the youth. In Algiers, the young people never collect to dance, converse, or amuse themselves with the innocent gaities of their age. Here are no theatres, balls, or concerts; and, even in the public duties of religion, the sexes never assemble together. An Algerine courtship would be as disagreeable to the hale youth of New England, as a common bundling would be disgusting to the Mussulman. No opportunity is afforded to the young suitor to search for those nameless bewitching qualities and attentions, which attach the American youth to his mistress, and form the basis of connubial bliss; nor is the young Algerine permitted, by a thousand tender assiduities, to win the affections of the future partner of his life. His choice can be only directed by the rank or respectability of the father of his intended bride. He never sees her face, until after the nuptial ceremony is performed; and even some days after she has been brought home to his own house. The old people frequently make the match, or, if it originates with the youth, he confides his wishes to his father or some respectable relation, who communicates the proposal to the lady's father. If he receives it favourably, the young couple are allowed to exchange some unmeaning messages, by an old nurse of the family. The bride's father or her next male kin, with the bridegroom, go before the Cadi and sign a contract of marriage, which is attested by the relatives on each side. The bridegroom then pays a stipulated sum to the bride's father; the nuptial ceremony is performed in private, and the bridegroom retires. After some days, the bride is richly arrayed, accompanied by females, and conveyed in a covered coach or waggon, gaudy with flowers, to her husband's house. Here she is immediately immured in the women's apartments, while the bridegroom and his friends share a convivial feast. After some ceremonies, the nature of which I could not discover, the bridegroom enters the women's apartment, and for the first time discovers whether his wife has a nose or eyes. Among the higher ranks, it is said, the bride, after the expiration of a month, goes to the public bath for women, is there received with great parade, and loaded with presents by her female relations, assembled on the occasion. The bridegroom also receives presents from his friends.

Within a limited time, the husband may break the contract, provided he will add another item to that already given, return his bride with all her paraphernalia; and, putting the holy alcoran to his breast, assert that he never benefited himself of the rights of an husband.

Notwithstanding the apparent restraint, the women are under, they are said to be attached to their husbands, and enjoy greater liberty than is generally conceived. I certainly saw many women in the streets, so muffled up, and so similar from their outward garment, that their nearest relatives could not distinguish one from another. The vulgar slaves conjecture that the women take great liberties in this general disguise.

Their funerals are decent but not ostentatious. I saw many. The corps, carried upon a bier, is preceded by the priests, chanting passages from the alcoran in a dolorous tone. Wherever the procession passes, the people join in this dirge. The relatives follow, with the folds of their turbans loosened. The bodies of the rich are deposited in vaults, those of the poor, in graves. A pillar of marble is erected over them, with an unblown[6] rose carved on the top for the unmarried.

At certain seasons, the women of the family join a procession in close habits, and proceed to the tomb or grave, and adorn it with garlands of flowers. When these processions pass, the slaves are obliged to throw themselves on the ground with their faces in the dust, and all, of whatever rank, cover their faces.

Chapter XXII.

O prone to grovelling errour, thus to quit
The firm foundations of a Saviour's love,
And build on stubble.

Author's *Manuscript Poems.*

Argument.

The Religion of the Algerines: Life of the Prophet Mahomet.

In describing the religious tenets of the Algerines, the attention is immediately drawn to Mahomet or Mahomed, the founder of their faith.

This fortunate impostor, like all other great characters in the drama of life, has been indignantly vilified by his opponents, and as ardently praised by his adherents. I shall endeavour to steer the middle course of impartiality; neither influenced by the biggoted aversion of Sales[1] and Prideaux,[2] or the specious praise of the *philosophic Boulanvilliers.*[3]

Mahomet was born in the five hundred and sixty ninth year of the christian era. He was descended from the Coreis,[4] one of the noblest of the Arabian tribes. His father, Abdalla, was a man of moderate fortune, and bestowed upon his son such an education as a parent in confined, if not impoverished circumstances, could confer. The Turks say, he could not write; because they pride themselves in decrying letters, and because the pious among them suppose his ignorance of letters a sufficient evidence of the divine original of the book, he published, as received from and written by the finger of Deity.

But when the Arabian authors record, that he was employed as a factor by his uncle Abutileb,[5] there can little doubt remain but that he was possessed of all the literary acquirements, necessary to accomplish him for his business. He has been stigmatized as a mere camel driver. He had the direction of camels it is true. The merchandize of Arabia was transported to different regions by carrivans of these useful animals, of a troop of which he was conductor; but there was as much difference between his station and employment, and that of a common camel driver, as between the supercargo of an India ship in our days, and the seaman before the mast. In his capacity of factor, he travelled into Syria, Palestine, and Egypt; and acquired the most useful knowledge in each country. He is represented as a man of a beautiful person, and commanding presence. By his engaging manners and remarkable attention to business, he became the factor of a rich Arabian merchant, after whose death he married his widow, the beautiful Cadija,[6] and came into the lawful possession of immense wealth, which awakened in him the most unbounded ambition. By the venerable custom of his nation, his political career was confined to his own tribe; and, the patriarchal being the prominent feature of the Arabian government, he could not hope to surmount the claims of elder families, even in his own tribe, the genealogies of which were accurately preserved. To be the founder and prophet of a new religion would secure a glorious preeminence, highly gratifying to his ambition, and not thwarting the pretensions of the tribes.

Mankind are apt to impute the most profound abilities to founders of religious systems, and other fortunate adventurers, when perhaps they owe their success more to a fortunate coincidence of circumstances, and their only merit is the sagacity to avail themselves of that tide in the affairs of men,[7] which leads to wealth and honour. Perhaps there never was a conjuncture more favourable for the introduction of a new religion than that, of which Mahomet availed himself. He was surrounded by Arian christians, whose darling creed is the unity of the Deity,[8] and who had been persecuted by the Athenasians into an abhorrence of almost every other christian tenet:[9] by Jews, who had fled from the vindictive Emperour Adrian,[10] and who, too willfully blind to see the accomplishment of their prophecies in the person of our Saviour, in the midst of exile were ready to contemn those prophecies, which had so long deluded them with a Messiah, who never came: and by Pagans, whose belief in a plurality of gods made them the ready proselytes of any novel system; and the more wise of whom were disgusted with the gross adsurdities of their own mythology. The system of Mahomet is said to have been calculated to attach all these. To gratify the Arian and the Jew, he maintained the unity of God; and, to please the Pagans, he adopted many of their external rites, as fastings, washings, &c. Certain it is, he spoke of Moses and the patriarchs, as messengers from heaven, and that he declared Jesus Christ to be the true Messias, and the exemplary pattern of a good life, a sentiment critically expressing the Arian opinion. The stories of Mahomet's having retired to a cave with a monk and a Jew to compile his book; and falling into fits of the epilepsy, persuading his disciples that these fits were trances in order to propagate his system more effectually, so often related by geography compilers, like the tales of Pope Joan[11] and the nag's head consecration of the English bishops,[12] are fit only to amuse the vulgar. It is certain, he secluded himself from company and assumed an austerity of manners, becoming the reformer of a vicious world. In his retirement, he commenced writing the alcoran. His first proselytes were of his own family, the next, of his near relatives. But the tribe of Corei were so familiar with the person and life of Mahomet that they despised his pretensions; and, fearful lest what they styled his mad enthusiasm should bring a stigma upon their tribe, they first attempted to reason him out of his supposed delusion; and, this failing, they sought to destroy him. But a special messenger of heaven, who, Mahomet says, measured ten million furlongs at every step, informed him of their design, and he fled to Medina, the inhabitants of which, being already prepossessed in favour of his doctrine, received him with great respect.*

He soon inspired them with the most implicit confidence in the divinity of his mission, and confirmed their faith by daily portions of the alcoran, which he declared was written by the finger of God, and transmitted to him immediately from heaven by archangels, commissioned for that important purpose. He declared himself the *Sent of God,* the sword of his almighty power, commissioned to enforce the unity of the divine essence, the unchangeableness of his eternal decrees, the future bliss of true believers, and the torment of the damned, among the nations. He boldly pronounced all those, who died fighting in his cause, to be entitled to the glory of martyrs in the heavenly paradise; and, availing himself of some of the antient feuds among the neighbouring tribes, caused his disciples in Medina to wage war upon their neighbours, and they invariably conquered, when he headed their troops. The tribe of Corei flattered by the honours, paid their kinsman, and confounded by the repeated reports of his victories, were soon proselyted, and become afterwards the most enthusiastic supporters of his power. In six hundred and twenty seven, he was crowned sovereign at Medina, like the divine Melchisedec, uniting in his person the high titles of prophet and king.[13] He subdued the greater part of Arabia, and obtained a respectable footing in Syria. He died at Medina in the year six hundred and thirty three, and in the sixty fourth year of his age. European writers, who have destroyed almost as many great personages by poison as the French have with the guillotine, have attributed his death to a dose administered by a monk. But when we consider his advanced age and public energies, we need not recur to any but natural means for the cause of his death.

---

* This flight was in the six hundred and twenty second year of the christian era, when Mahomet was fifty four years of age. The Mahometan of all sectaries commence their computation of time from this period, which they style the *hegira,* or flight.

Chapter XXIII.

See childish man neglecting reason's law,
Contend for trifles, differ for a straw.

Author's *Manuscript Poems.*

Argument.

The Sects of Omar and Ali.

Upon the decease of the prophet, his followers were almost confounded. They could scarce credit their senses. They fancied him
only in a swoon, and waited in respectful silence until he should
again arise to lead them to conquest and glory. His more confidential friends gathered around the corpse; and, being impressed with
the policy of immediately announcing his successour, they held a
fierce debate upon the subject. In the alcoran, they found no direction for the election, nor any successour to the caliphate pointed
out. They agreed to send for his wives and confidential domestics.
The youngest of his wives produced some writings, containing the
precious sayings of the prophet, which, she said, she had collected
for her own edification. To these were afterwards added such observations of the prophet, as his more intimate associates could recollect, or the policy of those in power invent. These were annexed
to the alcoran, and esteemed of equal authority. This compilation
was called the book of the companions of the apostle. In the writings, produced by his favourite wife, the prophet had directed his
great officers to elect his successour from among them, and assured

them that a portion of his own power would rest upon him. Abu-beker, a friend and relative, and successful leader of the forces of the prophet, by the persuasions of those around, immediately entered the public mosque; and, standing on the steps of the desk, from which the prophet used to deliver his oracles, he informed the multitude that God had indeed called the prophet to paradise, and that his kingly authority and apostolic powers rested upon him. To him succeeded Omar and Osman:[1] while the troops in Syria, conceiving that Ali,[2] their leader, was better entitled to succeed then either, elevated him also to the caliphate, though he refused the dignity until he was called by the voice of the people to succeed Osman. Hence sprang that great schism, which has divided the Mussulman world; but, though divided, as to the successour of the prophet, both parties were actuated by his principles and adhered to his creed. Omar and his successours turned their arms towards Europe; and, under the name of Saracens or Moors, possessed themselves of the greater part of Spain and the Mediterranean isles: while the friends of Ali, establishing themselves as sovereigns, made equal ravages upon Persia, and even to the great peninsula of India.

The Algerines are of the sect of Omar, which, like many other religious schisms, differs more in name, than in any fundamental point of creed or practice from that of Ali. The propriety of the translation of the alcoran into the Persian language, and the succession of the caliphate seem the great standards of their respective creeds.

CHAPTER XXIV.

Father of all! in ev'ry age,
    In ev'ry clime ador'd,
By saint, by savage, and by sage,
    Jehovah, Jove, or Lord.[1]

POPE.

ARGUMENT.

The Faith of the Algerines.

The Algerine doctors assert, that the language of the alcoran is so
ineffably pure, it can never be rendered into any other tongue. To
this they candidly impute the miserable, vitiated translations of the
christians, who they charge with having garbled the sacred book,
and degraded its sublime alegories and metaphors into absurd tales.
This is certain, the portions, I have heard chanted at funerals and
quoted in conversation, ever exhibited the purest morality and the
sublimest conceptions of the Deity. The fundamental doctrine of
the alcoran is the unity of God. The evil spirit, says the koran, is
subtly deluding men, into the belief that there are more gods than
one, that in the confusion of deities he may obtain a share of devotion; while the Supreme Being, pitying the delusions of man, has
sent Abraham, Moses, Soliman,[2] breathed forth the Messias of the
christian in a sigh of divine pity, and lastly sent Mahomet, the seal
of the prophets, to reclaim men to this essential truth. The next
fundamental points in the Mussulman creed are a belief in the
eternal decrees of God, in a resurrection and final judgment to bliss

or misery. Some hold with christians that the future punishment will be infinite, while others suppose that, when the souls of the wicked are purified by fire, they will be received into the favour of God. They adhere to many other points of practical duty: such as daily prayers, frequent ablutions, acts of charity and severe fastings; that of rhammadin,[3] is the principal, which is similar to the catholic lent, in abstinence, for the penitent abstains only from a particular kind of food, while he gluts himself with others perhaps more luscious. The alcoran also forbids games of chance, and the use of strong liquors; inculcates a tenderness for idiots, and a respect for age. The book of the companions of the apostle enjoins a pilgrimage to his tomb, to be made by the true believers once at least in their lives: but though they view the authority, which enjoined this tedious journey divine, yet they have contrived to evade its rigour by allowing the believer to perform it by proxy or attorney.

Upon the whole, there does not appear to be any articles in their faith, which incite them to immorality or can countenance the cruelties, they commit. Neither their alcoran nor their priests excite them to plunder, inslave or torment. The former expressly recommends charity, justice, and mercy towards their fellow men. I would not bring the sacred volume of our faith in any comparative view with the alcoran of Mahomet; but I cannot help noticing it as extraordinary, that the Mahometan should abominate the christian on account of his faith, and the christian detest the Mussulman for his creed; when the koran of the former acknowledges the divinity of the christian Messias, and the bible of the latter commands us to love our enemies. If each would follow the obvious dictates of his own scripture, he would cease to hate, abominate, and destroy the other.

Chapter XXV.

O here; quæ res
Nec modum habet neque consilium ratione modoque
Tractari non vult.[1]

Hor. *Sat.* 3. *Lib.* ii.

Argument.

*Why do not the Powers in Europe suppress the Algerine Depredations?
is a Question frequently asked in the United States.*

I answer, that this must be effected by a union of the European
maritime powers with the Grand Seignior; by a combination
among themselves; or by an individual exertion of some particular
state. A union of the European powers with the Grand Seignior
most probably would be attended with success; but this is not to be
expected; as it never can be the interest of the sublime Porte to suppress them, and the common faith of the Mussulman has more influence in uniting its professors than the creed of the christian, to
the disgrace of the *latter*: and, as the Grand Seignior's dominion
over the Algerines is little more than nominal, he is anxious to conciliate their favour by affording them his protection; considering
prudently, that though intractable, they are still a branch of the
Mussulman stock. Provoked by their insults, he has sometimes
withdrawn his protection, as was the case, when he by treaty with
the Venetians permitted their fleet to enter the Ottoman ports, for

the express purpose of destroying the Algerine gallies; but, it is obvious, the sublime Porte meant merely to chastise not to ruin them.

In the Grand Seignior's wars with the Europeans, the piratical states have rendered signal services, and he himself not unfrequently receives valuable douceurs for exerting his supposed influence over them, in favour of one or another of the contending powers of Europe. In the siege of Gibraltar by the Spaniards, during the late American war, that garrison received frequent supplies of provision from the Barbary Shore; but, by the application of Louis XVI. to the sublime Porte, the Grand Seignior influenced the Barbary states to prohibit those supplies; and the English consul was dismissed from one of them with the most pointed marks of contempt. While the Grand Seignior reaps such solid advantages from them, it is absurd to predicate upon his cooperation against them; neither can a union of the European powers be more fully anticipated. Jealousy as often actuates mighty nations, as weak individuals. Whoever turns the pages of history with profit, will perceive that sordid passion is the impulse of action to the greatest states. Commercial states are also actuated by avarice, a passion still more baneful in its effects. These excite war, and are the grand plenipotentiaries in the adjustment of the articles of peace. Hence it is, that, while every European power is solicitous to enrich and aggrandize itself, it can never join in any common project, the result of which, it is jealous, may advantage its neighbour; and is content to suffer injury, rather than its rival should share in a common good. Hence it is, that christian states, instead of uniting to vindicate their insulted faith, join the cross and the crescent in unholy alliance, and form degrading treaties with piratical powers; and, as the acme of political folly, present those very powers, as the purchase of their friendship, weapons to annoy themselves in the first war, that their avarice or caprice shall wage. But, if ever a confederacy of the European powers should be formed against the Algerines, experience affords us but slender hopes of its success; for, I will venture to assert, that from the confederacy of Ahab and Jehoshaphat, when they went up to battle to Ramoth Gilead,[2] to the treaty of Philnitz,[3] there never was a combination of princes or nations, who, by an actual union of their forces, attained the object of their coalition. If the political finger is pointed to the war of the allies of Queen Anne, and the conquests of the Duke of Marlborough,[4] as an exception, I likewise point to the distracting period, when that conqueror was superceded by the Duke of Ormond,[5] and the treaty of Utrecht[6] will confirm the opinion I have advanced.

The detail of the history of the Algerines evinces, that the arms of individual states can be attended with no decisive success. Indeed, the expense of an efficacious armament would defray the price of the Dey's friendship for years; and the powers of Europe submit to his insults and injuries from a principle of economy. An absolute conquest of the Algerine territory cannot be effected but by invasion from the interiour, through the cooperation of the Grand Seignior or the assistance of the other Barbary states. The former I have shewn cannot be predicated, and the latter, for obvious reasons, is as little to be expected. A permanent conquest of the city and port of Algiers cannot be effected, without the subjection of the interiour country. Temporary though spirited attacks, upon that city and port, have never answered any salutary purpose. They may be compared to the destruction of our seaports, in our revolutionary war. The port attacked bore so small a proportion to the whole, that its destruction rather served to irritate, than to weaken or subjugate. It should be considered, likewise, that the houses of the Algerines are built of slight and cheap materials; that upon the approach of an enemy the rich effects of the inhabitants are easily removed inland, while nothing remains but heavy fortifications to batter, and buildings, which can be readily restored, to destroy. The following anecdote will shew how sensible the Algerines themselves are of these advantages. When the French vice admiral, the Marquis du Quesne, made his first attack on Algiers, he sent an officer with a flag on shore, who magnified the force of his commander, and threatened to lay the city in ashes, if the demands of the marquis were not immediately complied with. The Dey, who had, upon the first approach of the enemy, removed the aged, the females and his richest effects, coolly inquired of the officer how much the levelling his city to ashes would cost. The officer, thinking to encrease the Dey's admiration of the power of the Grand Monarque, answered, two millions of livres. Tell your commander, said the Dey, if he will send me half the money I will burn the city to ashes myself.[7]

Chapter XXVI.

A pattern fit for modern knights
To copy out in frays and fights.[1]

Hudibras.

Argument.

An Algerine Law Suit.

An officer of police parades the city at uncertain hours, and in all directions, accompanied by an executioner and other attendants. The process of his court is entirely verbal. He examines into all breaches of the customs, all frauds, especially in weights and measures, all sudden assays, disputes concerning personal property, and compels the performance of contracts. He determines causes on the spot, and the delinquent is punished in his presence. The usual punishments, he inflicts, are fines, beating on the soles of the feet, dismemberment of the right hand; and, it is said, he has a power of taking life; but, in such case, an appeal lies to the Dey. If complaint is made to him of the military, the priests or officers of the court, navy, or customs, or against persons attached to the families of the consuls, envoys, or other representatives of foreign powers, upon suggestion, the cause is immediately reported to the Dey, who hears the same in person, or deputes some officer of rank to determine it, either from the civil, military, or religious orders, as the nature of the cause may require. In fact, this officer of police seldom judges any cause of great importance. The object of his commission seems to be the detection and punishment of common cheats, and to suppress broils among the vulgar; and, as he has the power to adapt the punishment to the enormity of the offence, he often exercises it capriciously, and, sometimes, ludicrously. I saw a baker, who, for selling bread under weight, was sentenced to walk the public market, three times each day, for three days in succession, with a small loaf, attached by a ring to each of his ears; and to cry aloud at short distances *"bread for the poor."* This excited the resentment of the rabble, who followed him with abundance of coarse ridicule. Besides this itinerant judge, there are many others, who never meddle with suits, unless they are brought formally before them, which is done by mere verbal complaint; they send for the parties and witnesses, and determine almost as summarily as the officer of police. I confess that, when I left the United States, the golden fee, the lengthy bill of cost, the law's delay, and the writings of Honestus,[2] had taught me to view the judicial proceedings of our country with a jaundiced eye; and, when I was made acquainted with the Algerine mode of distributive justice, I yearned to see a cause determined in a court, where instant decision relieved the anxiety, and saved the purses of the parties; and where no long winded attorney was suffered to perplex the judge with subtle argument or musty precedent. I was soon delighted with an excellent display of summary justice. Observing a collection of people upon a piazza, I leaned over the rails, and discovered that an Algerine cadi[3] or judge had just opened his court. The cadi was seated cross legged on a cushion with a slave, with a whip and batten on one side; and another with a drawn scimitar on the other. The plaintiff came forward and told his story. He charged a man, who was in custody, with having sold him a mule, which he said was sound, but which proved blind and lame. Several witnesses were then called, who proved the contract and the defects of the mule. The defendant was then called upon for his defence. He did not deny the fact, but pleaded the law of retaliation. He said, he was a good Mussulman, performed all the rites of their holy religion, had sent a proxy to the prophet's tomb at Medina, and maintained an idiot; that he never cheated any man before, but was justified in what he had done, for, ten years before, the plaintiff had cheated him worse in the sale of a dromedary, which proved broken winded. He proved this by several witnesses, and the plaintiff could not deny it. The judge immediately ordered the mule and the money paid for it to be produced. He then directed his attendants to seize the defendant, and give him fifty blows on the soles of his feet for this fraud. The plaintiff at every stroke applauded the cadi's justice to the skies; but, no sooner was the punishment inflicted, than, by a nod from the judge, the exulting plaintiff was seized and received the same number of blows with the batten for the old affair of the broken winded dromedary. The parties were then dismissed, without costs, and the judge ordered an officer to take the mule, sell it at publick outcry, and distribute the product, with the money deposited, in alms to the poor. The officer proceeded a few steps with the mule, and, I thought, the court had risen, when the cadi, supposing one of the witnesses had prevaricated in his testimony, called back the officer, who had charge of the mule, ordered the witness to receive twenty five blows of the batten, and be mounted on the back of the mule, with his face towards the tail, and be thus carried through the city, directing the mule to be stopped at every corner, where the culprit should exclaim; "before the enlightened, excellent, just, and merciful cadi Mir Karchan, in the trial of Osman Beker and Abu Isoul, I spake as I ride." The people around magnified Mir Karchan for this exemplary justice; and I present it to my fellow citizens. If it is generally pleasing, it may be easily introduced among us. Some obstinate people may be still attached to our customary modes of dispensing justice, and think that the advocates we see, and the precedents they quote, are but guards and enclosures round our judges, to prevent them from capriciously invading the rights of the citizens.

Chapter XXVII.

And though they say the LORD LIVETH, surely they swear falsely.[1]

JEREMIAH.

ARGUMENT.

A Mahometan Sermon.

I once had an opportunity of approaching unnoticed the window of one of the principal mosques. After the customary prayers, the priest pronounced the following discourse with a dignified elocution. It was received by his audience with a reverence, better becoming christians than infidels. It undoubtedly suffers from translation and the fickleness of my memory; but the manner, in which it was delivered, and the energy of many of the expressions made so strong an impression, that I think I have not materially varied from the sentiment. I present it to the candid reader, as a curious specimen of their pulpit eloquence; and as, perhaps, conveying a more satisfactory idea of their creed, than I have already attempted, in the account I have given of their religion. The attributes of Deity were the subject of the priest's discourse; and, after some exordium, he elevated his voice and exclaimed:

GOD ALONE IS IMMORTAL. Ibraham and Soliman[2] have slept with their fathers, Cadijah the first born of faith, Ayesha the beloved,[3] Omar the meek, Omri the benevolent, the companions of the apostle and the Sent of God himself, all died. But God most high, most holy, liveth forever. Infinities are to him, as the numerals of arithmetic to the sons of

Adam; the earth shall vanish before the decrees of his eternal destiny; but he liveth and reigneth forever.

GOD ALONE IS OMNISCIENT. Michael, whose wings are full of eyes, is blind before him, the dark night is unto him as the rays of the morning; for he noticeth the creeping of the small pismire in the dark night, upon the black stone, and apprehendeth the motion of an atom in the open air.

GOD ALONE IS OMNIPRESENT. He toucheth the immensity of space, as a point. He moveth in the depths of ocean, and mount Atlas is hidden by the sole of his foot. He breatheth fragrant odours to cheer the blessed in paradise, and enliveneth the pallid flame in the profoundest hell.

GOD ALONE IS OMNIPOTENT. He thought, and worlds were created; he frowneth, and they dissolve into thin smoke; he smileth, and the torments of the damned are suspended. The thunderings of Hermon are the whisperings of his voice; the rustling of his attire causeth lightning and an earthquake; and with the shadow of his garment he blotteth out the sun.

GOD ALONE IS MERCIFUL. When he forged his immutable decrees on the anvil of eternal wisdom, he tempered the miseries of the race of Ismael in the fountains of pity. When he laid the foundations of the world, he cast a look of benevolence into the abysses of futurity; and the adamantine pillars of eternal justice were softened by the beamings of his eyes. He dropt a tear upon the embryo miseries of unborn man; and that tear, falling through the immeasurable lapses of time, shall quench the glowing flames of the bottomless pit. He sent his prophet into the world to enlighten the darkness of the tribes; and hath prepared the pavilions of the Houri for the repose of the true believers.

GOD ALONE IS JUST. He chains the latent cause to the distant event; and binds them both immutably fast to the fitness of things. He decreed the unbeliever to wander amidst the whirlwinds of errour; and suited his soul to future torment. He promulgated the ineffable creed, and the germs of countless souls of believers, which existed in the contemplation of Deity, expanded at the sound. His justice refresheth the faithful, while the damned spirits confess it in despair.

GOD ALONE IS ONE. Ibraham the faithful knew it. Moses declared it amidst the thunderings of Sinai. Jesus pronounced it; and the messenger of God, the sword of his vengeance, filled the world with immutable truth.

Surely there is one God, IMMORTAL, OMNICIENT, OMNIPRESENT, OMNIPOTENT, most MERCIFUL, and JUST; and Mahomet is his apostle.

Lift your hands to the eternal, and pronounce the ineffable, adorable creed: THERE IS ONE GOD, AND MAHOMET IS HIS PROPHET.

Chapter XXVIII.

For sufference is the badge of all our tribe.[1]

SHAKESPEARE.

Argument.

Of the Jews.

I have thus given some succinct notices of the history, government, religion, habits, and manners of this ferocious race. I have interspersed reflections, which, I hope, will be received by the learned with candour; and shall now resume the thread of my more appropriate narrative.

By unremitted attention to the duties of my office, and some fortunate operations in surgery, I had now so far ingratiated myself with the director and physicians of the infirmary, that I was allowed to be absent any hours of the day, when my business in the hospital permitted, without rendering any especial reason for my absence. I wandered into all parts of the city, where strangers were permitted to walk, inspected every object I could, without giving umbrage. I sometimes strayed into that quarter of the city, principally inhabited by Jews. This cunning race, since their dispersion by Vespasian and Titus, have contrived to compensate themselves for the loss of Palestine, "by engrossing the wealth, and often the luxuries of every other land; and, wearied with the expectation of that heavenly king," who shall repossess them of the holy city, and put their enemies beneath their feet, now solace themselves with a Messiah, whose glory is enshrined in their coffers. Rigidly attached to their own customs, intermarrying among themselves, content to be apparently wretched and despised, that they may wallow in secret wealth; and secluded, in most countries, from holding landed property, and in almost all from filling offices of power and profit, they are generally received as meet instruments to do the mean drudgery of despotic courts. The wealth, which would render a subject too powerful, the despot can trust with an unambitious Jew; and confide secrets, which involve his own safety to a miserable Israelite, whom he can annihilate with a nod. The Jews transact almost all the Dey's private business, besides that of the negotiations of merchants. Nay, if an envoy from a foreign power comes to treat with the Dey, he may have the parade of a public audience; but, if he wishes to accomplish his embassy, he must employ a Jew: and, it is said, the Dey himself shares with the Jew the very sums paid him for his influence with this politic despot. The Jews are also the spies of the Dey, upon his subjects at home, and the channels of intelligence from foreign powers. They are therefore allowed to assemble in their synagogues; and have frequently an influence at the court of the Dey, with his great officers, and even before the civil judge, not to be accounted for from the morality of their conduct. Popular prejudice is generally against them; and the Dey often avails himself of it by heavy amercements for his protection. In the year one thousand six hundred and ninety, he threatened to extirpate the whole race in his dominions, and was finally appeased by a large contribution they raised and offered as an expiation of a supposed offence. It was commonly reported, that the Jews in Algiers, at that time, had procured a christian child, which they privately purified with much ceremony, fattened and prepared for a sacrifice, at their feast of the passover, as a substitute for the paschal lamb. This horrid tale, which should have been despised for its absurdity and inhumanity, the Dey affected to credit. He appointed several Mahometan priests to search the habitations of the Jews, immediately before the feast of the passover, who, discovering some bitter herbs and other customary preparations for the festival, affected to have found sufficient evidence against them; and the mob of Algiers, mad with rage and perhaps inflamed by the usurious exactions of particular Jews, rushed on furiously to pillage and destroy the wretched descendants of Jacob. Two houses were demolished, and several Jews assassinated before the arrival of the Dey's guards, who quickly dispersed this outrageous rabble. The Dey, who desired nothing less than the destruction of so useful a people, was soon appeased by a large present, and declared them innocent: and, such is the power of despotic governments, that the Jews were soon received into general favour; and the very men, who, the day before, proceeded to destroy the whole race, now saw, with tame inaction, several of their fellows executed for the attempt.

Chapter XXIX.

But endless is the tribe of human ills,
And sighs might sooner cease than cause to sigh.[1]

Young.

Argument.

The Arrival of other American Captives.

Returning from a jaunt into the city, I was immediately commanded to retire to my room, and not to quit it, till further orders, which it was impracticable to do, as the doors were fastened upon me. The next morning, my provisions were brought me, and the doors again carefully secured. Surprised at this imprisonment, I passed many restless hours in recurring to my past conduct, and perplexing myself in searching for some inadvertent offence, or in dreadful apprehension, lest the present imprisonment should be a prelude to future and more severe punishment. The stone quarry came to my imagination in all its horrours, and the frowns of Abdel Melic again pierced my soul. I attempted in vain to obtain from the slave, who brought me provisions, the cause of my confinement. He was probably ignorant; my solicitations were uniformly answered by a melancholy shake of the head. The next day, the director of the hospital appeared. To him I applied with great earnestness; but all the information he would give was, that it was by the Dey's order I was confined; and that he, with the physicians and my friend the

Mollah, were using all their influence to obtain my release. He counselled me to amuse myself in preparing and compounding drugs, and promised to see me again, as soon as he could bring any good news. About a week after, an officer of the court, with a city judge, entered my apartment, and informed me of the cause of my imprisonment. From them I learned, that several American vessels had been captured;[2] and, it was suspected, I had been conversing with my countrymen; and, from my superiour knowledge of the country, I might advise them how to escape. If a man is desirous to know how he loves his country, let him go far from home; if to know how he loves his countrymen, let him be with them in misery in a strange land. I wish not to make a vain display of my patriotism, but I will say, that my own misfortunes, upon this intelligence, were so absorbed in those of my unfortunate fellow citizens, thus delivered over to chains and torment, many of them perhaps separated from the tenderest domestic connexions and homes of ease, that, I thought, I could again have willingly endured the lashes of the slave driver, and sink myself beneath the burthens of slavery, to have saved them from an Algerine captivity. I could readily assure the Dey's officers, that I had not conversed with my miserable countrymen; but, while I spake, the idea of embracing a fellow citizen, a brother christian, perhaps some one, who came from the same state, or had been in the same town, or seen my dear parents, passed in rapid succession, and I was determined, betide what would, to seek them the first opportunity. We were soon joined by the Mollah, who repeatedly assured my examiners, that, though an infidel, I might be believed. By his solicitation, I was to be released; but not until I would bind myself by a solemn oath, administered after the christian manner, that I would never speak to any of the American slaves. When this oath was proposed, I doubted whether to take it; but, recollecting that, if I did not, I should be equally debarred from seeing them, and suffer a grievous confinement, which could do them no service, I consented and bound myself never directly or indirectly to attempt to visit or converse with my fellow citizens in slavery. It was, at the same time, intimated to me, that for the breach of this oath I might expect to be impaled alive.—Often, when I have drawn near the places of their confinement and labours, I have regretted my submitting to this oath, and once was almost tempted to break it, at seeing Captain O'Brien[3] at some distance.

Chapter XXX.

Now, by my hood, a gentile and no Jew.[1]

Shakespeare.

Argument.

The Author commences Acquaintance with Adonah Ben Benjamin, a Jew.

After I had taken this oath, the officers departed, and I was liberated. I was now more cautious in my rambles, avoided the notice of the Mussulmen inhabitants, and made more frequent visits to that part of the city, inhabited by Jews and foreigners. Refreshing myself with a glass of sherbet in an inferiour room, I was accosted by an old man, in mean attire, with a pack of handkerchiefs and some remnants of silk and muslins on his back. He asked me, if I was not the learned slave, and requested me to visit a sick son. I immediately resolved to go with him; rejoicing that Providence, in my low estate, had left me the power to be charitable. We traversed several streets and stopped at the door of a house, which, in appearance, well suited my conductor. It had but two windows towards the street, and those were closed up with rough boards, the cracks of which were stuffed with rags and straw. My conductor looked very cautiously about, and then, taking a key from his pocket, opened the door. We passed a dark entry, and, I confess, I shuddered, as the door closed upon me, reflecting that, perhaps, this man was employed to decoy me to some secret place, in order to assassinate me, by the direction of my superiours, who might wish to destroy me in this secret manner. But I had but little time for these gloomy reflections; for, opening another door, I was startled with a blaze of light, let into apartments splendidly furnished. My conductor now assumed an air of importance, requested me to repose myself on a silken couch, and retired. A young lady, who was veiled, of a graceful person and pleasing address, soon brought a plate of sweetmeats and a bottle of excellent wine. The old man soon reappeared; but, so changed in his habit and appearance, I could scarce recognize him. He was now arrayed in drawers of the finest linen, an embroidered vest, and loose gown of the richest Persian silk. He smiled at my surprise, shook me by the hand, and told me that he was a Jew; assuring me, that he was with his brethren under the protection of the Dey. The outward appearance of his house, and the meanness of his attire abroad were, he said, necessary to avoid envy and suspicion. But come, said he, I know all about you; I can confide in you. Come refresh yourself with a glass of this wine;—neither Moses nor your Messiah forbid the use of it. We ate of the collation, drank our wine liberally; and then he introduced me to his son, whom I found labouring under a violent ague. I administered some sudorifics, and left direction for the future treatment of my patient. Upon my departure, the Jew put a zequin into my hand, and made me promise to visit his son again; requesting me to seat myself in the place, he had found me, at the same hour, the next day but one afterwards; and, in passing through the dark entry, conjured me not to mention his domestic style of living. The name of this Jew was Adonah Ben Benjamin. I visited his son, according to appointment, and found him nearly restored to health. The father and son both expressed great gratitude; but the former told me he would not pay me for this visit in silver or gold, but with something more valuable, by his advice. Come and see me sometimes; I know this people well, and may render you more service than you expect. I afterwards visited this Jew frequently, and from him obtained much information. He told me, in much confidence, that soon after I was taken, a Jew and two Algerines made a tour of the United States, and sent home an accurate account of the American commerce;[2]

and that the Dey was so impressed with the idea of our wealth, that he would never permit the American slaves to be ransomed under a large premium, which must be accompanied with the usual presents, as a purchase of peace, and an annual tribute. Expressing my anxiety to recover my freedom, he advised me to write to some of the American agents in Europe. I accordingly addressed a letter to William Carmichael,[3] Esq; charge des affairs from the United States, at the count of Madrid, representing my deplorable circumstances, and the miserable estate of my fellow prisoners; praying the interference of our government, stating the probable mode of access to the Dey, and enclosing a letter to my parents. This my friend, the Jew, promised to convey; but, as I never received any answer from Mr. Carmichael, and my letters never found the way to my friends, I conclude, from the known humanity of that gentleman, my letters miscarried.

Sometime after, I heard that the United States had made application, through Mr. Lamb, for the redemption of their citizens, and I had hopes of liberty; intending, if that gentleman succeeded in his negotiations, to claim my right to be ransomed, as an American citizen, but his proposals were scouted with contempt. I have sometimes heard this gentleman censured for failing to accomplish the object of his mission, but very unjustly; as I well remember that I, who was much interested in his success, never blamed him at the time; and, I know, the ransom, he offered the Dey, was ridiculed in the common coffee houses, as extremely pitiful. The few Algerines, I conversed with, affected to represent it as insulting. It was reported, that he was empowered to offer only two hundred dollars per head for each prisoner indiscriminately,[4] when the common price was four thousand dollars per head for a captain of a vessel, and one thousand four hundred for a common fore mast sailor. When this unsuccessful attempt failed, the prisoners were treated with greater severity; doubtless with a design to affright the Americans into terms, more advantageous to the Dey.

Finding my hopes of release from the applications of my country to fade, I consulted the friendly Jew, who advised me to endeavour to pay my own ransom, which, he said, might be effected with

my savings from my practice by the mediation of a rich Jew, his relation. I accordingly put all my savings into Adonah Ben Benjamin's hands, which amounted to two hundred and eighty dollars,
and resolved to add to it all I could procure. To this intent I
hoarded up all I could obtain; denying myself the slender refresh-
ments of bathing and cooling liquors, to which I had been for some
time accustomed. The benevolent Hebrew, promising that, when I
had attained the sum requisite, within two or three hundred dollars, he himself would advance the remainder, no miser was ever
more engaged than I to increase my store. After a tedious interval,
my prospects brightened surprisingly. Some fortunate operations, I
performed, obtained me valuable presents; one to the amount of
fifty dollars. My stock, in the Jew's hands, had increased to nine
hundred dollars; and, to add to my good fortune, the Jew told me,
in great confidence, that, from the pleasing account of the United
States, which I had given him, for I always spoke of the privileges of
my native land with fervour, he was determined to remove with his
family thither. He said he would make up the deficiency in my ransom, and send me home by the first European vessel, with letters to
a Mr. Lopez, a Jew, who, he said, lived in Rhode Island or Massachusetts, to whom he had a recommendation from a relation, who
had been in America. To Mr. Lopez he intended to consign his
property. He accordingly procured his friend, whose name I did
not then learn, to agree about my ransom. He concluded the contract at two thousand dollars. My friends in the hospital expressed
sorrow at parting with me; and making me some pecuniary presents, I immediately added them to my stock, in the hands of the
Jew. In order to lessen the price of my ransom, the contractor had
told my master that he was to advance the money, and take my word
to remit it, upon my return to my friends. This story I confirmed. I
went to the Jew's house, who honestly produced all my savings; we
counted them together, and he added the remainder, tying the
money up in two large bags. We spent a happy hour, over a bottle of
his best wine: I, in anticipating the pleasure my parents and friends
would receive in recovering their son, who was lost, and the Jew in
framing plans of commerce in the United States, and in the enjoy-

ment of his riches in a country, where no despot should force from him his honest gains; and, what added to my enjoyment, was the information that a vessel was to sail for Gibraltar in two days, in which, he assured me, he would procure me a passage. I returned to the hospital, exulting in my happy prospects. I was quite beside myself with joy. I capered and danced as merrily, as my youthful acquaintance at a husking. Sometimes I would be lost in thought, and then burst suddenly into loud laughter. The next day towards evening, I hasted to the house of my friend the Jew, to see if he had engaged my passage, and to gratify myself with conversing upon my native land. Being intimate in the family, I was entrusted with a key of the front door. I opened it hastily, and passing the entry, knocked for admittance at the inner door, which was soon opened. But, instead of the accustomed splendour, all was gloomy; the windows darkened, and the family in tears. Poor Adonah Ben Benjamin had, that morning, been struck with an apoplexy, and slept with his fathers. I soon retired as sincere a mourner as the nearest kindred. I had indeed more reason to mourn than I conceived; for, upon applying to his son for his assistance in perfecting my freedom, which his good father had so happily begun, he professed the utmost ignorance of the whole transaction; declared that he did not know the name of the agent, his father had employed, and gave no credit to my account of the monies I had lodged with his father. I described the bags. He cooly answered, that the God of his father Abraham had blessed his father Adonah with many such bags. I left him, distracted with my disappointment. Sometimes I determined to relate the whole story to the director of the hospital, and apply for legal redress to a cadi; but the specimen I had of an Algerine law suit deterred me. I had been so inadvertent, as to countenance the story that a Jew was to advance the whole sum for me. If I had been a Mussulman, I might have attested to my story; but a slave is never admitted as an evidence in Algiers, the West Indies, or the Southern States. The disappointment of my hopes were soon known in the hospital, though the hand Adonah Ben Benjamin had in the contract remained a secret. The artful Jew, who had contracted for my ransom, fearing he should have to advance the money himself, spread a report that I was immensely rich in my own country. This coming to the ears of my master, he raised my ransom to six thousand dollars, which the wily Israelite declining to pay, the contract was dissolved. From my master I learned his name, and waited upon him, hoping to obtain some evidence of Adonah's having received my money, at least so far as to induce his son to restore it. But the Jew positively declared that Adonah never told him other, than that he was to advance the cash himself. Thus, from the brightest hopes of freedom, I was reduced to despair; my money lost; and my ransom raised. I bless a merciful God that I was preserved from the desperate folly of suicide. I never attempted my life; but, when I lay down, I often hoped that I might never awake again, in this world of misery. I grew dejected and my flesh wasted. The physicians recommended a journey into the country, which my master approved; for, since the report of my wealth in my native land, he viewed my life as valuable to him, as he doubted not my friends would one day ransom me at an exorbitant premium.

Chapter XXXI.

No gentle breathing breeze prepares the spring,
No birds within the desert regions sing.[1]

Philips.

Argument.

The Author, by Permission of his Master, travels to Medina, the burial Place of the Prophet Mahomet.

The director soon after proposed, that I should attend some merchants, as a surgeon in a voyage and journey to Medina, the burial, and Mecca, the birth place of the prophet Mahomet; assuring me, that I should be treated with respect, and indeed find some agreeable companions on the tour, as several of the merchants were infidels, like myself, and that any monies I might acquire, by itinerant practice, should be my own. I accepted this proposal with pleasure, and was soon leased to two Mussulman merchants, who gave a kind of bond for my safe return to my master. I had cash advanced me to purchase medicines, and a case of surgeon's instruments, which I was directed to stow in a large leather wallet. I took a kind leave of my patrons in the hospital, who bestowed many little presents of sweetmeats, dates, and oranges. I waited upon the good Mollah, who presented me with fifty dollars. I have charity to believe that this man, though an apostate, was sincere in his faith in the Mahometan creed. He pressed my hand at parting, gave me many salutary cautions, as to my conduct during the voyage; and said, while the tears started in his eyes, my friend, you have suffered much misfortune and misery in a short life; let me conjure you not to add the torments of the future to the miseries of the present world. But, added he, pausing, who shall alter the decrees of God? I flatter myself, that the scales of natal prejudice will yet fall from your eyes, and that your name was numbered among the faithful from all eternity.

Our company consisted of two Algerine merchants, or factors, twenty pilgrims, nine Jews, among whom was the son of my deceased friend Adonah, and two Greek traders from Chios, who carried with them several bales of silks and a quantity of mastic, to vend at Scandaroon, Grand Cairo and Medina. We took passage in a Xebec; and, coasting the African shore, soon passed the ruins of antient Carthage, the Bay of Tunis; and, weathering cape Bona, and steering south easterly, one morning hove in sight of the Island of Malta, inhabited by the knights of that name, who are sworn enemies of the Mahometan faith. I could perceive, that the sight of this island gave a sensible alarm to the crew and passengers. But the captain, or rather skipper, who was a blustering, rough renegado, affected great courage, and swore that, if he had but one cannon on board, he would run down and give a broad side to the infidel dogs. His bravery was soon put to the test; for, as the sun arose, we could discern plainly an armed vessel bearing down upon us. She overhauled us fast, and our skipper conjectured she bore the Maltese colours. All hands were now summoned to get out some light sails, and several oars were put out, at which the brave skipper tugged as lustily as the meanest of us. When the wind lulled and we gained of the vessel, he would run upon the quarters of the Xebec, and hollow; "Come on, you christian dogs, I am ready for you." I have some doubts, whether the vessel ever noticed us. If she did, she despised us; for she tacked and stood to the south west. This was no sooner perceived by our gallant commander, than he ordered the Xebec to lay too, and swore, that he would pursue the uncircumcised dogs, and board them; but he first would prudently ask the approbation of the passengers, who instantly determined one and all that their business was such, that they must insist upon the captain's making his best way to port. The captain consented, but not without much grumbling at his misfortune, in losing so fine a prize; and declared that, when he landed his passengers, he would directly quit the port and renew the chase. After a smart run, we dropt anchor in the port of Alexandria, called by the Turks Scandaroon.[2] This is the site of the antient Alexandria, founded by Alexander the great; though its present appearance would not induce an opinion of so magnificent a founder. It lies not far from the wester-most branch of the river Nile, by which, in ancient day, it was supplied with water. The antiquarian eye may possibly observe, in the scattered fragments of rocks, the vestiges of the ruins of its antient grandeur; but a vulgar traveller, from the appearance of the harbour, choked with sand, the miserable buildings, and more wretched inhabitants of the town, would not be led to conclude that this was the port, which rose triumphant on the ruins of Tyre and Carthage. We here hired camels; and, being joined by a number of pilgrims and traders, collected from various parts of the Levant, we proceeded towards Grand Cairo, the present capital of Egypt; and, after travelling three days, or rather three nights, for we generally reposed in the heat of the day, which is severe from one hour after the sun's rising until it sets, we came to a pretty town on the west bank of the Nile, called Gize,[3] and hence passed over on rafts to the city of Grand Cairo, called by the Turks Almizer; the suburbs of which extend to the river, but the principal town commences its proper boundaries, at about three miles east of the Nile. I was now within a comparatively short distance of two magnificent curiosities, I had ever been desirous of beholding. The city of Jerusalem was only about five day's journey to the south east,[4] and I had even caught a glimpse of the pyramids near Gize. I went with my masters and others to see a deep stoned pit, in the castle, called Joseph's well; and said to have been dug by the direction of that patriarch. I am not antiquarian enough to know the particular style of Joseph's well architecture; but the water was sweet and extremely cold. The Turks say that Potiphar's wife[5] did not cease to persecute Joseph with her love, after he was released from prison, and advanced to power; but the patriarch, being warned by a dream to dig this well, and invite her to drink of the water, which she had no sooner done, but one cup of it so effectually cooled her desires, that she was ever afterwards an eminent example of the most frigid chastity. In Grand Cairo, we were joined by many pilgrims from Palestine, and the adjacent countries. The third day, our carivan, which consisted of three hundred camels and dromedaries, set out for Medina, under the convoy of a troop of Mamaluke guards, a tawny, raw boned, ill clothed people. Some of the merchants, and even pilgrims made a handsome appearance in person, dress, and equipage. I was myself well mounted upon a camel, and carried with me only my leather wallet of drugs, which I dispensed freely among the pilgrims; my masters receiving the ordinary pay, while I collected many small sums, which the gratitude of my patients added to the usual fee. We passed near the north arm of the red sea, and then pursued our journey south, until we struck the same arm again, near the place where the learned Wortley Montague has concluded the Israelites, under the conduct of Moses, effected their passage.[6] The breadth of the sea here is great, and the waters deep and turbulent. The infidel may sneer, if he chooses; but, for my own part, I am convinced beyond a doubt, that, if the Israelites passed in this place, it must have been by the miraculous interposition of a divine power. I could not refrain from reflecting upon the infatuated temerity, which impelled the Egyptian king to follow them. Well does the Latin poet exclaim; *Quem Deus vult perdere, prius dementat.*[7] We then travelled east, until we came to a small village, called Tadah. Here we filled many goat skins with water, and laded our camels with them. In addition to my wallet, I received two goat skins or bags of water upon my camel. The weight, this useful animal will carry, is astonishing; and the facility and promptitude, with which he kneels to receive his rider and burthen, surprising. We now entered the confines of Arabia Petrea, very aptly denominated the rocky Arabia; for, journeying south east, we passed over many ridges of mountains, which appeared of solid rocks, while the vallies and plains between them were almost a quicksand. Not a tree, shrub, or vegetable is to be seen. In these vallies, the sun poured intolerable day, and its reflections from the land were insupportable. No refreshing breeze is here felt. The intelligent traveller often fears the rising of the wind, which blows such sultry gales, that man and beast often sink beneath them, "never to rise again" or, when agitated into a tempest, drive the sand with such tumultuous violence, as to overwhelm whole caravans. Such indeed were the stories told me, as I passed these dreary plains. The only inconvenience, I sustained, arose from the intense heat of the sun, and the chills of the night, which our thin garments were not calculated to exclude. On the third day, after we left Tadah, the water, which we transported on our camels, was nearly expended. These extraordinary animals had not drank but once, since our departure. Near the middle of the fourth day, I observed our camels snuff the air, and soon set off in a brisk trot, and just before night brought us to water. This was contained in only one deep well, dug, like a reversed pyramid, with steps to descend on every side, to the depth of one hundred feet; yet the sagacity of the camel had discovered this water at perhaps twenty miles distance. So my fellow travellers asserted; but I have since thought, whether these camels, from frequently passing this desert country, did not discover their approach to water, rather from the eye, noting familiar objects, than the actual scenting the water itself. A horse that has journeyed the whole day, will quicken his step at night, when, upon a familiar road, within some miles of an accustomed stable. Our escort delighted in the marvellous. Many a dreadful story did they tell of poisonous winds and overwhelming sands; and of the fierce wandering Arabs, who captured whole caravans, and eat their prisoners. Many a bloody battle had they fought with this cruel banditti, in which, according to their narratives, they always came off conquerours. Frequently were we alarmed, to be in readiness to combat their savage free bootees; though I never saw but two of the wild Arabs, in the whole of our journey. They joined us at a little village, east of Istamboul, and accosted us with great civility. They were dressed in blue frocks, girded round the waste with particoloured sashes, in which were stuck a pistol and a long knife. Their legs were bare, and sheepskin caps covered their heads.

Their complexions were sallow, but their garments and persons were clean. Indeed, their dress and address evinced them to be of a more civilized race than our guards, who affected to treat them with lofty hauteur; and, when they departed, assured us that they were spies, and that an attack from their countrymen might now be apprehended with certainty; if, said the leader of our escort, they are not terrified by finding you under our protection.

Chapter XXXII.

Procul! O procul! este profani.[1]

Virgil.

Argument.

The Author is blessed with the Sight and Touch of a most holy Mahometan Saint.

When we were within one day's journey of Medina, we halted for a longer time than usual; occasioned, as I found, by the arrival of a most holy saint. As I had never seen a saint, being bred, in a land, where even the relics of these holy men are not preserved, for I believe all New England cannot produce so much as a saint's rotten tooth or toe nail, I was solicitous to see and converse with this blessed personage. I soon discovered him, in the midst of about fifty pilgrims, some of whom were devoutly touching their foreheads with the hem of his garment, while others, still more devout, prostrated themselves on the ground, and kissed the prints of his footsteps in the sand. Though I was assured, that he was filled with divine love, and conferred felicity on all, who touched him; yet, to outward appearance, he was the most disgusting, contemptible object, I had ever seen. Figure to yourselves, my readers, a little decrepit, old man, made shorter by stooping, with a countenance, which exhibited a vacant stare, his head bald, his finger and toe nails as long as hawks' claws, his attire squalid, his face, neck, arms, and legs begrimed with dirt and swarming with vermin, and you will have some faint idea of this Mussulman saint. As I was too reason-able to expect that holiness existed in a man's exteriour, I waited to hear him speak; anticipating, from his lips, the profoundest wis-dom, delivered in the honied accents of the saints in bliss. At length he spake; and his speech betrayed him, a mere idiot. While this as-tonished me, it raised the respect of his admirers, who estimated his sanctity in an inverse ratio to the weakness of his intellects. If they could have ascertained, that he was born an idiot, I verily believe, they would have adored him; for the Mahometans are taught by their alcoran, that the souls of saints are often lodged in the bodies of idiots; and these pious souls, being so intent on the joys of para-dise, is the true reason, that the actions of their bodies are so little suited to the manners of this world. This saint however did not as-pire to the sanctity of a genuine idiot; though, I fancy, his modesty injured his preferment, for he certainly had very fair pretensions. It was resolved, that the holy man should go with us; and, to my great mortification and disgust, he was mounted behind me on the same camel; my Mahometan friends probably conceiving, that he would so far communicate his sanctity by contact, as that it might affect my conversion to their faith. Whatever were their motives, in the embraces of this nauseous being, with the people prostrating them-selves in reverence on each side, I made my entry into the city of Medina.

Chapter XXXIII.

There appears to be nothing in their nature above the power of the Devil.[1]

EDWARDS *on Religious Affections.*

ARGUMENT.

The Author visits the City of Medina: Description of the Prophet's Tomb, and principal Mosque.

Medina Tadlardh, erroneously called Medina Talmabi,[2] is situated in Arabia Deserta, about forty five miles east from the borders of the red sea. To this place, as has been before related, the prophet fled, when driven from Mecca his birth place; and here he was buried, and his remains still are preserved, in a silver coffin, ornamented with a golden crescent, enriched with jewels, covered with cloth of gold, supported upon silver tassels, and shadowed by a canopy, embroidered with silk and gold thread upon silver tissue. This canopy is renewed annually, by the bashaw of Egypt; though other bashaws, and great men among the Turks, often assist in the expense, or augment the value of the yearly present, by silver lamps and other ornaments. The whole are contained in a magnificent mosque, in which are suspended innumerable gold and silver lamps, some of which are kept continually burning, and all are lighted on certain public occasions; and even upon the approach of some dignified pilgrim. I had not acquired sufficient holiness, from my blessed companion, to be permitted to enter this sanctified building. The Arabians are profusely extravagant, in the titles they bestow on the city of Medina; calling it the most holy, most renowned, most excellent city; the sanctuary of the blessed fugitive; model of the refulgent city in the celestial paradise; and some of the great vulgar suppose, that when the world shall be destroyed, this city, with the prophet's remains, will be transported by angels, with all its inhabitants, to paradise. We tarried there but a few hours, as the great object of the devotions of the pilgrims was Mecca. Pilgrimages are performed to both places; but those to Medina are not indispensably necessary; being directed by the book of the companions of the apostles, while those to Mecca are enjoined by the alcoran itself. The former are supposed meritorious, the latter necessary to salvation. I had the curiosity to inquire respecting the prophet's coffin being suspended in the air by a load stone, and was assured that this was a mere christian obloquy, as no pretensions of any such suspension were ever made.

CHAPTER XXXIV.

The heaven of heavens cannot contain thee.[1]

BIBLE.

ARGUMENT.

The Author visits Mecca: Description of the Al Kaaba, or House of God.[2]

Being freed from my blessed companion, I had an agreeable journey from Medina to Mecca, which is the most ancient city in all Arabia; situated about two hundred miles south east of Medina, twenty one degrees and forty five minutes north latitude, and one hundred and sixteen degrees east longitude, from Philadelphia, according to late American calculations. I saw the great mosque in the centre of Mecca, which it is said, far surpasses in grandeur that of Sancta Sophia in Constantinople. It certainly is a very august building, the roof of which is refulgent; but even the inhabitants smiled at my credulity, when I observed that I had read it was covered with plated gold. This mosque contains within its limits the grand object of the Mussulman's pilgrimage; the *Al Kaaba*, or house of God, said to have been built by the hands of the patriarch Abraham; to confirm which the Arabian priests shew a black stone, upon which they say Abraham laid his son Isaac, when he had bound him in preparation for his intended sacrifice. This stone and building were great objects of veneration, before the mission of the prophet, and he artfully availed himself of this popular prejudice, in rendering the highest respect to the holy house, in his life time, and enjoining upon his followers, without distinction among males, to visit it once in their lives. The advent of the prophet was said to be announced from the four corners of the house, which exhibit the four cardinal points. Few pilgrims are permitted to enter this sacred, venerable building; but, after travelling, some of them perhaps a thousand miles, they are content to prostrate themselves in the courts, which surround it. Few Mahometans perform this pilgrimage in person; those who do are highly respected. This pilgrimage was enjoined, by the prophet, to be performed in person; but, when he laid this injunction, it is not probable he anticipated the extensive spread of his doctrines. So long as his disciples were limited by the boundaries of Arabia, or had only extended themselves over a part of Syria, this pious journey was practicable and easy; but, when the crescent rose triumphant on the sea coast, and most of the interiour of Africa, when it shone with splendour in Persia, Tartary, and Turkey, and even adorned the Moorish minarit in Spain, actual pilgrimage was deemed impracticable; and the faithful were allowed to visit the Kaaba by deputy. The ingenuity of more modern times has alleviated this religious burthen still further, by allowing the deputy to substitute other attornies under him. Thus for example: the pious Mussulman in Belgrade will employ a friend at Constantinople, who will empower another friend at Scandaroon to procure a confidential friend at Grand Cairo to go in the name of him at Belgrade, and perform his pilgrimage to Mecca. Certificates of these several substitutions are preserved, and the lazy Mussulman hopes by this finesse to reap the rewards of the faithful in paradise.

Chapter XXXV.

Sweeter than the harmonica or lute,
Or lyre swept by the master's pliant hand;
Soft as the hymns of infant seraphim,
Are the young sighings of a contrite heart.

Author's *Manuscript Poems.*

Argument.

The Author returns to Scandaroon: Finds Adonah's Son sick: His Contrition: Is restored to Health.

After tarrying sixteen days at Mecca, during which time my masters fasted, prayed, performed their devotions at the Kaaba, and sold their merchandize, we retraced the same rout to Scandaroon. Here we found the son of Adonah Ben Benjamin, who had been detained in this place by sickness, so weakened from a tedious slow fever that his life was despaired of. He expressed great joy, at our return, and begged my professional assistance; assuring me, that he esteemed his present disorder a judicial punishment from the God of his fathers, for the injury he had done me; candidly confessing, that he knew of his father's having received my money, which he would restore upon our return to Algiers, if I would effect his recovery. He prevailed upon my masters that I should abide in the house with him, during their absence, as they were engaged upon a trading tour to a place called Gingè, upon the river Nile. I exerted all my skill, both as a physician and nurse. Perhaps my attention in the latter capacity, assisted by his youth, was of more service than my prescriptions. Be that as it may, he recovered rapidly, and in ten days was able to walk the streets; but I could not help noticing with sorrow, that as his strength increased, his gratitude and promises to refund my money decreased.

Chapter XXXVI.

O what a goodly outside falshood hath![1]

Shakespeare.

Argument.

The Gratitude of a Jew.

One day, walking on the beach, the Jew looked me steadily in the face; and, laying his hand upon my shoulder, said I owe you my life, I owe you money, which you cannot oblige me to pay. You think, a Jew will always deceive in money matters. You are mistaken. You shall not wait for your pay in Algiers; I will pay you here in Alexandria. I owe you one thousand dollars on my father's account. Now, what do you demand for restoring me to health? Nothing replied I, overjoyed at his probity; restore me my money, and you are welcome to my services. This must not be, said the son of Adonah, I have done wickedly, but mean not only to pay you, but satisfy my own conscience. I will allow you in addition to the one thousand dollars, two thousand more for your assistance, as a physician; and then will advance three thousand more, which I will take your word to repay me, when you are able. I was astonished. I seized his hand and felt his pulse, to discover if he was not delirious. His pulse were regular, and I knew his ability to perform his promise. We will meet here on the morrow, and I will pay you. I met him the next day, and he was not ready to make payment. I now began to doubt his promises, and blame myself for the delusions of hope. By his appointment I met him the third day, on a retired part of the beach, westward from the port. We now saw a man approaching us. That man, said the Jew, will pay you. You well understand, my friend, that your ransom is fixed at six thousand dollars. Now, whoever gives you your liberty, really pays you that sum. I have engaged the person, who is approaching, and who is the master of a small vessel, to transport you to Gibraltar, whence you may find your way home. The man now joined us and confirmed the words of the Jew, for whom he professed a great friendship. It was concluded, that I should come to that spot immediately after dark, where I should find a small boat waiting to carry me on board the vessel. The master of the vessel declaring, that he run a great risk, in assisting in my escape; but was willing to do it out of commiseration for me, and friendship for the Jew; and reminded me, that I had better pick up all my property, and bring it with me. I hastened home with the Jew, and collected all the property I could with propriety call my own; which consisted of a few clothes, and to the amount of three hundred and twenty dollars in cash. As soon as it was dark, the Jew accompanied me to the beach, and then took an affectionate leave of me, presenting me with the value of ten dollars, as a loan, gravely remarking, that now I owed him three thousand and ten dollars, which he hoped I would transport to him as soon as I arrived in America. The Jew quitted me, and I soon discovered the approach of the boat, which I stept into with a light heart, congratulating myself, that I was again A FREE MAN. The boat soon rowed along side of a vessel, that was laying to for us. I jumped on board, and was directly seized by two men, who bound me and hurried me below deck; and, after robbing me of all my property, left me in the dark to my own reflections. I had been so long the sport of cruel fortune, that these were not so severe, as my sympathising readers may conjecture. Repeated misfortunes blunt sensibility. I perceived that I had been played a villanous trick, and exchanged a tolerable slavery, for one perhaps more insupportable; but should have been perfectly resigned to my fate, if the dread of being returned to Algiers and suffering the dreadful punishment, already related, had not presented itself. In the morning, I requested to see the captain; and, by his orders, was brought upon deck; to my surprise, it was not the same person who had decoyed me on board. I was confounded. I intended to have expostulated; but could I tell a stranger, a man, who appeared a Mussulman by his garb, that I was a runaway slave? While I was perplexing myself what to say, the man, who had decoyed me on board, appeared. He was a passenger, and claimed me as his slave, having purchased me, as he said, for four hundred zequins of a Jew, my former master, and meant to carry me with him to Tunis. I was now awakened to all the horrours of my situation. I dared not irritate my new master by contradictions, and acquiesced in his story in dumb despair. On the eighth day, after we departed from Scandaroon, the vessel made cape Bona, and expected soon to anchor in the port of Tunis. My master had a Portuguese slave on board, who slept in the birth with me. He spoke a little broken English, having been formerly a sailor on board a vessel of that nation. He gave me the most alarming apprehensions of the cruelty of our master, but flattered me by saying that the Tunise in general were more mild with their slaves than the Algerines, and allowed a freer intercourse with the European merchants; and, by their interference, we might obtain our liberty. While my fellow slave slept, I lay agonizing with the dread of entering the port of Tunis. Often did I wish that some friendly rock or kindly leak would sink me, and my misfortunes, in perpetual oblivion; and I was nigh being gratified in my desperate wishes; for, the same night, a tremendous storm arose, and the gale struck us with such violence, that our sails were instantly slittered into rags. We could not shew a yard of canvass, and were obliged to scud under bare poles. The night was excessively dark; and, to increase our distress, our ballast shifted and we were obliged to cut away our masts by the board, to save us from foundering. The vessel righted, but being strong and light, and the hatchways being well secured, our captain was only fearful of being driven on some christian coast. The next night, the wind lulled; and the morning after, the sun arose clear, and we found ourselves off the coast of Sardinia, and within gun shot of an armed vessel. She proved to be a Portuguese frigate. To the confusion and dismay of our captain and passenger, and to the great joy of myself and fellow slave. The frigate hoisted her colours, manned her boats, and boarded us. No sooner was his national flag displayed, than the overjoyed Portuguese ran below and liberated me from my fetters, hugged me in raptures, and hauling me upon deck, the first man we met was our master, whom he saluted with a kick, and then spit in his face. I must confess that this reverse of fortune made me feel for the wretched Mussulman, who stood quivering with apprehensions of instant death; nor could I refrain from preventing the Portuguese from avenging himself for the cruelties, he had suffered, under this barbarian. The boats soon boarded us, and secured the captain and crew, whom they treated with as much bitter contempt, as my fellow had exercised toward our late master. This poor fellow soon introduced me to his countrymen, with a brief account of my country and misfortunes.

Chapter XXXVII.

How glorious now, how changed since yesterday.

Anon.

Argument.

Conclusion.

The Portuguese officers treated me with politeness; and, when they were rifling the vessel, requested me to select my property from the plunder. I was then sent on board the frigate. The captain expressed much joy, at being the means of my deliverance, and told me, that the Portuguese had a sincere regard for the Americans; and that he had received express orders to protect our commerce from the Barbary corsairs. The prisoners were brought on board and confined below; and, after every thing valuable was taken from the prize, the ship stood for the straits of Gibraltar, leaving a boat to fire the Tunise vessel. I never received more civility than from the officers of this frigate. In compliment to them, I was obliged to throw my Mahometan dress over the ship's side; for they furnished me with every necessary, and many ornamental articles of European clothing. The surgeon was particularly attentive. I lent him some assistance among the sick, his mate being unwell; and, among other presents, he gave me a handsome pocket case of surgical instruments. After a pleasant voyage, we anchored in port Logos, in the southern extremity of Portugal.[1] Here I received the agreeable intelligence, that the United States were about commencing a treaty with the Dey of Algiers, by the agency of Joseph Donaldson, jun. Esq;[2] which would liberate my unhappy fellow citizens, and secure the American commerce from future depredations. Without landing, I had the good fortune to obtain a passage on board an English merchantman, bound for Bristol, Captain Joseph Joceline, commander. We had a prosperous voyage to the land's end; and, very fortunately for me, just off the little isle of Lundy, spake with a brigantine, bound to Chesapeak Bay, Captain John Harris, commander. In thirty two days, we made Cape Charles, the north chop of the Chesapeak, and I prevailed upon the captain to set me on shore; and, on the third day of May, one thousand seven hundred and ninety five, I landed in my native country,[3] after an absence of seven years and one month; about six years of which I had been a slave. I purchased a horse, and hastened home to my parents, who received me as one risen from the dead. I shall not attempt to describe their emotions, or my own raptures. I had suffered hunger, sickness, fatigue, insult, stripes, wounds, and every other cruel injury; and was now under the roof of the kindest and tenderest of parents. I had been degraded to a slave, and was now advanced to a citizen of the freest country in the universe. I had been lost to my parents, friends, and country; and now found, in the embraces and congratulations of the former, and the rights and protection of the latter, a rich compensation for all past miseries. From some minutes I preserved, I compiled these memoirs; and, by the solicitations of some respectable friends, have been induced to submit them to the public. A long disuse of my native tongue, will apologize to the learned reader for any inaccuracies.

I now mean to unite myself to some amiable woman, to pursue my practice, as a physician; which, I hope, will be attended with more success than when essayed with the inexperience and giddiness of youth. To contribute cheerfully to the support of our excellent government, which I have learnt to adore, in schools of despotism; and thus secure to myself the enviable character of an useful physician, a good father and worthy FEDERAL citizen.

My ardent wish is, that my fellow citizens may profit by my misfortunes. If they peruse these pages with attention they will perceive the necessity of uniting our federal strength to enforce a due respect among other nations. Let us, one and all, endeavour to sustain the general government. Let no foreign emissaries inflame us against one nation, by raking into the ashes of long extinguished enmity or delude us into the extravagant schemes of another, by recurring to fancied gratitude.[4] Our first object is union among ourselves. For to no nation besides the United States can that antient saying be more emphatically applied; BY UNITING WE STAND, BY DIVIDING WE FALL.

Notes

Even for a Harvard-educated lawyer, Royall Tyler was exceptionally well read. For the most part, these notes merely identify his sources. Where Tyler refers to a text not readily accessible today, I have provided slightly more detail. Proper names easily found in a standard dictionary, atlas, or desk encyclopedia are not explained here.

The standard biography is G. Thomas Tanselle's *Royall Tyler* (Cambridge, Mass.: Harvard University Press, 1967). Tanselle has inventoried the substantive differences between the first and last editions of *The Algerine Captive* published during Tyler's lifetime in "Early American Fiction in England: The Case of *The Algerine Captive,*" *Papers of the Bibliographical Society of America* 59 (October–December 1965): 367–84.

The Contrast is widely anthologized; Tyler's other dramatic works may be found in *Four Plays,* edited by Arthur Wallace Peach and George Floyd Newbrough (Princeton, N.J.: Princeton University Press, 1941). Marius B. Péladeau has edited two collections of Tyler's works: *The Verse of Royall Tyler* (Charlottesville: University Press of Virginia, 1968) and *The Prose of Royall Tyler* (Rutland, Vt.: Charles E. Tuttle, 1972). There is no modern edition of *A Yankey in London* (New York: Isaac Riley, 1809).

For discussions of Tyler in the context of early American literature, see Cathy Davidson, *Revolution and the Word* (New York: Oxford University Press, 1986), chapter 7, and Robert A. Ferguson, *Law and Letters in Ameri-*

can Culture (Cambridge, Mass.: Harvard University Press, 1984), chapter 4.
For a concise history of America's encounter with the Barbary pirates, see
Gary E. Wilson, "American Hostages in Moslem Nations, 1784–1796: The
Public Response," *Journal of the Early Republic* 2 (Summer 1982): 123–41.
Robert J. Allison's *The Crescent Obscured: The United States and the Muslim
World, 1776–1815* (New York: Oxford University Press, 1995) gives a more
detailed account of the crisis and America's cultural and literary reaction
to it. Nine Barbary captivity narratives by Americans are reprinted in Paul
Baepler, ed., *White Slaves, African Masters: An Anthology of American Barbary
Captivity Narratives* (Chicago: University of Chicago Press, 1999), although
most were published after Tyler's novel appeared.

1. *By your patience, . . . course:* See *Othello* I.iii.89–91.

DEDICATION

1. *David Humphreys:* The soldier, diplomat, and poet David Humphreys
   (1752–1818) served as an aide-de-camp to George Washington during
   the Revolutionary War and as a trusted diplomat afterward. In 1793,
   while serving as minister to Portugal, Humphreys was put in charge of
   negotiating for the release of Americans held captive in Algiers. When
   he appealed in newspapers for charitable contributions, Americans
   responded enthusiastically, and Humphreys was able to send each prisoner a hat, a suit of clothes, and a monthly allowance for food. Washington's administration was embarrassed, however, that private citizens
   had taken on a public responsibility. The final details of the hostages'
   release were arranged by the diplomats Joseph Donaldson Jr. and Joel
   Barlow in 1796. After serving as minister plenipotentiary to Spain,
   Humphreys introduced merino sheep to America in 1802.
2. *a Poet and the Biographer of a Hero:* Humphreys and his fellow Yale
   alumni Timothy Dwight, John Trumbull, and Joel Barlow were
   known as the Connecticut Wits. Humphreys was author of *The Anarchiad: A Poem on the Restoration of Chaos and Substantial Night* (1787) and
   Essay on the Life of the Honorable Major-General Israel Putnam (1788).

PREFACE

1. *Levi Ames:* A broadside entitled *The Last Words and Dying Speech of Levi
   Ames, Executed at Boston, Octo. 21, 1773, for Burglary, Taken from His Own*

Mouth, and Published at His Desire, as a Solemn Warning to All, More Particularly Young People was published in Salem in 1773.

2. *some dreary somebody's Day of Doom:* The Puritan minister Michael Wigglesworth (1631–1705) kept a diary concerning his religious doubts and sexual cravings and wrote *The Day of Doom* (1662), a poem about the Last Judgment.

3. *Brydone:* the English traveler Patrick Brydone (1736–1818), author of *A Tour through Sicily and Malta* (1774).

4. *Bruce:* the Scottish explorer James Bruce (1730–94), author of *Travels to Discover the Source of the Nile* (1790).

5. *Mrs. Ratcliffe:* Ann Radcliffe (1764–1823), author of the popular Gothic novel *The Mysteries of Udolpho* (1794).

6. *the young lady, mentioned by Addison in his Spectator:* Joseph Addison and Richard Steele collaborated on *The Spectator,* a series that combined essays and fiction, between 1711 and 1714. But Tyler probably came across this anecdote in *The Posthumous Works of a Late Celebrated Genius, Deceased* (1770), a book spuriously attributed to Laurence Sterne, in fact written by Richard Griffith: "52. A lady of my acquaintance told me one day, in great joy, that she had got a parcel of the most delightful *novels* to read, that she had ever met with before. They call them Plutarch's Lives, said she. — I happened, unfortunately, to inform her ladyship, that they were deemed to be *authentic histories.* — Upon which her countenance fell, and she never read another line in them." Volume 2, pp. 233–34. Thanks to David A. Brewer of Ohio State University for finding this source.

VOLUME I

CHAPTER I

1. *Think of this, . . . time:* See *Macbeth* III.iv.95–97.

2. Captain John Underhill: Upon immigrating to Boston in 1630, John Underhill (1597–1672) became captain of the militia. He led Massachusetts troops in the Pequot War of 1636 and 1637. Soon after, he was caught up in the Antinomian controversy, a conflict between Massachusetts Bay Colony authorities and a group of more independent-minded Puritans who felt that personal experience of God's grace superseded any human law. In 1637, Underhill was charged with sedi-

tion for supporting John Wheelwright, a minister suspected of disdaining worldly authority. Underhill retracted his support for Wheelwright, but a woman then testified that during a shipboard voyage with her, Underhill had boasted of an unmediated experience of God's love—namely, an assurance of salvation had come to him one day while smoking his pipe. He was banished in 1638. The following year, he fled to New Hampshire to avoid prosecution for adultery. He lived out his later years in Connecticut, the Dutch colony of New Amsterdam, and Long Island.

3. *the Reverend Jeremy Belknap:* Jeremy Belknap (1733–98) wrote *History of New-Hampshire* (1791–92), one of Tyler's sources for this chapter.

4. *the Earl of Leicester:* Robert Dudley (1532?–88), earl of Leicester.

5. *the Earl of Essex:* Robert Devereux (1566–1601), earl of Essex, was the earl of Leicester's stepson. He became a popular hero after he took Cádiz in 1596.

6. *Tyronne:* Essex fell out of favor with Elizabeth when he agreed to a truce with the Irish rebel Hugh O'Neill (1540?–1616), earl of Tyrone.

7. *the petty insurrection, which cost Essex his head:* Encouraged by Puritan ministers to believe that the people would rise up if he appealed to them, Essex led a brief, doomed rebellion against Elizabeth.

8. *Reverend Mr. Robinson, . . . Governour Carver, Elder Brewster:* John Robinson (1576–1625) was pastor of the Pilgrim community at Leiden, where John Carver (1576–1621) and William Brewster (1567–1644) were his parishioners. Carver and Brewster sailed on the *Mayflower* to Plymouth Colony, where Carver became the first governor and Brewster the leading preacher. Robinson remained in Leiden.

9. *Governour Winthrop:* John Winthrop (1588–1649) was the first governor of the Massachusetts Bay Colony.

10. *Ann Hutchinson:* At weekly prayer meetings in her home, Anne Hutchinson (1591–1643) insisted that salvation could be had only by God's grace and not at all by human works, a belief condemned by Winthrop and others as Antinomianism, or lawlessness. In 1637 she was banished from Massachusetts Bay Colony and settled in Aquidneck Island, now part of Rhode Island.

11. *That the government . . . conversion:* The quote appears in Belknap's *History,* volume 1, chapter 2.

12. *Roger Williams:* The religious maverick Roger Williams (1603?–83)

rebuked Massachusetts Bay Colony for lingering allegiance to the Church of England, wrongful seizure of Indian land, and confusion of church and state. He was banished in 1636 and afterward founded Rhode Island.

13. *the pious Wheelwright:* The Puritan minister John Wheelwright (1592–1679) was associated with the Antinomian beliefs of his sister-in-law Anne Hutchinson—mistakenly, he later claimed—and banished from the Massachusetts Bay Colony from 1637 to 1644.

14. *William Aspinwall and John Coggeshell:* For writing a petition to the General Court in support of Wheelwright, William Aspinwall (b. 1605) was banished from the Massachusetts Bay Colony in 1637. For defending the same petition, John Coggeshall (1599–1647) was disfranchised. Coggeshall immigrated to Rhode Island in 1638 and became president of the Providence Plantations in 1647.

15. *the candid American author, above named:* that is, Jeremy Belknap.

16. *Whosoever looketh on . . . heart:* See Matthew 5:28.

CHAPTER II

1. *Hugh Peters:* The clergyman Hugh Peter (1598–1660) helped write the Massachusetts Bay Colony's legal code, assisted in the prosecution of Anne Hutchinson, and was executed during the Restoration for his service to Cromwell as chaplain and propagandist.

2. *MASTER HANSERD KNOLLYS:* The historical John Underhill took the side of the Baptist pastor Hansard Knollys (1598–1691) in his feud with another clergyman in Dover, New Hampshire.

3. *Mr. Hilton:* Edward Hilton (1596–1670?) founded Dover, the first permanent settlement in New Hampshire.

4. *Roger Harlakenden:* Harlakenden came to Massachusetts Bay Colony in 1635 and served on the governor's council from 1636 to 1638.

5. *Sir Harry Vane, the governour, Dudley, Haines, with masters Cotton, Shepherd, and Hugh Peters:* Henry Vane (1613–62), Thomas Dudley (1576–1653), and John Haynes (1594–1654) were governors of the Massachusetts Bay Colony. John Cotton (1584–1652) and Thomas Shepard (1605–49) were prominent Puritan clergymen.

6. *Gregory Nazianzen:* Saint Gregory of Nazianzus (c.328–89).

7. *how these prowde . . . cummine:* See Matthew 23:23.

8. *William Blaxton:* Until the Puritans landed in Boston Harbor, William Blackstone (1595–1675) lived in a cottage where Beacon Hill now stands; his cows grazed on the future site of the Boston Common. The quote attributed to him in the text is genuine.

9. *brother Fish:* According to Belknap's *History,* in 1639 John Underhill "sent thirteen armed men to Exeter to rescue out of the officer's hand one Fish, who had been taken into custody for speaking against the king."

10. 4th month: April.

11. *like the sons . . . nakedness:* See Genesis 9:23.

CHAPTER III

1. *The Devil offered . . . territory:* A paraphrase of Ethan Allen's response to a British attempt to buy his allegiance (*A Narrative of Colonel Ethan Allen's Captivity,* 1779).

2. *the Pequod wars:* In 1636 and 1637, Massachusetts, Plymouth, and Connecticut retaliated for a trader's murder by all but destroying the Pequot tribe. John Underhill wrote an account of the war entitled *Newes from America* (1638).

3. *Albany, then possessed by the Dutch, under the name of Amboyna:* The settlement was known as Beverwyck at the time.

4. *the famous Colonel Church:* In King Philip's War (1675–76), Benjamin Church (1639–1718) led Plymouth Colony's forces.

CHAPTER IV

1. *William Phipps:* William Phips (or Phipps) (1651–95), first royal governor of Massachusetts.

2. *Mather's Magnalia:* Cotton Mather first wrote about Phips in *Pietas in Patriam: The Life of His Excellency Sir William Phips, Knt.* (1697) and reprinted the account in *Magnalia Christi Americana* (1702).

CHAPTER V

1. *'Tis education forms . . . inclined:* Alexander Pope, *Epistles to Several Persons,* "Epistle 1, to Sir Richard Temple, Lord Cobham" (1734), lines 149–50.

2. *Dilworth's spelling book:* Thomas Dilworth's *A New Guide to the English Tongue: in five parts,* widely used and often reprinted.

3. *the great Mr. Whitfield:* George Whitefield (1714–70), the best-known preacher of the Great Awakening, the American religious revival movement of the eighteenth century.

4. *Valentine and Orson:* The anonymous romance *Valentine and Orson, The Two Sonnes of the Emperour of Greece* was frequently reprinted in Britain and America and was popular as a children's book.

5. *he stuck a skewer through Apollyon's eye in the picture, to help Christian beat him:* See John Bunyan, *Pilgrim's Progress,* part 1, stage 4.

6. *the Adamses in oratory:* President John Adams (1737–1826) and his second cousin Samuel Adams (1722–1803).

7. *cæsura:* an interruption in the rhythm of a line of poetry, caused when a word ends within a metrical foot. Classicists used to devote much time and energy to distinguishing between kinds of caesura.

8. *a Witherspoon in divinity:* John Witherspoon (1723–94) became president of the College of New Jersey (later Princeton University) in 1768 and brought Scottish common-sense philosophy to America.

CHAPTER VI

1. *Heteroclita sunto:* The section on irregular nouns in William Lily's *Short Introduction of Grammar* begins with the lines "Quae genus aut flexum variant, quaecunque novato / ritu deficiunt, superantve, Heteroclita sunto," which is translated in an English trot included with the book as follows: "Let these nouns be heteroclites [i.e., irregularly inflected], which do vary gender or declension, and whatsoever do want or have overmuch after a new order."

2. cognata tempora: tense systems.

3. *Virgil Delphini and Schrevelius's Lexicon:* Charles de la Rue originally prepared his annotated edition of Virgil for the dauphin, or heir apparent, of France. Though they dated from the seventeenth century, both the Delphine Virgil and Schrevelius's Lexicon (a Greek dictionary compiled by Cornelis Schrevel) were common schoolbooks well into the nineteenth century.

4. *after the manner of Virgil . . . in the georgics:* See Virgil, *Georgics,* book 4, lines 281ff.

CHAPTER VII

1. *Delightful task!...breast:* James Thomson, *The Seasons* (1730), "Spring," line 1152ff.

2. *a false concord:* a failure of words to agree in case, gender, or number even though the rules of grammar require them to (e.g., "they is").

3. bundling: In the New England courtship ritual known as bundling, lovers went to bed together with their clothes on. By the late eighteenth century the custom was on the wane and often joked about, as in the 1785 ballad "A New Bundling Song": "For some we may with truth suppose, / Bundle in bed with all their clothes. / But bundler's clothes are no defence, / Unruly horses push the fence." See Henry Reed Stiles, *Bundling: Its Origin, Progress and Decline in America* (1928).

4. got the bag: was rejected as a suitor.

5. papish: papist.

6. *Dr. Watts's version of the Psalms:* Isaac Watts, *Psalms of David* (1719).

7. *the version of Sternhold and Hopkins:* Thomas Sternhold and John Hopkins, *Certayne Psalmes Chosen out of the Psalter of David, and Drawen into English Metre* (1549).

8. Gradus ad Parnassum: a Latin thesaurus compiled by Paul Aler in the early eighteenth century.

CHAPTER VIII

1. *Search then the ruling passion:* Alexander Pope, *Epistles to Several Persons,* "Epistle 1, to Sir Richard Temple, Lord Cobham" (1734), line 174.

2. *played at duck and drake:* skimmed flat stones across water.

3. *funk:* smoke.

4. *Bunyan's Holy War, the Life of Colonel Gardner, and the Religious Courtship:* John Bunyan, *The Holy War, Made by Shaddai upon Diabolus, for the Regaining of the Metropolis of the World; Or, The Losing and Taking Again of the Town of Mansoul* (1682); Philip Doddridge, *Some Remarkable Passages in the Life of the Honourable Col. James Gardiner, Who Was Slain at the Battle of Preston-Pans September 21, 1745;* and Daniel Defoe, *Religious Courtship: Being Historical Discourses, on the Necessity of Marrying Religious Husbands and Wives Only...* (1722).

5. *Burn's Justice abridged:* Richard Burn, *Burn's Justice, An Abridgment of Burn's Justice of the Peace and Parish Officer* (1773).

6. *Buchan's Family Physician, Culpepper's Midwifery, and Turner's Surgery:* William Buchan, *Buchan's Family Physician;* Nicholas Culpeper, *Directory for Midwives;* and Daniel Turner, *Art of Surgery.*

CHAPTER IX

1. *He, from thick . . . day:* Alexander Pope, *Messiah, a Sacred Ecologue, in Imitation of Virgil's Pollio* (1712), lines 39–40.

2. *materia medica:* drugs and other substances used to treat illness.

3. *couching for the gutta serena:* Tyler seems to be conflating two illnesses. In the treatment known as couching, a doctor removed a cataract by inserting a needle into the eye and pushing the lens downward. Gutta serena, also known as amaurosis, was a loss of sight caused by a disease of the optic nerve.

4. *volatiles:* smelling salts.

CHAPTER X

1. Sanderson: Nicholas Saunderson (1682–1739) was a professor of mathematics at Cambridge University and the author of *Elements of Algebra* (1740).

2. the celebrated Doctor Moyes: During his 1785 visit to Boston, Henry Moyes, a blind chemistry professor from Manchester, England, boarded with Tyler's future father-in-law. Tyler assisted him during his lectures. See *Grandmother Tyler's Book: The Recollections of Mary Palmer Tyler (Mrs. Royall Tyler), 1775–1866* (New York: G. P. Putnam's, 1925), 95–97, and "Education of the Blind," *North American Review* 37 (July 1833): 20–59.

CHAPTER XI

1. *None are so . . . Fool:* See *Love's Labour's Lost,* V.ii.69–72.

2. *it was quaker meeting:* People were sitting in silence waiting for someone to speak.

3. *the Reverend Mr. K——:* perhaps Samuel Kirkland (1741–1808), who ministered to several tribes of the Iroquois nation.

4. *Elliot:* John Eliot (1604–90) preached to the Algonquin Indians in their own language and translated the Bible for them.

5. *ox eyed:* in Greek, *boôpis;* see *Iliad,* book 1, line 551.

CHAPTER XII

1. *Honour's a sacred . . . not:* Joseph Addison, *Cato: A Tragedy,* II.i.427–30.

2. *on 'change:* at the Exchange (that is, among creditable gentlemen).

CHAPTER XIII

1. *The flower of learning, and the bloom of wit:* Edward Young, *Love of Fame, the Universal Passion,* satire 2, line 58.

2. *lawn and sarcenet:* fine linen and silk.

3. *Stackhouse's Body of Divinity:* Thomas Stackhouse, *A Complete Body of Speculative and Practical Divinity* (1729).

4. *Glass's works, not on cookery, but the benignant works of John Glass, the father of Sandiman, and the Sandimanians:* Hannah Glasse wrote *The Art of Cookery Made Plain and Easy.* John Glas (1695–1773) founded a sect, eventually named after his disciple and son-in-law, Robert Sandeman, that emphasized communal living and the autonomy of individual congregations.

5. *a book, called Rolling Belly Lettres:* Charles Rollin, *The Method of Teaching and Studying the Belles Lettres.*

6. *Virgil's traveller, treading on the snake in the grass:* See Virgil, *Georgics,* book 4, line 461.

CHAPTER XIV

1. *A Babylonish dialect, . . . affect:* Samuel Butler, *Hudibras,* part 1, canto 1, lines 93–94.

2. *Cullen, Munroe, Boerhaave, and Hunter:* the medical authorities William Cullen (1710–90), Alexander Monro (1697–1767), Hermann Boerhaave (1668–1738), and John Hunter (1728–93).

3. *my learned friend, Doctor Kitteridge:* perhaps Thomas Kittredge (1746–1818), who served as surgeon of Colonel James Frye's regiment at the Battle of Bunker Hill.

CHAPTER XV

1. *Well skill'd . . . ray:* John Milton, *A Mask Presented at Ludlow-Castle, 1634,* lines 619–21.
2. *a Dispensatory:* a book of instructions for preparing medicinal substances.
3. *Cullen's First Lines:* William Cullen, *First Lines of the Practice of Physic* (U.S. edition, 1781).
4. *Paracelsus:* The given name of the Swiss physician and alchemist Paracelsus (1493–1541) was Theophrastus Bombastus von Hohenheim.

CHAPTER XVI

1. *The lady Baussiere rode on:* Laurence Sterne, *Tristram Shandy,* volume 5, chapter 1.
2. *the late Dr. Joseph Gardner:* Joseph Gardner (1752–94), a physician and member of the Continental Congress.
3. *these remarks will be published by themselves in a future edition:* Tyler died before finishing his revision, entitled "The Bay Boy." The chapters he did complete are printed in *The Prose of Royall Tyler,* ed. Marius Péladeau (Charles E. Tuttle, 1972), 21–174.

CHAPTER XVII

1. *A hornet's sting, . . . wing:* Anna Letitia Barbauld, "The Invitation," lines 157–58.
2. *a Raynal or Buffon:* The French scholars of natural history Guillaume-Thomas-François, abbé Raynal (1713–96), and Georges-Louis Leclerc, comte de Buffon (1707–88).

CHAPTER XVIII

1. *Asclepiades boasted that . . . physician:* François Rabelais, *Gargantua and Pantagruel,* book 4, author's prologue.
2. *a tympany:* a distended abdomen.

CHAPTER XIX

1. *Here phials, . . . declare:* Samuel Garth, *The Dispensary,* canto 1, lines 99–104.

2. *the savin bush:* an evergreen shrub with purple berries, whose dried leaves were taken as an abortifacient.

3. *listed:* edged with a strip of cloth.

4. *pill cochia:* Extract of colocynth, a relative of the watermelon, acts as a strong cathartic.

5. *troy:* system of weights used for gems and precious metals.

6. *the English Ratcliffe:* The English physician John Radcliffe (1650–1714) treated several monarchs and was known for his wit.

7. *rose cancers:* a cancer of the breast or face with the appearance of an opening rose.

8. *white swellings:* chronic swelling of the knee; tuberculosis of the bone.

9. *flip:* A warm drink made of beer and liquor, sweetened with sugar and sometimes whipped with an egg.

CHAPTER XX

1. *Around bright trophies . . . slay:* Samuel Garth, *The Dispensary,* canto 5, lines 126–27.

2. *ring-bones, wind galls, and spavins:* diseases that afflict horses' legs.

3. *peripneumony:* pneumonia.

4. *Omne quod exit . . . nomen:* another quotation from Lily's Latin grammar, literally, "Every noun which endeth in *um,* whether Greek or Latin, is the neuter gender, so a noun undeclined."

5. *the learned doctors Hudibras and Mc'Fingal:* Hudibras was the hero of a satirical poem by Samuel Butler; Tory M'Fingal was the hero of a similar poem by John Trumbull (1750–1831).

6. *the great Crookshank's church history:* a pun on the last name of William Crookshank, author of *The History of the State and Sufferings of the Church of Scotland, from the Restoration to the Revolution* (1762).

7. *Chesselden:* The English surgeon William Cheselden (1688–1752) wrote a treatise on the removal of kidney stones.

8. *Tully:* Cicero.

9. *Propria quæ maribus:* The section of Lily's Latin grammar concerning the gender of nouns begins, "Propria quae maribus tribuuntur, mascula dicas: / ut sunt divorum; Mars, Bacchus, Apollo . . ." ("Thou mayest call proper names, which are attributed to the male kind, masculines: as be the names of the heathenish gods; Mars the god of battle, Bacchus the god of wine, Apollo the god of wisdom . . .").

10. *struggling about red ears at a husking:* Traditionally, a person who found a red ear of corn at a husking was entitled to kiss whomever he or she liked.

11. *If he could be led to substitute the aquatic draughts of Doctor Sangrado, as a succedaneum for the diffusible stimuli of Brown:* if he would drink water instead of alcohol.

Chapter XXI

1. *For man's relief . . . heaven:* The verse is probably Tyler's.
2. *Pringle:* The English physician John Pringle (1707–82) was best known for his writings on military medicine and sanitation.
3. *play twenty rubbers of all fours:* All fours is a card game. A rubber is a set of three games.

Chapter XXII

1. *To kinder skies, . . . turn:* Oliver Goldsmith, *The Traveller; or, A Prospect of Society,* lines 239–40.

Chapter XXIII

1. *One not vers'd . . . rules:* Alexander Pope, *Imitations of Horace,* book 2, satire 2, lines 9–10.
2. *Governour Jay, of New York:* John Jay (1745–1829).
3. *the late Governour Livingston, of New Jersey:* William Livingston (1723–90).
4. *Mr. R——— M———:* perhaps the financier Robert Morris (1735–1806).

Chapter XXIV

1. *supple jack:* a species of woody vine (*Berchemia scandens*).
2. *I said I will take heed unto my ways, . . . wicked:* See Psalms 39:1.
3. *hassoc:* a cushion on which worshipers may kneel in church.

Chapter XXV

1. *Hope springs eternal . . . blast:* Alexander Pope, *Essay on Man,* epistle 1, lines 95–96.

2. *Mr. J———n:* perhaps Thomas Jefferson.

3. *the Downs:* an anchorage in the English Channel.

CHAPTER XXVI

1. *Now mark a spot . . . wise:* William Cowper, *The Task,* book 1 ("The Sofa"), lines 725–28.

2. *How poor, how rich, . . . gods:* adapted from Edward Young, *The Complaint, or Night Thoughts on Life, Death, and Immortality,* night 1, lines 68ff.

CHAPTER XXVII

1. *Thus has he, . . . are out:* Hamlet V.ii.189–95.

2. *the son of a late patriotic American governour:* The painter John Trumbull (1756–1843), son of Connecticut governor Jonathan Trumbull, was a friend of Tyler's.

CHAPTER XXVIII

1. *He could distinguish . . . OWL:* Samuel Butler, *Hudibras,* canto 1, lines 67–74.

2. *Peter Pindar:* the satirist John Wolcot (1738–1819).

CHAPTER XXIX

1. *an eloquent Bolingbroke:* The statesman Henry Saint-John, the first viscount Bolingbroke (1678–1751), supplied the philosophy that Alexander Pope turned into verse in his *Essay on Man.*

2. *the fiery Hotspur:* a character in Shakespeare's *King Henry IV, Part 1.*

3. *footnote: Mr. Johnson, a respectable bookseller in St. Paul's church yard, London.* Joseph Johnson (1738–1809) was a bookseller and the publisher of Joseph Priestley, William Cowper, Erasmus Darwin, and Mary Wollstonecraft. Johnson printed loose pages of Thomas Paine's *Rights of Man* (1791) but became so nervous about the potential political reaction that Paine had to find another publisher to bind them.

4. *an epigram of Peter Pindar's . . . the DEVIL'S IN PAINE:* Peter Pindar wrote a number of poems about Paine, but this verse is probably Tyler's.

CHAPTER XXX

1. *Man hard of heart ... ill!:* Edward Young, *The Complaint, or Night Thoughts on Life, Death, and Immortality,* night 3, lines 210–17.
2. *malmsey:* a strong, sweet wine.
3. *tent wines:* a weak, dark red Spanish wine, often used in Communion.
4. *Fuertuventura:* Fuerteventura is the second largest of the Canary Islands and the one closest to Africa.
5. *the little island of Goree:* Gorée is part of Senegal today.
6. *Loango city, upon a small well peopled island near the coast of Congo:* near present-day Pointe-Noire, Congo.
7. *Cacongo:* a coastal town in present-day Angola.

CHAPTER XXXI

1. *Can thus ... pains?:* John Milton, *Paradise Lost,* book 11, lines 507–11.

CHAPTER XXXII

1. *Chains are the portion ... dungeon:* William Cowper, *The Task,* book 5, lines 581–82.
2. *If Abraham had indeed sent Lazarus to the rich man, in torment:* See Luke 16:19–25.

VOLUME II

CHAPTER I

1. *There dwell the most ... escape:* William Cowper, *The Task,* book 5, lines 397–99.
2. *the Dey's troops or cologlies: Kulughli,* also spelled *koulouglis,* were the descendants of Ottoman Turks who had married local women.
3. *Mufti:* Muslim jurist.
4. *Hadgi's:* hajjis; Muslims who have made a pilgrimage to Mecca.
5. *the present Dey, Vizier Hassen Bashaw:* From 1766 to 1791 the dey of Algiers was Muhammad ibn Uthman. Baba Hassan ruled from 1791 to 1798.
6. *the chieux or secretary:* This is probably a conflation of two distinct terms. In Algiers, the dey's personal secretaries were called *khujas.* The *kahya,* responsible for administering justice to Moors, was the deputy

of the *agha;* the *agha* was the captain-general of the janissaries. See Charles-André Julien, *History of North Africa* (London: Routledge, 1970), 321–22. In *A Compleat History of the Piratical States of Barbary* (London: R. Griffiths, 1750), J. Morgan writes that "The *Chaoux* are Messengers of the King's House," charged with carrying out arrests of Turks on the dey's orders. Morgan spells the office of the agha's deputy *"Chaya"* (pages 184, 194). In *A Short Account of Algiers,* Mathew Carey refers to "the Chiayah or secretary of the bashaw of Tripoli" (page 33) and "twenty four Chiah bassas or colonels subordinate to the aga" (page 14). By the term *chieux,* Tyler might mean either *khuja/chaoux/chiayah* or *kahya/chaya/chiah.*

CHAPTER II

1. *the kumrah, a wretched looking, though serviceable animal in that country, propagated by a jack upon a cow:* In *Travels, or Observations, Relating to Several Parts of Barbary and the Levant* (1638), Thomas Shaw makes mention of "the kumrah, as the Algerines call a little serviceable beast of burden, begot betwixt an ass and a cow. That which I saw at Algiers, where it was not looked upon as a rarity, was single hoofed like the ass, but distinguished from it in having a sleeker skin, with the tail and the head (though without horns) in fashion of the dam's" (volume 1, part 3, chapter 2, section 1). The *kumrah* also appears in James Wilson Stevens, *An Historical and Geographical Account of Algiers* (Philadelphia: Hogan & M'Elroy, 1797), 134.

2. *attornment:* transference of homage; acknowledgment of a new feudal lord.

3. *Charles the twelfth of Sweden has however been stigmatized by the historian, as a madman, for opposing the insulting Turk, when a prisoner, though assisted by nearly two hundred brave men:* Charles XII (1682–1718), king of Sweden, had encouraged Turkey to go to war against Russia. After Turkey and Russia made peace, he refused to leave Bessarabia. In 1713 a Turkish army evicted him by force. He was then imprisoned for a year.

CHAPTER III

1. *True, I talk of dreams, . . . south: Romeo and Juliet,* I.iv.97–103.
2. *the works of a Behn and a Colman:* Aphra Behn's novel *Oronooko; or, the History of the Royal Slave* (1688) and perhaps George Colman's play *Turk and No Turk* (1785).

CHAPTER IV

1. *One day . . . YOUNG'S REVENGE:* Edward Young, *The Revenge: A Tragedy* (1721), I.i.36–40.
2. *the barrenness of a RACHEL is sometimes compensated to the husband, by the fertility of a BILHAH:* See Genesis 30:2–5.
3. *the river Saffran:* In *Travels, or Observations, Relating to Several Parts of Barbary and the Levant* (1738), Thomas Shaw mentions a River Masaffran that debouches just to the west of the city of Algiers. "The name of Masaffran," Shaw writes, "was probably attributed to it from the tawny or saffron colour of its water" (volume 1, part 1, chapter 3).
4. *a mattoc:* a farming tool whose head combines a hoe and a pick.

CHAPTER V

1. *A christian is . . . tell:* Edward Young, *Night Thoughts on Life, Death, and Immortality,* night 4, lines 788–93.
2. *a Renegado:* a Christian who has converted to Islam. In Algiers, most corsairs were renegades, and they rivaled the Turks for political control of the country.
3. *"what shall it profit you, if you gain the whole world and lose your own soul, or what shall a man give in exchange for his soul":* See Mark 8:36–37.
4. *the Mahometan imposture:* Humphrey Prideaux's book *The True Nature of Imposture, Fully Displayed in the Life of Mahomet* (1697; U.S. edition, 1798) popularized in the West the notion of Muhammad as a deliberate fraud who conspired to invent a religion for his own advantage. Of the inspirations that led to the Koran, for example, Prideaux writes: "In the thirty-eighth year of his age [Mahomet] withdrew himself from his former conversation, and affecting an Eremetical life, used every morning to withdraw himself into a solitary cave, near Mecca, called the Cave of Hira, and there continued all day, exercising himself, as he

pretended, in prayers, fastings, and holy meditations; and there it is supposed he first had his consults with those accomplices, by whose help he made the Alcoran" (U.S. edition, p. 11).

CHAPTER VI

1. *Hear I, or . . . plume!!:* Edward Young, *The Complaint, or Night Thoughts on Life, Death, and Immortality,* night 4, lines 651–53.
2. *the tefta:* unidentified; perhaps a variant spelling of "taffeta."
3. *The Indian of North America surprised the European physician, by a process founded on similar principles:* For additional contemporary descriptions of the Native American sweat bath, see Elizabeth A. Fenn, *Pox Americana: The Great Smallpox Epidemic of 1775–82* (Farrar, Straus and Giroux, 2001), 24–25.
4. *Sydenham:* The English physician Thomas Sydenham (1624–89) brought a new emphasis on empirical study to medicine and pioneered the use of cinchona bark in agues.
5. *a preparation of gum, called the balm of Mecca:* The aromatic resin from a tree of the genus *Commiphora* was used as an antiseptic and to treat wounds. It was also known as balm of Gilead.
6. *"the liberal shepherds give a grosser name":* See *Hamlet,* IV.vii.170.

CHAPTER VII

1. *But pardon, . . . object:* Shakespeare, *King Henry V,* prologue, lines 8–11.
2. *the Wolga:* the Volga River.
3. *Tien:* T'ien (or *Tian*) means "heaven" in Chinese and is the name of the supreme power in ancient Chinese religion.
4. *Cradled with the Parsees of Indostan, you had adored fire:* Fire has a special symbolic importance in the Persian religion of Zoroastrianism.
5. *alcoran:* the Koran.
6. *Omar and Abubeker:* Umar ibn al-Khattab and Abu Bakr were close friends of Muhammad's; he married daughters of both men. After the prophet's death, Abu Bakr became the first caliph; Umar became the second.
7. *thundering of Hermon:* Hermon was a mountain ridge on the border between Syria and Lebanon.

8. *Bismillahi Rrahmani Rrhahimi:* This is a rough transcription of the Arabic for the English phrase that immediately follows in the text.

CHAPTER VIII

1. *Et cest lingue, . . . Hotchpot:* This is a paraphrase of Edward Coke's *First Part of the Institutes of the Laws of England; or, A Commentary upon Littleton,* book 3, section 268, which reads as follows: "Et cest terme (Hotchpot) nest forsque un terme similitudinarie, et est a tant adire, cestascavoir, de mitterles terres en Frankmariage, et les auters terres en fee simple ensemble . . ." ("And this term (Hotchpot) is but a term similitudinary, and is as much to say, as to put the lands in Frankmarriage, and the other Lands in Fee simple together . . ."). In the section just prior to it, Littleton observes that "it seemeth that this word (Hotchpot) is in English, A Pudding, for in this Pudding is not commonly put one thing alone, but one thing with other things together."
2. HASTY PUDDING: cornmeal mush.

CHAPTER IX

1. *the river Sanaga:* the Senegal River.

CHAPTER X

1. *O beasts, of pity void! . . . head:* See William Somerville, "The Chace," lines 204–5.

CHAPTER XI

1. *If perchance thy home . . . born:* Mark Akenside, "Inscription VI. For a Column at Runnymede," lines 11–16.
2. *hectic:* a fever associated with tuberculosis and characterized by dry skin and a flushed face.

CHAPTER XII

1. *Oft have I prov'd . . . please:* Robert Blair, *The Grave,* lines 92–94.
2. *quinquina or jesuits bark:* The bark of the cinchona contains quinine and can reduce fever.
3. *I made a decoction, as near to Huxham's, as the ingredients I could procure*

would admit: The English physician John Huxham (1692–1768) wrote a well-known book on fevers. "Huxham's tincture" was a mix of cinchona bark, "bitter orange peel, serpentary root, saffron, and cochineal mixed in spirit" (Norman Moore, "John Huxham," *Dictionary of National Biography,* ed. Stephen and Lee [Oxford University Press, 1938], 10:364).

CHAPTER XIII

1. *os frontis:* forehead.
2. *Ismaelism:* a word formerly used as a synonym for Islam; the Arabs are said to be descended from Abraham's son Ishmael. (Today the term has a different meaning and describes a distinct group of Shiite Muslims.)

CHAPTER XIV

1. *a pulse glass:* Tyler describes the medical device accurately. When a pulse-glass was held in the hand, the alcohol inside it visibly responded to the holder's pulse.
2. *the bark:* cinchona bark; see note 2 to Volume II, Chapter XII, on "quinquina."

CHAPTER XV

1. *the ancient Mauritinia Massilia:* Mauretania was the Latin name for northwest Africa. The Massyli were a powerful tribe located in northern Algeria; in the second century B.C., their power rivaled that of Carthage.
2. *Bruce, an Englishman:* See note 4 to Preface.
3. *the American edition of Guthrie's Geography:* William Guthrie, *A New System of Modern Geography* (Philadelphia: Mathew Carey, 1793–95).
4. *the celebrated Belisarius:* In the service of the Emperor Justinian I, the Byzantine general Belisarius (c.505–65) defeated the Vandals of Africa.
5. *the kingdom of Tefilet:* Tafilalt, now an oasis in southeastern Morocco, was the center of an independent kingdom from the eighth to the tenth centuries.
6. *Dr. Shaw:* Thomas Shaw (1692–1751) was the author of *Travels, or Ob-*

servations, Relating to Several Parts of Barbary and the Levant (1738), an important source for Tyler of information about Algiers.

7. *the enlightened historian:* For details of early Algerian history, Tyler's ultimate source is William Robertson's *History of the Reign of the Emperor Charles V* (1769), books 5 and 6. Tyler seems to have come to Robertson, however, by way of Mathew Carey, *A Short Account of Algiers, Containing a Description of the Climate of that Country, of the Manners and Customs of the Inhabitants, and of Their Several Wars against Spain, France, England, Holland, Venice, and Other Powers of Europe, from the Usurpation of Barbarossa and the Invasion of the Emperor Charles V to the Present Time* (1794).

8. *Horric:* the Turkish pirate Aruj, also known as Barbarossa I (1473?–1518).

9. *Hayraddin:* Khayr al-Din (1483?–1546), also known as Barbarossa II, was the younger brother of Aruj. To consolidate his control of Algiers, he allied himself with the Ottoman sultan Selim I.

10. *Eutimi, then king of Algiers:* Selim al-Tumi, the sheik of Algiers, asked Aruj to help him drive the Spanish from the city. To repay the favor, Aruj had Selim al-Tumi strangled in his bath and declared himself sultan.

11. *the Oran:* a port city west of Algiers.

12. *the neighbouring king of Temecien:* Abu Hammu III was then the ruler of Tlemcen, an ancient city in northwestern Algeria and capital of the Abd al-Wadid kingdom.

13. *the brave Marquis de Comeres, the Spanish governour of Oran:* Tyler is still depending on Carey's *Short Account of Algiers* for his historical information, but here Carey's source appears to be J. Morgan's *A Compleat History of the Piratical States of Barbary* (London: R. Griffiths, 1750), which identifies this figure as "the Marquis *de Gomarez,* Governor of *Oran*" (page 28).

14. *the Grand Seignior:* The Ottoman sultan Selim I (1467–1520) was also known by the title "the Sublime Porte."

15. *Andrew Doria:* the Genoese admiral Andrea Doria (1466–1560).

16. *a mole:* a breakwater; it was built by Khayr al-Din in 1529 and required constant maintenance.

17. *succeeded by Hassan Aga, a renegado from Sardinia:* Hasan Agha (d. 1549?) became Khayr al-Din's caliph in Algiers in 1536.

18. *Another Hassan, son to the second Barbarossa:* Hassan Pasha (d. 1572) was the son of Khayr al-Din and ruled Algiers from 1544 to 1567. He defeated the Spanish at Mostaganem in 1558.

19. *the Count de Alcandara:* perhaps Martin Alfonso de Córdoba, first count of Alcaudète.

20. *his successor, Mahomet:* the successor to Hassan Pasha was Muhammad, son of Salih Re'is. He pacified the Turkish janissaries by allowing them to privateer. After only a year, he was succeeded by Eulj Ali, also known as Kilij Ali, who ruled Algiers from 1568 to 1587.

21. *Scandaroon in Syria, an Ottoman city:* Iskenderun, formerly Alexadretta, a port city in southern Turkey.

22. *in sixteen hundred and twenty three, threw off their dependence on the sublime Porte:* Throughout the sixteenth and seventeenth centuries, the pashas of Algiers, who were appointed by the Turkish sultan and supported by Turkish janissaries, steadily lost power to the divan, an Algerian council dominated by renegades and corsairs. Nonetheless, the Regency of Algiers continued to profess at least a nominal allegiance to Turkey into the eighteenth century.

23. *Hali Pinchinin:* Originally from Italy, the pirate Ali Bitchnin, also known as Picenino, owned two palaces in Algiers.

24. *the rich chapel of our lady of Loretto:* The fresco-filled church in Loreto, Italy, is said to contain the house of the Virgin Mary.

25. *Valona:* present-day Vlorë, Albania.

26. *the Marquis du Quesne:* the French naval officer Abraham Duquesne (1610–88).

27. *bomb ketches:* ketches (two-masted sailing vessels) equipped with mortars for bombing.

28. *Mezemorto the Dey's admiral:* the corsair captain Hadjidji Husayn Pasha, also known as Mezzomorto (d. 1701).

29. *the Count O'Reilly:* the Irish-born Spanish general Alexander O'Reilly (1725–94).

30. *the United States ... concluded a treaty with this piratical state on the fifth of September, one thousand seven hundred and ninety five:* America agreed to pay more than $700,000, and the dey of Algiers released more than one hundred American hostages and promised not to seize any new ones. The text of the treaty was published in James Wilson Stevens, *An*

Historical and Geographical Account of Algiers (Philadelphia: Hogan & M'Elroy, 1797).

CHAPTER XVIII

1. *May these add ... damnation: Timon of Athens* III.i.52–53.

CHAPTER XXI

1. *Prætulerim scriptor delirus . . . fallant:* "I should prefer to be thought a foolish and clumsy scribbler, if only my failings please, or at least escape me." Horace, *Epistles,* book 2, epistle 2, lines 126–27 (trans. H. Rushton Fairclough [Cambridge, Harvard University Press, 1929]).
2. *chatty B— or bungling Ben:* The newspaperman Benjamin Franklin Bache (1769–98) was more respected for his vehemently partisan Republican opinions than for his accuracy as a reporter. His grandfather was Benjamin Franklin (1706–90); perhaps Tyler describes him as bungling because in his *Autobiography* Franklin identifies the principal "errata" of his life as if it were a text he had tried to correct. (For these identifications and for those in the next note, see Marius Péladeau, ed., *The Poetry of Royall Tyler* [University Press of Virginia, 1968], 75.)
3. *Tedious as Doctor P—nce, or rather / As Samuel, Increase, Cotton M—r:* Thomas Prince (1687–1758) was minister of Boston's Old South Church and author of several histories of New England. The Mathers were the best-known family of Puritan preachers and writers; Increase (1639–1723) was the father of Cotton (1663–1728), who was the father of Samuel (1706–85).
4. *cit Genet:* France's revolutionary government sent Edmond Genet (1763–1834) to the United States with instructions to recruit Americans for attacks on Florida, Mexico, and Canada. He confirmed the Federalists' worst fears about France and embarrassed the francophile Republicans. After causing much anxiety and bluster, his mission collapsed.
5. *Chastelreux:* the travel writer François Jean marquis de Chastellux (1734–88).
6. *unblown:* not yet blossomed.

CHAPTER XXII

1. *Sales:* George Sale (1699?–1736) translated the Koran into English in 1734. He prefaced his translation with a "Preliminary Discourse" that examined Islam and Muhammad's life in detail. Tyler's description of Sale as "bigoted" was a minority opinion; elsewhere Tyler himself refers to the "liberality of the good Sale."

2. *Prideaux:* Humphrey Prideaux; see note 4 to Volume II, Chapter V.

3. *the specious praise of the* philosophic Boulanvilliers: Henri, comte de Boulainvilliers (1658–1722) wrote a *Life of Mohamet* that was translated into English in 1731.

4. *the Coreis:* The Quraysh were a wealthy tribe of traders.

5. *Abutileb:* Abu Talib was Muhammad's protector as well as his uncle.

6. *beautiful Cadija:* Khadija was Muhammad's first wife; he survived her by more than a decade.

7. *tide in the affairs of men:* See *Julius Caesar* IV.iii.217.

8. *Arian christians, whose darling creed is the unity of the Deity:* In fact, the heretic Arius (c.250–336) taught that Christ was distinct from God, who created him.

9. *persecuted by the Athenasians into an abhorrence of almost every other christian tenet:* Athanasius (c.293–373), bishop of Alexandria, insisted on the orthodox doctrine of the Nicene Creed, which holds that Christ is of the same substance as the Father.

10. *Jews, who had fled from the vindictive Emperour Adrian:* After the Roman emperor Hadrian banned circumcision and excluded the Jews from Jerusalem, he faced an uprising led by Bar Kokhba that lasted from 132 to 135.

11. *Pope Joan:* a legendary female pope, who supposedly took office in 855 and went into labor during a ceremonial procession.

12. *the nag's head consecration of the English bishops:* According to this legend, the chain of consecration on which Anglican orders are based was broken in 1559 by John Scory (d. 1585) at the Nag's Head Inn in Chepeside. Instead of following the accepted ritual, Scory is said to have "consecrated" merely by touching a Bible to the new bishops' heads and saying, "Take thou authority to preach the word of God."

13. *like the divine Melchisedec, uniting in his person the high titles of prophet and king:* See Genesis 14:18–20 and Hebrews 7:1–28.

CHAPTER XXIII

1. *Osman:* Uthman ibn Affan was an early convert to Islam and became the third caliph.
2. *Ali:* Ali ibn Abi Talib was Muhammad's cousin and ward. He became the fourth caliph.

CHAPTER XXIV

1. *Father of all!. . . Lord:* Alexander Pope, "The Universal Prayer, Deo Opt. Max.," lines 1–4.
2. *Soliman:* Solomon.
3. *rhammadin:* Ramadan.

CHAPTER XXV

1. *O here; quæ res . . . vult:* "My master, a thing that admits of neither method nor sense cannot be handled by rule and method." Horace, *Satires,* book 2, satire 3, lines 265–67 (trans. H. Rushton Fairclough [Cambridge, Mass.: Harvard University Press, 1929]).
2. *the confederacy of Ahab and Jehoshaphat, when they went up to battle to Ramoth Gilead:* See 1 Kings 22:1–6.
3. *the treaty of Philnitz:* In 1791 Austria and Prussia vowed to restore Louis XVI to the throne of France if other European powers would support them.
4. *the war of the allies of Queen Anne, and the conquests of the Duke of Marlborough:* John Churchill, the first duke of Marlborough (1650–1722), won many victories in the War of the Spanish Succession, in which Great Britain was allied with Holland and Austria. The war marked the decline of the French empire and the rise of the British.
5. *the Duke of Ormond:* James Butler, duke of Ormonde (1665–1745), succeeded Marlborough as commander of British forces in the War of the Spanish Succession. But he later became involved in Jacobite attempts to put the son of the Stuart king James II on the British throne. He was impeached in 1715 and went into exile.
6. *the treaty of Utrecht:* England and Holland signed the Peace of Utrecht in 1713, leaving Austria to continue its war against France alone.
7. *I will burn the city to ashes myself:* In *A Short Account of Algiers* (1794),

Mathew Carey writes that "The trite tale of a dey of Algiers having offered to burn the city for fifty thousand pounds, is a despicable newspaper fiction" (page 39).

CHAPTER XXVI

1. *A pattern fit . . . fights:* Samuel Butler, *Hudibras,* part 1, canto 2, lines 13–14.
2. *the writings of Honestus:* In 1786, writing under the cognomen "Honestus," Benjamin Austin (1752–1820) attacked the power of lawyers in a series of letters published in Boston's *Independent Chronicle.* He went on to become an ardently Republican politician.
3. *an Algerine cadi:* a judge in an Islamic court; usually spelled *qadi.*

CHAPTER XXVII

1. *And though they say the Lord* LIVETH, *surely they swear falsely:* Jeremiah 5:2.
2. *Ibraham and Soliman:* the Old Testament patriarchs Abraham and Solomon.
3. *Ayesha the beloved:* Aisha, daughter of Abu Bakr, was Muhammad's favorite wife after Khadija.

CHAPTER XXVIII

1. *For sufference is . . . tribe: The Merchant of Venice* I.iii.108.

CHAPTER XXIX

1. *But endless is . . . sigh:* Edward Young, *The Complaint, or Night Thoughts on Life, Death, and Immortality,* night 1, lines 283–84.
2. *several American vessels had been captured:* Since Underhill was captured in November 1788, this probably refers to the Algerian capture of twelve American ships and more than one hundred sailors in October and November 1793.
3. *Captain O'Brien:* Richard O'Brien, captain of the American merchant ship *Dauphin,* was captured along with fourteen of his crew on July 31, 1785.

CHAPTER XXX

1. *Now, by my hood, . . . Jew: The Merchant of Venice* II.vi.51.
2. *soon after I was taken, a Jew and two Algerines made a tour of the United States, and sent home an accurate account of the American commerce:* This may be a reference to two men and a woman who were expelled from Virginia in 1786. They were carrying documents in Hebrew that aroused suspicion; Governor Patrick Henry worried that they might be spies from Algiers. See Robert J. Allison, *The Crescent Obscured: The United States and the Muslim World, 1776–1815* (New York: Oxford, 1995), 3–6.
3. *William Carmichael:* Carmichael (d. 1795) served as an American diplomat in Spain from 1780 to 1794.
4. *It was reported, that [Lamb] was empowered to offer only two hundred dollars per head for each prisoner indiscriminately:* In April 1786, John Lamb offered the dey of Algiers $50,000 in exchange for the release of twenty-one American hostages. Unfortunately, John Adams and Thomas Jefferson had instructed Lamb to spend no more than two hundred dollars per captive. Congress refused to pay the higher amount, and negotiations collapsed.

CHAPTER XXXI

1. *No gentle breathing . . . sing:* Ambrose Philips, "To the Earl of Dorset," lines 11–12.
2. *the port of Alexandria, called by the Turks Scandaroon:* Present-day Alexandria, an Egyptian port city, is also known as Al-Iskandariyah.
3. *Gize:* Giza (Al Jizah).
4. *The city of Jerusalem was only about five day's journey to the south east:* probably a misprint for "northeast."
5. *Potiphar's wife:* See Genesis 39:1–23.
6. *until we struck the same arm [of the Red Sea] again, near the place where the learned Wortley Montague has concluded the Israelites, under the conduct of Moses, effected their passage:* In a letter to William Williamson dated December 2, 1765, Edward Wortley Montague wrote:

I sat out from Cairo by the road known by the name of Tauricke Ben Israel; after twenty-four hours travelling, at about three miles an hour, we passed by an opening in the mountains on our right hand, viz. the mountains Maxattee.

There are two more roads, one to the northward of this, which the Mecca pilgrims go, and one to the south between the mountains, but never travelled, (as it does not lead to Suez, which is thirty hours march from Cairo,). Through this breach the children of *Israel* are said to have entered the mountains; and not to have taken the most southern road, which I think most probable; for those valleys, to judge by what are now seen, could not be passable for *Pharaoh*'s chariots. This breach, the inhabitants told me, leads directly to a plain called Badeah, which, in Arabic, signifies something new or extraordinary, as the beginning of every thing is new which was not before known.

At Suez I found an opportunity of going to Tor, by sea, which I gladly embraced; that by going nearer the place, at which the Israelites are supposed to have entered the gulph, and having a view from the sea as well as that of the opposite shore, I might be a little better able to form a judgment about it; besides, I was willing to have the views, bearings, and soundings, which I took.

When we were opposite to Badeah, it seemed to me (for I was not on shore) a plain capable of containing the Israelites, with a small elevation in the middle of it. I saw something too like ruins; the captains and pilots told me, that this was the place where the Israelites entered the sea, and the ruins were those of a convent (I suppose built on the spot in commemoration of the fact;) they added that there was good water there.

The Life, Travels and Adventures of Edward Wortley Montague, Esq. (Boston: John W. Folsom, 1794), 129–30.

7. *Well does the Latin poet exclaim;* Quem Deus vult perdere, prius dementat: "Whom the Gods would destroy they first make mad," in Longfellow's famous translation. The Latin saying is anonymous; the Greek version is attributed to Euripides.

Chapter XXXII

1. *Procul! O procul! este profani:* "Away, O souls profane! Stand far away!" Virgil, *Aeneid,* book 6, line 258.

Chapter XXXIII

1. *There appears to be nothing in their nature above the power of the Devil:* Jonathan Edwards, *A Treatise Concerning Religious Affections,* part 3, section 1. Edwards is discussing sensory experiences that are associated with religion and make a vivid impression on a person's imagination.

2. *Medina Tadlardh, erroneously called Medina Talmabi:* The Arabic name

for the Saudi Arabia holy city is Medinat an-Nabi, which means "city of the Prophet."

Chapter XXXIV

1. *The heaven of heavens cannot contain thee:* 1 Kings 8:27.
2. the Al Kaaba, or House of God: The Kaaba, a cube-shaped shrine, contains a sacred black stone and is Islam's holiest site.

Chapter XXXVI

1. *O what a goodly outside falshood hath!:* Shakespeare, *The Merchant of Venice* I.iii.100.

Chapter XXXVII

1. *port Logos, in the southern extremity of Portugal:* Lagos.
2. *Joseph Donaldson, jun. Esq.:* Donaldson was appointed deputy to Algiers in the spring of 1795.
3. *on the third day of May, one thousand seven hundred and ninety five, I landed in my native country:* Most of the American hostages in Algiers did not return home until February 1797.
4. *Let no foreign emissaries inflame us against one nation, by raking into the ashes of long extinguished enmity or delude us into the extravagant schemes of another, by recurring to fancied gratitude:* perhaps a reference to Edmond Genet; see note 4 to Volume II, Chapter XXI.

A Note on the Type

The principal text of this Modern Library edition
was set in a digitized version of Janson, a typeface that
dates from about 1690 and was cut by Nicholas Kis,
a Hungarian working in Amsterdam. The original matrices have
survived and are held by the Stempel foundry in Germany.
Hermann Zapf redesigned some of the weights and sizes for
Stempel, basing his revisions on the original design.

MODERN LIBRARY IS ONLINE AT
WWW.MODERNLIBRARY.COM

MODERN LIBRARY ONLINE IS YOUR GUIDE TO CLASSIC LITERATURE ON THE WEB

THE MODERN LIBRARY E-NEWSLETTER

Our free e-mail newsletter is sent to subscribers, and features sample chapters, interviews with and essays by our authors, upcoming books, special promotions, announcements, and news.

To subscribe to the Modern Library e-newsletter, send a blank e-mail to: join-modernlibrary@list.randomhouse.com or visit www.modernlibrary.com

THE MODERN LIBRARY WEBSITE

Check out the Modern Library website at www.modernlibrary.com for:

- The Modern Library e-newsletter
- A list of our current and upcoming titles and series
- Reading Group Guides and exclusive author spotlights
- Special features with information on the classics and other paperback series
- Excerpts from new releases and other titles
- A list of our e-books and information on where to buy them
- The Modern Library Editorial Board's 100 Best Novels and 100 Best Nonfiction Books of the Twentieth Century written in the English language
- News and announcements

Questions? E-mail us at modernlibrary@randomhouse.com
For questions about examination or desk copies, please visit the Random House Academic Resources site at www.randomhouse.com/academic